Unleashing Colter's Hell

Sean Smith

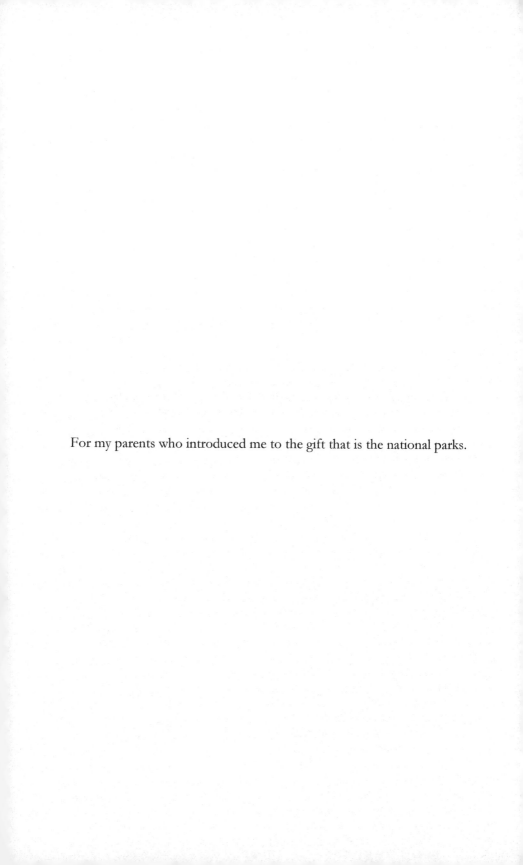

For my parents who introduced me to the gift that is the national parks.

ACKNOWLEDGMENTS

I'd like to acknowledge the assistance of several people in the writing of this book. Eric Penz and Craig Kellermann for their editing help, David Robinson, Liz Borg, Cinda Waldbuesser, Jacqueline Crucet, Lynn Davis, Paul Roach, Tommy Hough, Tom Hill, Chip Jenkins, Debbie Bird, Jim DiPeso, as well as my wife and family for their encouragement and support.

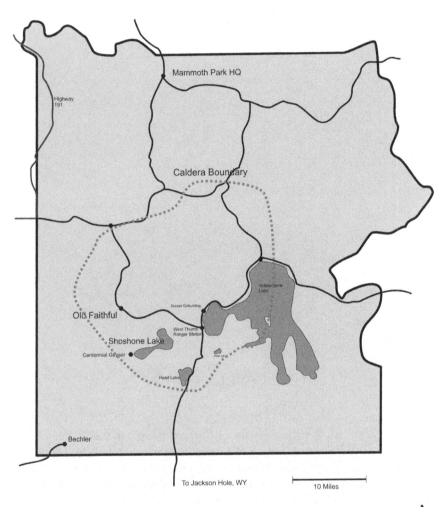

Mammoth Park HQ

Highway
191

Caldera Boundary

Yellowstone
Lake

Old Faithful

Sinclair Outbuilding

West Thumb
Ranger Station

Shoshone Lake

Centennial Geyser

Heart Lake

Bechler

To Jackson Hole, WY

10 Miles

N

Yellowstone National Park

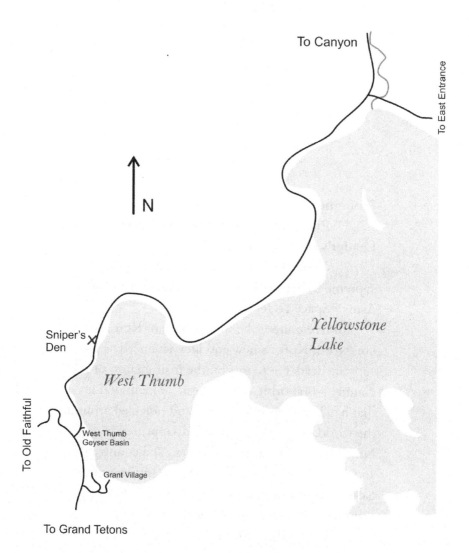

Prologue
Pyongyang North Korea, Supreme Leader's office: April, 25, Morning

General Chun Yong Huh sat outside the supreme leader's office. Chun headed the Grand Army's Space Defense Division.

In five minutes he was to present Kim Jong Un, North Korea's new and inexperienced supreme leader, a report on the malfunction of the country's first orbital rocket test. A malfunction that had been reported widely and ridiculed around the world. In the past, people disappeared in North Korea for far less offenses. The country's soccer goalie had been shot for his embarrassing, lackluster performance in the recent World Cup. But that was under Un's father, Kim Jong Il.

Under Il, a visit to this office would have made Chun nervous. But not this morning. Things had changed in North Korea.

And so the general sat outside the leader's office on a bench he'd sat on countless times before and that was just as hard, but surprisingly not as uncomfortable. *Had Un changed the bench somehow?* Chun wondered. He doubted it. More likely it was the bench on the other side of the door he was about to walk through that was

different. He wore his dress uniform covered with
medals and ribbons, several of which the supreme
leader's father had personally pinned to his chest.
A stern-faced, muscle-bound army secretary with a
haircut as clipped as his demeanor occupied the
desk next to the office's entrance. The secretary's
look betrayed not a hint of any emotion. His
square jaw and features could have been cut from
stone. He appeared to be doing nothing more
than looking forward. The secretary's phone
buzzed. Without taking his gaze off Chun, he
picked up the receiver and put it to his ear.

"Right away," he grunted. Placing it back
on the cradle, he said, "You may go in."

Chun entered the supreme leader's office.
He had been in this room numerous times before.
It was cavernous. North Korea's publicly revered
but not yet feared new leader, Kim Jong Un,
looked diminutive and yet the spitting image of
Kim Il Sung, Un's paternal grandfather, as he sat at
the far end of the room behind an intricately
carved, antique desk. Chun had fought alongside
Sung, the founder of North Korea's Stalinist
philosophy, during the Korean War. After Sung's
death in 1994, Chun's allegiance had immediately
transferred to his son, Kim Jong Il. His allegiance
was now expected to pass once again to Un. Chun
had met Un once while the future North Korean
leader had studied abroad in Switzerland. Chun
had found Un to be a fun loving, fit, young man at
that time. No longer. He'd turned into an
overweight, round faced, thirty-something, carbon
copy of his grandfather. Too many five star
dinners followed by late night partying, Chun

5

guessed. This new supreme leader was soft.

Chun surmised that Un was likely also over his head. In his early thirties, the new leader of the communist North had no experience leading a nation. He had been selected to lead by default. Il, his father, had been forced to anoint Un his successor when his eldest son shamed himself, and worse, North Korea, by trying to sneak into Tokyo Disneyland with a fake passport. Il's next oldest son was rumored to be gay. Il's prejudice couldn't allow him to turn over the reins of power to a son who slept with men. It would leave the new leader open to blackmail. That left Un to take over. Kim Jong Il made the decision to make Un his successor based on the assumption he'd have plenty of time to groom him for leadership. But that plan went out the window when Kim Jong Il unexpectedly died, thrusting Un into the role of supreme leader. He'd had to learn on the job and it showed. Un's first several steps in office had been awful. He placed a moratorium on the country's nuclear program while also suspending their long range missile project. Un wasn't old enough to realize that these were the only things keeping the American hordes at bay. Compounding the insult, he begged the west for food aid, all but admitting the country was incapable of taking care of its people. Kim Il Sung was surely rolling in his grave.

And now the satellite launch had been a failure. What was that American saying, three strikes and you're out? Un clearly had three strikes and needed to be taken out of the game. But how and when were the huge questions.

Un's office was a mix of four cultures--
Russian, Chinese, Korean and, surprisingly,
American. Large, red hammer and sickle Soviet
flags hung from flag poles in a far corner of the
room. Pictures of Kim Jong Il and Sung with
former Soviet leaders, such as Khrushchev and
Brezhnev, hung there as well. Reminders of North
Korea's communist beginnings. Chun was glad to
see those hadn't been removed. At least not yet.

Chinese paintings, tokens of friendship
from the Chinese Ambassador, also adorned the
walls. North Korean folk art, including ancient
pottery, stood on bases in strategic spots
throughout the room. Chun was certain they had
been stolen from their rightful owners, but here in
North Korea anything the supreme leader did was
legal. Yet, most surprising was the American
influence on the room. A brand-new computer
with oversized monitors sat on top of the leader's
desk. Things were changing in North Korea.
Chun expected this. However, he hadn't expected
the western movie pictures. Images of modern
Hollywood movie stars dotted the wall and
intermixed with portraits of Un with other world
leaders. A large poster of Mickey Mouse, signed
by Walt Disney himself, held a special flood-lit
section of the wall near posters of Michael Jordan
and Dennis Rodman.

A strange collection. Chun surmised that it
accurately reflected the psyche of its main
occupant.

The immense room made the country's
new leader look small, more childlike.

Chun's shoes clicked on the marble floor,

echoing along the oak walls as he walked the length of the office. The only other sound was the faint ticking of a clock. Several large flat screen televisions displaying capitalist propaganda broadcasts covered one wall, but there was no sound, just the flickering glow of what passed for news in the West.

Chun approached Kim Jong Un, bowed, and placed a thick bound report on the desk. He stepped back and straightened. For what seemed like several minutes, Kim Jong Un studied the report. Purposefully, the supreme leader leafed through hundreds of pages. Chun knew the slower Un reviewed this report the more he was supposed to squirm. Not this time. Not from Un. Chun had witnessed Il use the technique of patience, contemplation, and quiet to unnerve his subordinates to great result. Never let your friends or opponents know your true emotions, your true intentions, the previous supreme leader had drilled into his inner circle of generals. So it was likely Un, the man thrust into the spotlight, never really knew his father's true feelings or intentions. But Chun had known them and knew that Il would retch at what his son was doing to the once great North Korea.

Chun continued to study the new leader as he pored over countless charts, figures, images, and text crammed into the document. Yet its significance could be summed up in a single paragraph.

The March launch of the nation's Unha 3 rocket had not made earth's orbit. The rocket's primary stage fuel

*system had failed roughly seventy three seconds into the
launch, destroying the entire missile, including the weather
satellite payload. Debris had rained from the sky off Korea's
coast over a thirty square mile section of the northern Pacific
Ocean.*

Chun watched as Un looked up from the
report. Un read the question on the mind of his
Army officer.

"No, general, this won't be seen as a
violation of our agreement with the Americans,"
Un said with no contextual explanation. "I only
agreed to the Americans' terms to buy time, to
forestall the revolution of our starving people.
However, I never agreed to stop North Korea's
orbital rocket program, nor give up a single bomb
of our current stock of nuclear weapons. North
Korea gave up nothing, staved off revolt, and
captured significant international good will."

"I appreciate the simplicity of the
misdirection. North Korea, under both Il and
Sung, had pulled this many times before." Chun
retorted. The mention of Un's father and
grandfather was an obvious, but hopefully not too
obvious, questioning of Un's resourcefulness.
"But the more important question is how many
times will the Americans buy the good faith of the
North Korean government?"

Un ignored these questions it seemed as a
slight smile crept across the supreme leader's face.
"I recognize the world considers the dramatic
explosion of our rocket as a failure of the Korean
system and its engineering capabilities." CNN and
Fox News, Un knew, had already jumped to

conclusions in hour-long special reports on the launch failure, and had made assertions that this was North Korea's most advanced military technology. Little did they know.

"Under my father's leadership, North Korea spent untold treasure and lives to achieve the goal of space flight. My father was convinced space flight, intercontinental rocket launches, would defend North Korea forever. But this is untrue. Until the United States is destroyed, North Korea's future would always be under threat."

"Yes, the western world will be quick to judge this apparent failure, assuming North Korea's goal was to launch a rocket into space." The smile slipped from Un's face like a snake slipping from his hole to strike. "But their assumption is wholly inaccurate."

A look of surprise came across Chun's face. Could he have misjudged Un?

"I do not share my father's amazement of the West's gullibility and failure to look beneath the surface appearance of our actions." Un went on. "Even the western perception of North Korea's past and present leaders has been incorrect. For example, Western conventional wisdom had been that my father was mad, ruthless, and, most of all, determined to do anything to insure the continuation of the North Korean system." Un's black eyes seemed to narrow as they scrutinized Chun. "You and I both know otherwise. My father inherited this country, yet, like many who inherit a fortune or company, my father had no grand vision for its future, beyond that of choosing its successor. And picking me as

the next Korean leader was the only right thing my
father actually did."

Speaking such truths under Kim Jong Il
would have sent one to Gullah or worse. But Il
was dead and it appeared so was the ban on
speaking ill of the former leader. Perhaps the time
to act was coming sooner than thought.

Chun was pulled out of his thoughts as Un
went on. "I know the western perception of me is
quite different. I've heard the West perceives that
I'm ill-prepared, inexperienced, and weak. That
I'm not ready to lead a nuclear power. My youth
makes me pliable and vulnerable to manipulation.

Chun agreed with the West on this and
nearly said as much. It was obvious that Un was
even more of a figure-head leader than his father.
A military coup was inevitable. Chun had read the
stories in the New York Times and other western
media outlets. He was even privy to secret CIA
psych reports.

The time to act was now.

"They are all wrong," Un stated coldly,
looking straight at Chun. "My father was believed
strong, but was truly weak. I'm different from my
father. I do not want to be a caretaker leader,
living off the accomplishments of my celebrated
grandfather. Instead, I'll complete my grandfather's
legacy. Where Il had failed to bring a socialist
revolution to the world through the destruction of
the United States, I will succeed.

Chun had stopped listening. The new
supreme leader was obviously delusional.
However, the boy leader was right on one point. Il
had failed to move North Korea into its rightful

place in the world. But it was Chun who would bring a new North Korea to the world.

Un got up from his desk and walked around the room. "I have a plan. A plan to exploit America's Achilles' heel. Its ignorance of how the world truly worked, its arrogance in assuming all shared the same values, will be its downfall. I unlike my father, not only know this but I'm strong enough to act on it."

Kim Jong Un returned to his chair, swiveling it, turning his back to his rocket scientist. Chun watched the new leader as he looked out floor-to-ceiling windows strategically placed to look down on the people's parade ground below. Chun couldn't help but feel a new day was coming. North Korea's enemies would soon feel her wrath.

Un turned back to face the rocket scientist while pressing a button on his phone. The secretary outside the office door answered. Kim Jong Un ordered a tea and returned his attention to Chun's report.

Chun looked on as Un read that most of the wreckage from the massive rocket had been recovered by the United States' Navy. This had impressed Chun. The rocket had shattered into millions of pieces, which rained down on the North Pacific and was scattered for miles. U.S. destroyers and other surface ships raced to the crash zone seemingly before the missile debris hit the water. Through the North Korean's intelligence network, Chun knew the wreckage had been flown to a secret military base in Nevada for dissection and analysis.

Upon reading this Un chuckled quietly.

This laughter seemed odd and out of place to Chun. The Americans and their allies would learn nothing from the wreckage. In fact, they would likely conclude the Korean missile program was fifteen years behind its actual status.

Sweat began to form on Chun's forehead as Un turned page after page. Throughout the crash zone, dozens of vessels plowed the waters, some so close the crews could practically jump from one deck to another. Western media reported several fishing boats and private craft had pulled debris from the sea's surface and had dispatched divers to recover the fragments below. The Americans had moved surprisingly quickly to recover any parts.

Chun thought he heard the supreme leader say something. Perfect? Had North Korea's supreme leader just said perfect?

In any recovery effort, however, some pieces of the puzzle were always missing. This was no different. A small fishing vessel, which seemed not worth noting, had been strategically positioned to recover an important piece of wreckage. A part of the rocket's actual payload that was big enough to achieve North Korea's ultimate goal and small enough to fit within the average suitcase.

Chun watched the leader turn to the last page. If he had been presenting this report to Un's father he would be trembling. He had feared giving Kim Jong Il bad news. And this report was bad news. Its final analysis: the rocket launch deemed a "complete failure." In the past, Chun had been struck by Kim Jong Il for far less minor offenses. No blow came from North Korea's dear

13

leader this time. Oddly, Chun never thought he'd miss Kim Jong Il's leadership. The constant terror used to keep order was hard to live with. But he did miss the order and in a sense the terror. For while Il ruled through fear, he did bring order and purpose to North Korea. Chun felt this purpose was slipping away.

Instead, Kim Jong Un chuckled and mumbled the words, "Complete failure."

The supreme leader stared hard at Chun, saying nothing for several moments.

Tick, tick, tick. The clock seemed to get louder.

"Even a bee sting in the right place can take down a bear," Un finally said.

"Excuse me?" Chun replied, confused.

"Never mind," Un said . "You are excused."

Chun audibly sighed. Spinning on his heels, he turned toward the door. *The boy leader is truly weak*, Chun thought. His fellow generals were right, Un's rule wouldn't last. Un's father never would have let such a public failure go unpunished.

It occurred to Chun that perhaps the military could use Un. But to what end? Yes, bringing South Korea to heel was a goal. She must be punished for her defiance of her northern masters. But after that? Korea was a peninsula, boxed in by the sea on three sides and China to the north. Where and how could it extend its empire? If Korea was to truly achieve its world potential, it would have to expand. Japan perhaps? Koreans had not forgotten about the humiliation, rape, and destruction the Japanese inflicted upon their people during World War II. Chun hated Japan, perhaps more than he hated the United States. Yes, Japan too would have to pay. After that? Maybe the idiot Chinese and Russians would be put under the boot of Korea's million man army. These two supposed super powers regularly slighted the Koreans, treating the country like an illegitimate child. They too should be made to suffer. That was plenty. Achieving Korean reunification and Japanese subjugation would take generations. But perhaps Chun would be the one to begin the process. Yes. He, Chun Yung Hun, would usher in Korea's rightful place in the world. Kim Jong Il was dead. Kim Jong Un was a joke. Chun could see that now.

Chun walked briskly toward the exit. He had plans to make.

The double doors at the far end of the office swung open before Chun reached them. Two armed guards blocked his progress, grabbing the missile defense chief before he knew what was happening. Chun was gripped by panic as he realized he was not to see the dawn. He knew he would be shot within the hour. "One must keep up appearances," Un said as his chief defense officer was led out the door to his fate.

Chapter 1
Yellowstone National Park, Grant
Village Ranger District: May 1, Late Morning

Grayson Cole had been a National Park ranger for nearly fifteen years and thought he had seen it all. Oblivious photographers who stepped too far forward or too far backward for the perfect shot, only to find themselves falling end over end down steep ravines. From scantily dressed teenagers in flip flops and booty shorts with wicked sunburns or multiple mosquito bites to frantic mothers and wild-eyed children separated and later reunited. Yes, he'd seen it all.

How many times had he been asked where the restrooms were located? What to do? Where to eat? What time? How long? How much?

It was his "flat hat", of course. The universal symbol of the park ranger adopted more than a hundred years ago when the U.S. Army patrolled national parks was what gave Cole authority and respect and invited all sorts of questions and all sorts of interest. There was also the fact that, now in his late thirties, he had been promoted to a coveted law enforcement position. It was his green and gray uniform, clip-on tie, golden badge, and the lettering on the side of his government-issued SUV that inspired all types of people to ask all sorts of questions and prompted typically shy people to slide up for souvenir photos they would proudly display for their friends at home. His uniform and marked truck caused other people – the kind of people who may have glove boxes full of traffic tickets or campers who may not have paid the park's modest campsite fees – to avert their eyes and *really* study the scenery at his approach.

Today, as lunchtime approached, Cole slowly patrolled the western shore of Yellowstone Lake. A few wispy high altitude clouds streaked an otherwise clear blue sky. The Absaroka Mountains were in the distance, a light dusting of new snow crowning their summits. Even though it was late spring, the snow was a reminder that winter never really left Yellowstone.

He studied the ridge line and the way the sun hits it just so. Daily, sometimes several times a day, Cole was awed by the sheer beauty and wonder of the park. Whether it was the way the air smelled when saturated with the scent of new wildflowers or how the steam from the geysers gave the park a mystical feel at sunset, there was always something to catch his imagination. Today, he was thinking about the rather incongruous history of the park. How could anyone have named this placed Colter's *Hell?*

John Colter, the first white explorer of the Yellowstone region, had been part of the Lewis and Clark expedition but left the Corps of Discovery on its return east. Colter had been with the expedition since it set out, but on the return trip his reservation about returning to civilization grew. The thought of living among weak, soft easterners turned his stomach. No, he'd stay out west. The corps had merely scratched the surface of the new western lands and Colter wanted to see more of it. He wanted to see it for himself. He had heard stories of entire mountain ranges made of glass, strange beasts, and canyons so wide one could yell *wake up* before going to bed and be awoken in the morning by the echo. But it was the tales told by the Native Americans that traveled with Lewis and Clark of a "cursed land" in the heart of the Rocky Mountains that most piqued his interest. Colter was determined to see it.

His curiosity was richly rewarded. Colter spent the next several years traversing the Wyoming wilderness, and was the first white man to see Yellowstone's Grand Canyon, its geyser basins, and heavily forested landscape. Colter was most impressed by the area's bison herds, herds that could take days to pass through.

Perhaps it was being chased by Indians who had stripped him naked before ordering him to run for his life, but Colter too eventually returned to civilization. Back in society, this original mountain man recounted his years in the wilderness, telling tales of Yellowstone's massive rivers, bountiful wildlife, and deep canyons. However, it was his startling account of the area's countless geysers, mud pots and hot pools that few easterners could believe. They dubbed the area Colter's Hell. The name stuck.

It wasn't until 1871, when Ferdinand Hayden led the first government sponsored Yellowstone expedition that proved much of Colter's account accurate. A year later, thanks to the testimony of Hayden and the paintings of world famous artist Thomas Moran, Congress established Yellowstone as the world's first national park.

Unknown to Colter, Hayden, and others at

the time of Yellowstone's establishment, "Hell"
proved an apt name for the area, given the volcano
that lay at the park's heart. It wasn't an ordinary
volcano, rather something modern scientists call a
super volcano with the ability to literally unleash
hell on earth. Even the smallest of Yellowstone's
eruptions dwarfed that of Mount St. Helens in
1980. Ash from these explosions, tens of feet
deep, has been found as far away as Arkansas and
Tennessee.

Thankfully that was all in Yellowstone's
past, its distant past. Humans had never seen its
volcanic fury and would not likely survive any
modern eruption.

Cole pulled his SUV into the parking lot of
the West Thumb Geyser Basin, a popular place for
hikers, families, and picnickers. Located on the far
western edge of Yellowstone Lake, the park's
largest lake, the West Thumb Basin is a thermal
area, an area full of spouting geysers, bubbling
mud pots, and picturesque hot pools made
accessible by a mile of wooden boardwalk.
Although its display was as spectacular as Old
Faithful, there were never large crowds. Cole got
out of the truck holding a walkie-talkie. Sure
enough, there was the male tourist his dispatcher
had called about, a thirty-something photographer
standing perilously close to a scalding hot geyser.
What had the guy been thinking when he stepped
off the boardwalk? That those warnings were just
decoration, or maybe only meant for the local
fauna?

A few years back, an oblivious group of
thirty Wisconsin tourists had brashly stepped off

the boardwalk at Old Faithful and walked directly up to the geyser's cone. Fortunately, it had been between eruptions, which occurred roughly every ninety minutes and propelled boiling water and steam a hundred fifty feet into the air. Had their timing been less lucky they could have all been boiled alive. Numerous signs and displays warned visitors to stay on marked trails and boardwalks yet somehow, and all too frequently, common sense seemed to take a vacation with some vacationers— like this guy.

The Park Service reacted to going off trail very seriously to protect plants and wildlife as well as the millions of visitors who made their way to western Wyoming each year. The wayward Wisconsin travelers, all of them, received citations and $200 fines, which surely weren't the nice mementos they may have hoped to take home.

Cole walked along the boardwalk toward the clueless tourist, concerned about his safety. Later he would write the guy a ticket. For now, he needed to get as close to the wayward man as possible without leaving the safety of the trail. He also needed to radio the park paramedics and get them to West Thumb – pronto. He spoke quietly and calmly into the radio, then returned it to the holder on his belt.

Cole called out to the tourist who was now even further off trail. "Stop right there," he ordered. The man took no notice as he adjusted the lens of his camera. "Sir! Stop right there," he repeated. This time the man looked up from his viewfinder toward Cole.

"What is it, Smokey?"

Clearly the guy didn't have a clue.

"Can I get you to stay where you are please?" Cole answered, with obvious concern in his voice. The man continued to pursue his subject, a nearby female elk with her fawn. The mother and fawn paid the tourist no heed, but Cole knew this could change at any moment. Most park visitors rightly came concerned about bears. Popular culture had done bears a disservice, portraying them either as warm adorable teddy bears or man eating horrifying beasts. The truth obviously was somewhere in between. But this public perception normally assured all but the craziest gave bears a wide berth. A few well publicized maulings had reinforced the public's fear. Never mind that in the past hundred years fewer than twenty people had been killed by North American bears while in comparison to the twenty people a *year* killed by domestic dogs.

However, few visitors came with any respect for Yellowstone's deer, elk, and bison populations. As a result, more people were injured each year by elk and bison than by bears—and would likely always be that way. People didn't expect Bambi to have an attitude. For that matter, many didn't even get the distinction between Bambi, a deer, and elk or bison. But if provoked, a thousand pound elk, or worse, two thousand pound bison, could maim or kill someone just as bad as a bear. Even though they would be just as dead, Cole guessed people feared these animals less because an elk or bison wasn't likely to eat them after their death.

"Stand still. Very still. Did you see the

signs about not leaving the trail?" Cole asked.

"Of course, but I thought that meant for hiking. I didn't think it applied to taking pictures of wildlife," the man replied.

"When the sign says don't leave the trail, it applies to *everyone*," Cole explained. "You see those geysers and hot springs right over there?"

The man nodded growing annoyed.

And how could he not see them, Cole thought. The bubbling and steaming hot springs were mere feet away. "The boiling water in those thermal features is brought to the surface by fractures and cracks in the earth's crust, an underground plumbing system of sorts."

The man looked at the geyser a few feet away.

"You see," Cole continued, "the problem is the Park Service doesn't know the exact location of all the cracks."

The errant tourist continued to adjust his camera, still not comprehending Cole's point.

"Making matters worse," Cole went on, "the pipes may be only a few inches below the surface. It's quite possible you are standing over millions of gallons of boiling hot water right now and all that separates you from that cauldron is a few inches of top soil."

Just then a nearby geyser erupted with a deep-throated roar, projecting boiling water at least twenty feet into the air. The elk and fawn bolted, heading off into a wooded glen. Hot mist rained down on the man.

The tourist now grasped the danger. Dropping his camera, he stammered, "Wha, wha, what should I do?"

"Well, there's no need to panic," Cole assured him. "I'll need you to carefully collect your camera and gear and join me here on the boardwalk."

The man snapped into action, jamming everything into his camera bag. Several wires and a roll of film protruded from the bag's compartments.

"Good. Now slowly begin walking over to where I'm standing," Cole commanded.

The man did as he was told, eyes wide with alarm.

"Now take a step forward and test the ground in front of you," Cole directed.

Like a soldier in a minefield, the tourist lifted his right leg very deliberately, extending his foot. Closing his eyes as if expecting to step on a bomb, he gingerly stepped forward. The soil crunched but held firm.

"Good job. Let's do it again," Cole encouraged.

The man repeated the process, transferring his weight from one foot to the other. He moved slowly, certain he could feel the ground weakening, but it held.

After five minutes of repeated baby steps, the stress began to affect the man. The park's extreme altitude and thin atmosphere weren't helping either. From his red face and labored breathing it was obvious he was struggling.

Another geyser erupted, again covering the man with a hot steamy mist.

Unable to handle the pressure of standing

up and being exposed any longer, the man got down on his belly and began to soldier-crawl the remaining distance. The ground was soaked in water, creating a large mud hole. The man struggled across the ground, covering himself in the sticky, stinky mud. Cole knew expensive outdoor clothing was likely ruined.

The length between the trespassing tourist and the boardwalk had been roughly 10 yards, yet it might as well have been a mile. It took him nearly 20 minutes to make it back to safety. By the time he reached the boardwalk a small crowd of curious onlookers had formed near Cole, captivated by the apparent life and death drama playing out before them. When the straying tourist finally reached the boardwalk, he collapsed like a pile of wet clothes, exhausted and mentally drained.

The park paramedics arrived just as the man buckled.

The first EMT on the scene went straight to the tourist, the other to Cole. "So, what's it this time?" she asked.

"This Ansel Adams wanna-be went off the boardwalk into the geyser field. It took twenty minutes for him to crawl back to the trail." Cole pointed to the tourist, who lay on the boardwalk with his eyes closed.

"Crawl? What the hell for?" she asked, a look of shock on her face.

"He didn't want to break through the crust into the geyser plumbing." Cole pointed to a spot just an arm's length or two away.

The other paramedic knelt next to the

downed tourist, applied an oxygen mask and gave his partner the thumbs up, mouthing, "He'll be OK."

The paramedic had a confused look on her face. "Grayson, that's an old road bed. The ground under there is solid as bedrock. It can hold a herd of bison. You know that."

Cole began to head back down the boardwalk toward his parked vehicle. After he was sure he was out of earshot of the downed hiker, he turned and winked. "Perhaps, but our photographer is not likely to go off trail again."

Chapter 2
Yellowstone National Park, Mammoth Hot Springs Natural Resource Laboratory, May 3, Mid-Afternoon

Dr. Jessica Drummond was Yellowstone National Park's natural resource management chief. The thirty-something mother of two was responsible for a staff of ten and for managing, as she liked to tell visitors, everything under the sun at Yellowstone. This was basically true. The resource management department managed the parks wildlife including its two hundred-plus grizzly bears, its millions of acres of forests, and thousands of miles of creeks, streams, rivers and lakes. She even had a hand in managing the role fire played in the park.

Dr. Drummond pinched herself daily about the good fortune that landed her the park service's premier resources management job. Drummond's job made her a hot commodity for television interviews and conference speaking engagements.

The general public's interest in Yellowstone never seemed to wane. The park had the ability to touch nearly everyone who visited it. It was as if Walt Disney had designed the park himself. If Disney had designed the park he couldn't have done better than Yellowstone. The world's first national park had it all. Spectacular scenery, towering waterfalls, massive canyons, and abundant wildlife all combined to give it a special place in America's heart.

She also knew the park's quaint historic buildings harkened back to a more romantic time.

Throw in the otherworldly aspects of the park, its geysers and hot springs, and one had the nearly perfect Disney-created environment with a new vista or discovery around every corner.

But Walt hadn't designed Yellowstone. The park wasn't Disneyland. Yellowstone was, in fact, a super volcano and beneath the park's postcard setting lay a killer capable of unleashing Armageddon.

During her countless speaking engagements and interactions with the park's visitors, it was apparent to Drummond that most humans went about their life blissfully unaware that beneath their feet was a superheated cauldron of immense pressure, and in some places molten rock. This hot core was left over from the formation of the planet billions of years ago. This heat is what made and continues to make life possible on the planet. Early volcanic eruptions spewed billions of tons of water vapor and oxygen and other gases. These elements seeded our oceans and atmosphere, preparing the way for single cell organisms to develop. Other planets, such as Mars, had similar histories. Their landscape was littered with the evidence of past volcanic eruptions. But their volcanoes were devoid of life today. Why?

The answer lay in the size of the other rocky planets. Mars, for example, was a small planet, roughly two-thirds the size of earth. Today it was desolate and devoid of surface water, with only a wispy remnant atmosphere consisting of mainly carbon dioxide. The red planet was too hostile to support life, or at least human life.

Like two muffins cooling after being taken out of the oven Mars, being the smaller muffin, cooled more quickly. Once Mars' core had frozen, the source of the planet's volcanic activity ceased. Thus no more gases going into the atmosphere, no more water or oxygen thrown to the surface where it could support life. It was only a matter of time, say a few billion years, for what remained of the Martian oceans to boil away and its atmosphere to bleed off into space. Today satellite images and probes provided hints of its possible glorious life supporting past.

This would be the earth's future, Drummond understood. But not today.

The Earth, being larger, took longer to cool. Its core still burns hot, powering the planet's volcanoes and feeding its atmosphere, oceans and sustaining life.

It has only been in the last hundred years that scientists have really come to grasp *why* volcanoes exist. The *where* they exist was equally perplexing. Early scientists discovered that volcanoes weren't randomly spread around the planet. Rather they were limited on earth to distinct hotspots or zones. The Pacific's ring of fire was the best known of these hot spots.

The question was why? Why were volcanoes concentrated in these select places?

Ancient cultures believed volcanic eruptions were the wars of angry gods. Northwest Native Americans saw the eruption of their snowcapped mountains as the fighting of jealous or furious lovers.

Modern science has replaced volcanoes'

myths with cold, hard scientific facts. It wasn't until the 1950's that German scientist Alfred Wegner's proposed theory of plate tectonics was truly accepted, finally answering the question. The earth's surface or crust, Wegner imagined, was much like the broken shell of an egg. The shell pieces float and ride on a super-heated core. In some places where a bit of shell bumps up against another, one piece is forced down under the other, known as a subduction zone. As the bit of shell is driven deeper into the core, it is subjected to intense heat and pressure, melting it. That melted rock, like hot air in a room, rises up through the overriding piece of shell, breaking through as volcanic eruptions.

The eruption's force depends on seemingly benign material known as silica. Silica, the microscopic ingredient in glass, in the volcano's magma determines whether an eruption will be quiet or violent. Silica affects how easily gases locked in the subterranean mantle escape. When the amounts of silica are minor, the trapped gas is emitted with less force and what follows are deemed quiet eruptions. Hawaiian volcanoes have very little silica. On the other hand, add more silica to a volcano's magma and violent eruptions take place. The magma of the volcanoes in the Pacific Northwest is heavily leaden with the little bits of glass. Thus more violent and explosive eruptions occur, such as the eruption of St. Helens in 1980.

Anthropologists believe modern humans have existed for roughly one hundred thousand years. During that time, society has evolved and learned to live with their fiery mountains.

Civilizations around the globe, from Asia to
Europe and to the Americas, have grown up in the
shadow of these monsters, learning to live with
their deadly neighbors. Yet, in a few instances the
relationship has turned deadly. Cities of Pompeii,
Italy and Thera, Greece were wiped entirely from
the face of the earth, killing hundreds of
thousands.

The Mount St. Helens eruption, the most
recent in the continental United States, took fifty-
seven souls. A minuscule number of human lives
given the two or three million people who live
within a few hundred miles of its crater.

All volcanoes have eruption cycles.
Eruptions literally take the fuel out of the
mountain. It takes time for the mountain to refill.
Volcanoes, such as Mount St. Helens, have a
roughly two hundred year eruption cycle, giving
humans plenty of time to develop and adapt to its
patterns.

Yellowstone wasn't Mount St. Helens,
Drummond knew. Its eruption cycle was
thousands of times longer. No modern human, at
least not one who could read, write, or really even
communicate, had seen its fury. Yet, the land in
the western United States tells the tale. West of
Yellowstone, in Idaho and Oregon, are hints of its
timeline. Large craters dozens of miles across are
spread in a line across these two states. Scientists,
before the theory of plate tectonics, thought them
to be vents from separate volcanoes. But as
humans deepened their understanding of the
earth's crust and its movement it became clear
these craters were evidence of past eruptions from

a single vent. It was assumed there was a hot spot
or magma chamber under the North American
plate's rocky mountain wilderness. This plate
moves west over the fixed hot spot at about the
same rate as finger nails grow. Like a slow moving
conveyor belt, the plate ceaselessly inches west.
Meanwhile, the hotspot fills with melted rock.
Pressure builds to unimaginable limits, heaving and
pushing the earth's surface upward until it cracks.
Gas and ash burst from these cracks, triggering
cataclysmic eruptions.

The source of these eruptions, the magma
chamber, is massive, larger than any chamber
previously known to modern science. Stretching
from Wyoming and Montana to well into Idaho
and diving hundreds of miles into the earth's crust,
the Yellowstone chamber has enough molten rock
to fuel an eruption for months, some say even
years.

But why here? Why the northwest corner
of Wyoming? Most volcanoes are clustered on the
edges of the tectonic plates. However,
Yellowstone is located on the interior of a plate.
Modern science appears to have solved this
mystery as well. Using seismic waves scientists
were able to measure Yellowstone's magma
chamber. They found that its chamber taps into a
magma plume that has risen to mere miles below
the earth's surface. The source of this super
volcano is not the result of two plates colliding as
is the case with most volcanoes, but rather a
massive vent of magma that effectively forced its
way up through the center of the plate.

The previous Yellowstone craters, like a

black pearl necklace, stretch two hundred fifty miles to the west. Volcanologists using sophisticated models calculate the interval between blasts by analyzing the distance between the craters. The rough estimate is six hundred thousand years. Thus modern humans have never experienced its blast. They have no experience of its power.

In most places around the world, the volcanic monster was adequately caged or at least understood. The molten rock of most volcanoes was dozens of miles below the surface. But at Yellowstone it has found a crack, a way to the surface. Hints of its destructive potential are sprinkled throughout the park, like clues left behind by a serial killer--geysers here and mud pots there.

Beneath Yellowstone's surface, the earth's temperature quickly rises. Rising molten rock from a mantle plume protrudes toward the surface like the red-hot tongue of a giant dragon. The tongue heats the surrounding rock. Rainwater falling on the Yellowstone landscape seeps into the park's broken and fractured ground, working its way toward the dragon's lair. The water becomes superheated, rushing back to the surface in awe-inspiring spouts of boiling water. A single drop of water falling on the park today may take up to a thousand years to burst to the surface in one of the park's geysers or hot springs.

Traveling deeper still, the solid rock is melted, forming the magma chamber for the super volcano. In most areas of the country this molten rock is deep within the earth. A typical car trip to the hellish underworld would take hours. At Yellowstone the drive takes minutes. Scientists using sophisticated computers and monitors were surprised and horrified to discover the Yellowstone magma chamber extends hundreds of miles beneath the surface. This massive dragon's belly could produce hell on earth. Walt Disney even in his wildest dreams could not have fantasized a more terrifying monster. Like warm air rising to the ceiling of a room, the molten rock in the magma plume moves toward the earth's surface, pushing up the crust, causing cracks, bulges, and, more importantly, earthquakes.

Some believe the dragon dead, its fury not seen in millennia. It was not dead. It was very much alive. What Drummond didn't know was that it was about to emerge from its hellish lair.

A small L shaped needle snapped and scratched a spiked line on the seismograph's drum of white graph paper. "Hey, we've got another one," shouted Tom Reynolds, Yellowstone's chief volcanologist, as he pointed at the seismograph. Tall and lanky, a classic computer nerd, Tom paced the small cluttered lab.

Drummond put down her mug of herbal tea, got up from her chair and approached the still twitching seismograph. Yellowstone still used an analog seismograph even though digital machines were far more accurate. She was old school and liked the look and feel of what might be considered vintage equipment. And quite frankly, she liked the sound of the scratching needle on paper. The scratching reminded her of a quill pen on paper, as if someone were writing a letter. The importance of the letter could be determined merely by the fervor of the needle's scraping.

Drummond had spent years in school studying earthquakes triggered by the movement of molten rock. She was now stationed in the most prolific place for potential volcanic action. Lectures, long lectures on the history of Yellowstone quakes, were her forte. And always she was asked, *When? When will this place blow?*

She studied the location of each quake, the type of crust that was impacted, and the depth of the epicenter, all of which indicated the size of the quake. But truth be told, nothing was more reliable in determining quake size or scope than the simple scratch, scratch of the seismograph. The more scratching, the larger the quake. It was that simple. Although surely she wouldn't tell that to the universities and corporations who paid her modest honorariums and speaking fees for her seismic presentations. At thirty-three she was well-regarded and respected, a fact that may have been assisted by her prematurely graying hair that was always pulled back in a ponytail.

"Wow. That's the third big quake this week," she said. "Let's take a look at the monitors to see how deep it is."

Dr. Drummond knew these earthquakes could be trouble. Tremors in the park were up sharply the past several weeks. Molten rock was obviously moving under the park. *Could this spell the beginning of an eruption cycle? How would we know,* she thought. Her gut told her the recent events were unprecedented. Something strange was happening at the park. The Shoshone Lake and

Norris Geyser Basin had seen significant rumblings. If she had to guess, a Yellowstone eruption was more likely today than yesterday. But did that mean there would be an eruption tomorrow? Should the park be evacuated? Should the western United States be evacuated? Where would the people go? How far would the people have to get to be safe? The 1980 eruption of Mount St. Helens devastated lands up to 18 miles from the volcano. The Yellowstone volcano was hundreds of times bigger. The Yellowstone blast zone could be catastrophic, leaving much of America uninhabitable for decades. Would anyplace be safe?

These questions swirled through Drummond's head, but they weren't for her to answer. Thank God. Her job was to collect information, analyze it to the best of her ability, and present it to people higher up the government ladder. Occasionally, some decision makers like a park superintendent would ask her opinion, but she knew the decision lay elsewhere. Reynolds and Drummond walked to the other side of the lab and sat at the Sinclair Vulcan 2020 computer, a state-of-the-art monitoring system designed for a single purpose, to track and monitor Yellowstone earthquakes. Designed by Sinclair Enterprises, the multi-million dollar computer seemed out of place in what resembled a high school chemistry lab. Dated typewriters, old-fashioned microscopes, bulky radios and other antique research equipment littered the room's hodge-podge of desks and tables. Research papers, an analog phone, and spiral notebooks covered Drummond's work station. The public would be shocked to know how antiquated most of the Park Service's monitoring tools actually were.

The sheer cost of the Vulcan computer and more than a hundred monitoring stations located throughout the park emphasized the importance of this technology. The super volcano beneath Yellowstone plunged seven hundred miles toward the earth's core. If unleashed it could smother half a dozen western states in scalding hot lava while decimating the rest of the United States with thick toxic ash. So there it sat, the Vulcan, designed to track and monitor the movement of the super volcano's molten heart.

Scanning the Vulcan's readout, Drummond and Reynolds could see the quake's epicenter below Shoshone Lake near the newly formed Centennial Geyser Basin. This was troubling. Drummond let out a long whistle. "From these readings it's obvious the magma chamber is expanding, swelling upward. What do you think, Tom?" Before he could answer, she continued. "Look here." She pointed to the running ticker at the bottom of the monitor. "Geyser activity is up five percent throughout the park. Water temperatures are up an average of 2 degrees. Ground displacement is up throughout the caldera. A massive dome is growing."

"What do we do?" Reynolds asked, obvious worry spreading across his face.

"This is above our pay grade," Dr. Drummond admitted. "I think it's time we saw the Park Superintendent."

Chapter 3
White House Oval House, Washington
D.C.: May 12, Early Morning

It was shaping up to be a beautiful spring day in
the nation's capital. Sunlight was just starting to
glide over the white marble of the Lincoln
Memorial. The last reminders of winter snow had
melted weeks before. It had been a long hard
winter, and green was just returning to the White
House's southern lawn. Beyond the Washington
Monument, Japanese Cherry trees around the
Potomac tidal basin were just a few weeks away
from blooming. Vehicles of every sort could be
seen zooming over the city's streets. Across town
countless government employees, lobbyists, and
business owners were starting their day. Yet, for
one man, the day's business was well underway.

John Paine sat behind the iconic desk
within the Oval Office. Smithsonian curators had
told him the massive desk was the same that Teddy
Roosevelt had used during his presidential years in
the White House.

President Paine, in his late 50s, was going
gray. His graying, however, was mild compared to
previous occupants of the office. For that he was
thankful. He chalked it up to his love of being the
chief executive. The media also noted and
commented on this exuberance, sometimes with
kudos, but on the conservative stations generally
with some suspicion.

Not even yet the official start of his day
and the president had already loosened his tie. It
was going to be a long morning. He wouldn't have

to make a public appearance until this afternoon, so he would forego the tie for now.

John Paine had a vision for the country, one that included a fair shake for the American citizen, a healthy skepticism of the accumulation of private power, and a focus on domestic policy over foreign. President Paine believed in his vision of America, and if the previous election was any indication so did the American public. And on their behalf he was willing to fight for that vision. Paine was a student of history and knew successful social change, such as civil rights or women's suffrage, came from leaders who held a strong vision and fought for it. Leaders such as Martin Luther King were revered today for their unbending commitment to a cause, not for their willingness to compromise. Paine understood that compromise was necessary in some political fights, but on the big matters, the ones that really mattered, the public would reward a fighter even if that fighter lost.

The extreme right had learned this lesson. The Tea Party movement had a vision, a bad one, but a vision. They believed in it and would not compromise on its legislative agenda. That was the secret of their success.

Today's liberal leaders had forgotten this secret. Over the past thirty years they traded the push for social change for access to power, the theory being that liberals would be able to effect more change from within. At first this access opened many doors, doors that allowed one to mingle with powerful men and women. It also opened doors to endless cocktail parties and black-tie galas, fundraisers and receptions. The access felt good, powerful, intoxicating. A drug really. Regrettably, intoxication wears off and with it its ability to hide unfortunate realities. To maintain the power high, the powerful required the liberal leaders to tone down their drive, their passion for social change. The parties quickly transformed from providing a means to change to serving as a drug to avoid troubling truths.

This tradeoff had additional costs. With access to power came an expectation to be mainstream, corporate. A mainstream corporation at America's heart was built to protect stability, to avoid risk. But social progress was never made by avoiding risk, it required risk.

Paine knew this. Paine knew it was better to fight for what was best for the country and lose, than win what wasn't. This didn't make the president popular with the opposition, or even some in his own party, but the president was clear he wasn't in office to win popularity contests. He was in office to secure progressive social change. He believed in winning elections and the president was willing to do all things legal to triumph in political fights. Paine had realized these things were not mutually exclusive.

This position caused waves. But in reality what the opposition had the most trouble with were Paine's principled stands on issues he deeply believed were in America's best interest. How could he do otherwise? He was uncompromising. Paine called it moral. This stance struck some in Washington as naïve. Others called his unbending position as dirty. So be it. Others called him

America's North Star for his fixed position on core matters. He liked that. He liked being president as well.

President Paine was always skeptical of previous occupants of this office who publicly proclaimed their dislike for the job. President Paine never really believed these pronouncements. No one who ever served as president didn't love it. Those men *wanted* to be president and many more did as well.

Paine enjoyed the perks. Yet, despite the trappings and pampering, President Paine had not changed since first entering the office. He kept a laser-like focus on his purpose, which was inscribed on a small desk plaque—*Lead the nation*. Staying focused on this purpose helped him find the joy in the job. He was President of the United States. Only forty five men had held this title, the most elite fraternity ever. He pinched himself on a regular basis. There were bad days, but there were far more good ones.

John Paine also loved politics and he knew, despite assertions to the contrary, all previous occupants enjoyed the political battle too. If they didn't, they really shouldn't have been in the White House. The American public deserved no less.

The president's day was shaping up like many others. It was 7 a.m. and he had just finished his first morning meeting, a briefing by Garrett Thomas, Secretary of Defense (DOD), and Stephen Watson, Director of the CIA, on the failed Korean rocket launch and the results of the recovery effort. Both the DOD and CIA agreed that the North Korean missile launch appeared to be an utter failure. However, since the missile was based on apparently antiquated technology the result was not surprising. Yet, critical rocket components had not been recovered, making a complete analysis impossible. Despite this, the DOD and CIA's best guess was that North Korea did not have the ability to hit the mainland United States with nuclear or conventional tipped weapons. They could strike Hawaii or Alaska perhaps, but not California.

"That's good news," the president stated, leaning back in his chair. "Keep me informed, though, of any changes. I don't trust Un. It's possible we are being played."

Paine stood, so did his advisors. Watson and Thomas exited through the oval office's main exit. The president headed toward the glass door leading out into the Rose Garden. He gazed out upon the south lawn, grass starting to poke up through the last of the winter snow. The president had grown up in the west. He was used to the wide open spaces of the Rocky Mountain west. The White House's backyard was now his outdoors and he didn't even get out there all that often. Well, except when he was walking to Marine One or rolling eggs during Easter. He enjoyed the south lawn, but it just wasn't a truly wild place. Yes, according to the Park Service, at one time the White House grounds had the highest concentration of ground squirrels of any park. So, the executive mansion had that going for it. That still didn't make it a wild place. Unfortunately too many Americans, especially many congressmen and senators, considered places like the south lawn or the capital mall, the stretch of grass between the Lincoln Memorial and the capitol dome, wild space. To these people the Wyoming backcountry might as well have been the dark side of the moon.

A robin flitted about the budding White House oaks. A sense of melancholy came over the president. He missed the Rocky Mountains. He missed open spaces, and in turn lands devoid of civilization's heavy hand. It occurred to the president that there were more people living within a five minutes' drive of the White House than in all of Montana. The president was always amazed that so many people would want to live in proximity to each other. He was glad they did because that meant there was space left for places like Yellowstone. But he also considered that Wyoming and other wild places existed because good men and women worked in Washington D.C. Until the country moved its capital to Laramie or Denver he'd have to live among millions of people to protect places like the national parks.

The Oval Office door was pushed open. Stephanie Van Dyke, his personal secretary, poked her head in. "Sorry to bother you, sir, but Secretary Matson is here for your next appointment."

The president was pulled from his thoughts. Turning back toward his desk, Paine saw one of his best friends, Phillip Matson, walk through the door.

Matson was Secretary of Interior, responsible for managing nearly one third of the United States. The Interior Secretary's portfolio included oversight of the nation's wildlife reserves,

reclamation lands, and national parks, including
Yellowstone. It was one of the most diverse
assignments in the federal government, a job that
required his oversight of issues as diverse as
endangered species management, reclamation of
large western areas such as that around Grand
Coulee dam, and regulation of surface mining. But
it was the oversight of the national parks that Paine
knew Matson enjoyed the most.

Matson was 61 years old and had spent
much of his adult life in public service. The
secretary was slightly overweight from a few too
many Washington cocktail parties. His round face
and receding hairline were evidence that his looks
had seen better days. Like the president, Secretary
Matson believed government could be a positive
force in people's lives. Matson had jumped at the
chance to lead the Department of Interior when
President Paine had approached the Washington
native about the job. Matson had then been the
Governor of Washington State. His
administration had enacted progressive reforms
including sweeping state conservation measures
which caught the eye of presidential candidate
Paine five years back. Resistance to Matson
joining the Paine Administration had come from a
few senators, mainly those from Idaho and
Nevada, who claimed the progressive Governor
couldn't represent *western issues* since he wasn't truly
from the West. Matson knew that being from the
west was code for states that valued ranching,
mining, and timber interests over all others.
Matson saw it more as bending over. During his
confirmation hearing, Governor Matson had

reminded these senators that the Evergreen State lies on the United States' *west* coast. Moreover, given Washington State's unique location in the union, Matson considered all states but Oregon, California, Alaska and Hawaii as being part of the East. The press and public ate it up and all but ended opposition to his confirmation.

The secretary walked into the office and extended his right hand. The two men shook hands. "Hey Phil, great to see you again," the president said warmly. "Can I get you anything?"

"Coffee would be great," Matson replied. The president nodded to a Navy steward who set off to get the refreshments.

Both men took a seat on the Oval Office's couch. Matson had a sense of awe come over him every time he entered the Oval Office. Great men, FDR, JFK, and Reagan, had worked in this room. History had been made and changed countless times in this office. The strategy for defeating the Nazis and the Soviets had been plotted in this very room.

It was hard not to be taken over by the sweep of history, to not be overwhelmed by its scope and the life-and-death matters debated and settled in this room. Matson was really glad he wasn't president. He was especially glad he wasn't required to make a decision about the information he was about to present to the president.

The threat was different than any other danger confronting the country. It had the potential to destroy the country at any time, and there was no good solution. No real answer to this threat. This wasn't the American way. Americans

were an optimistic bunch. They believed every
problem had a solution and given enough time
they would find it. Unfortunately, the real world
didn't operate this way. There were some
problems that had no good solution.

The American public, as much as they
denied it, had come to expect the federal
government to find a solution to nearly every
problem. If the stock market crashed, the
Securities and Exchange Commission would enact
new regulations to correct the markets. If the gulf
coast became fouled with millions of gallons of
spilled crude oil, the Coast Guard would clean up
the mess. If a strain of a previously unknown virus
swept across the planet, the Centers for Disease
Control would isolate the contagion and cure it. It
had always been and always would be.

There are some problems the federal
government and the American public couldn't
fight. Matson knew the best that could be done
was to manage the damage. He would never tell
the public this, but things like giant catastrophic
forest fires or asteroid strikes fit this category.
Matson had fought wildfires out in Washington in
his youth. Over the past one hundred years the
public had come to expect the Forest Service and
the Park Service to fight all wildfires. The feds
had gotten extremely efficient at suppressing fire.
The unofficial firefighting motto was, *out by the next
day*. But that efficiency led to a dangerous buildup
of fuels, laying the seeds for the catastrophic fires
of today. Matson, with the help of conservation
organizations, was slowly changing public policy,
reintroducing fire to the forests. The payoff,

unfortunately for a public used to problems being solved now, won't be realized for a couple generations. Matson knew though that the payoff would be realized, and that's how he withstood the slings and arrows of Congress and detractors.

Sadly, Matson understood there were some problems beyond even the people's ability to solve, even for the foreseeable future. Matson knew the American psyche was penetrated with the optimistic belief that problems created by humans could be solved by humans. Matson believed this mantra as well. Human problems in general tended to have understandable causes and solutions. Sometimes the solutions were difficult, but there was a course of action. Timeframes for human-caused problems were manageable and easily dividable by election cycle. But what about problems, threats, not created by people? Humans may not have the ability to comprehend the true threat, let alone the correct course of action. Even if humanity grasped the problem and the solution, the ability to act on that solution may require technology that wouldn't be developed for generations. Not being able to act, and to act now, is unacceptable to Americans. If the first American commandment was that all problems can be solved, then the second was, don't sit there, do something, even if that something was akin to pissing on a house fire. The public expected the president to pee. The greatest risk to the president wasn't trying and failing, it was not trying, even if that action took scarce resources needed elsewhere to actually meet the challenge.

President Paine suspected from the look

on his friend's face the information the secretary carried today was one of those non-human caused problems. It wasn't some foreign force threatening invasion. Paine almost wished that was the case. Fighting all the world's armies and even a few alien ones at the same time would be an easier challenge than the one he feared Matson was about to present. Yet, unknown to the commander in chief he was about to learn the country faced an even larger threat to national security. Perhaps the greatest threat the country had ever faced.

When the Yellowstone Superintendent alerted Secretary Matson just a few days ago about the growing Yellowstone threat, Secretary Matson had seriously considered not telling the president. There really wasn't anything Paine could do if the danger became a reality, at least not yet. So, what was the point of passing on the information, Matson had asked himself. Would he needlessly burden the man with a problem he could do little or nothing about? Paine was in a testing election fight and needed to devote as much of his mental ability to winning the November vote.

Ultimately, Matson decided the president must be told, if for no other reason than to begin preparations should the menace be delayed. But this was of little comfort, wasn't it? Delay was really all they could hope for. The threat would be realized. If not today, and maybe not tomorrow, but it was coming. If the country--no, the world, really--had some time, say five hundred years, then humans might be ready to weather the coming disaster. *Might* was the operative word. Humanity had never faced a threat like this. But another five centuries should be enough. By that time some technology may have been developed to prevent the disaster, or more likely, humans will have colonized Mars or some other planet to hedge the threat to humanity's survival.

Yet, the Park Service reports of the past day had tipped the scale toward alerting the president. Things had taken a turn for the worse at the world's first national park.

The president could see the secretary take a deep breath, as if about to jump off an extremely high dive. The president hoped for both their sake the water wasn't too deep.

"So what's on the agenda for today, I hope it has something to do with the Yellowstone wolf recovery," President Paine prodded, hoping to preempt today's meeting with good news. The Yellowstone wolf recovery had been one of the nation's most successful endangered species programs and President Paine had played a small part in the process when he served as senator from Montana.

"Unfortunately, no," Matson replied. "Although the wolves are doing quite well, so well in fact that Idaho and Montana are clamoring to shoot them as fast as they leave the park. They've filed several federal lawsuits to end the program. All legal efforts have failed. The DOI will continue to vigorously defend the wolves."

"Glad to hear it." Paine said.

The Navy steward returned with a silver serving tray of coffee. He placed it on the coffee table, poured cups for the president and the secretary, then left. Matson dropped a sugar cube into his coffee and took a drink.

"While I'm not here to talk about Yellowstone's wolves, I do have a number of items to discuss." At that the secretary handed the president an agenda that included discussion of the state of several western wildfires, hard rock mining reform, and tsunami threats to several western tribes.

At the completion of the agenda, the secretary asked if he could discuss an additional item. Yellowstone Park. The president nodded as Matson spread a large topographical map of the nation's first park on the Roosevelt desk.

"Less than a week ago, National Park volcanologists recorded a troubling series of shallow earthquakes under Yellowstone Lake, near the West Thumb Geyser Basin. Roughly here." Matson pointed to a western bay of the large alpine lake.

"As you know, earthquakes in the greater Yellowstone ecosystem are a fairly common occurrence. The park has a 3.0 magnitude earthquake nearly every week. However, what makes these unique is their sheer number and that they are centered near the earth's surface, about 3 miles down. I won't bore you with the details," Matson continued, "but a swarm of shallow earthquakes means the park's magma chamber is moving." That got the president's attention. He nearly spit out his coffee in the process.

Having served Montana for three terms in the Senate, the president was well aware the park was a super volcano with a violent and horrifying history of cataclysmic eruptions, eruptions that on average produced thousands of metric tons of ash.

"It gets worse," Matson went on. "The volcano's magma chamber is larger than first thought." Matson placed a computer generated image of the volcano's core in front of the president. "Originally, scientists believed it stretched roughly one hundred fifty miles to the west. New research out of the University of Utah shows the subterranean plume actually stretches over four hundred miles, well into the state of Idaho."

The president just stared at the secretary, thinking. "Oh my God," finally escaped his lips. He was no volcanologist but he knew that moving molten magma would likely be one indicator of a pending eruption.

"Park Service personnel recently discovered a new geyser basin," the secretary continued. "It's roughly centered near Shoshone Lake, about here on your map." Matson took another drink of coffee before going on. "The new basin is being unofficially named the Centennial Basin after the Park Service's pending 100th birthday."

The president nodded his approval. "I like it."

Secretary Matson went on, "Park Service scientists believe something unprecedented in recent history is happening. As I stated, earthquake frequency is up significantly, geyser activity and intensity has increased, yet here is what is most interesting."

The secretary handed the president a large satellite picture of Yellowstone Lake. "The blue lines ringing the lake represent the historic lakeshores. Here is the most recent lakeshore line. From all indications the lake shore is moving south." That didn't strike the president as particularly strange. Water bodies and their shorelines moved all the time. As the president knew, Lake Michigan's shoreline had moved several miles over the past thousand years.

The secretary could see that the president wasn't grasping the significance. He made it plainer. "Sir, these two shorelines are only two weeks apart.

"Two weeks. How can that be?"

"Our best guess is the park's magma chamber is moving up and displacing the northern portion of the lake, pushing the water to the south. It's what happens when one lifts the side of a pool, the water moves to the other end."

"So, if I've got this right, Yellowstone is experiencing a swarm of earthquakes, increased geyser activity, and a massive lake is being lifted at one end?"

"Correct."

The president got to the point. "Does the National Park Service and the United States Geological Survey believe an eruption is imminent?"

"No, however. . . ," the secretary trailed off.

"And?" The president was getting angry.

"However," and here is why Matson ultimately decided to tell the president of the Yellowstone threat, "any unanticipated event, say a massive earthquake or large meteor strike, could create crust fractures triggering an eruption. This is highly unlikely though."

"Okay. Sum it up. What are we looking at?" the president asked.

"Best case. If Yellowstone were to erupt today as it did six hundred thirty thousand years ago," the secretary paused and referred to a Park Service report to make sure he got the next information right. "An eruption that could last weeks or months. Burial of roughly a third of the United States in tens of feet of ash. Buildings would be crushed. Depending upon prevailing winds, total destruction of the Midwest's food production. And climate change the likes of which the planet has not seen in hundreds of thousands of years. Millions of people will be killed outright or starve to death in the ensuing weeks after the eruption. In a nutshell, it would destroy the country."

"That's the *best* case," the president asked sarcastically. "Okay, what's the worst case?"

"An eruption could destroy civilization as we know it."

Chapter 4
Spokane Washington, Red Lion Hotel Parking Lot: May 26, Night

A hooded figure sat waiting in his idling car, parked at the far, deserted end of the Spokane Red Lion's parking lot. It was dark and the car's occupant, Jamil Ali Hussain, was cold. He was also excited. The last dozen or so years had led him to this night. All the sacrifice, all the stress, and all the time within enemy territory were coming to an end.

Hussain was in his thirties, but his recent time in America behind enemy lines had aged him. He was tired and ready to go home. America's stench, vice, and corruption were getting to him. But it was almost over. Allah would provide him strength.

Hussain was al Qaeda. He was the very kind of operative the United States government feared lived within the continental United States, a sleeper agent awaiting activation orders. Tonight he would be activated.

Hussain had converted to Islam later in life, but once exposed to the one true faith his zeal burned bright. His devotion to Allah was solidified after he witnessed the countless slaughters of school children, wedding parties, and bystanders at the hands of western soldiers. In every instance American brass apologized, stating that mistakes had been made. However, it made little difference to those killed and their families. Further, these apologies never seemed to change American behavior, so there was a never ending slaughter of

innocents. With Allah's help, Hussain would end
this injustice.

After the United States' invasion of Iraq,
Hussain fought against coalition forces in
Afghanistan where he distinguished himself. His
bravery and heroism eventually caught the eye of
Osama Bin Laden.

Hussain would be groomed to be the
perfect sleeper agent. An agent that, once inserted
into America, would disappear among its
perversion and depravity. Hussain's handlers made
their potential sleeper agent study American
history. *"To destroy an enemy's future, one must
understand his past,"* they taught. Hussain dove into
the assignment with abandon.

A small shack became Hussain's history
classroom. Its exterior was well maintained, with a
manicured lawn and fresh coat of paint. The
inside was another story. Rotting boards littered
the floor, the drywall was damaged, and wall paint
was chipped or missing. The whole room smelled
of decaying wood and dirt. Hussain couldn't help
but suspect the building was a metaphor for the
United States. During his time in the *school room*
Hussain had been taught the romantic version of
American history. All its leaders--Thomas
Jefferson, George Washington, Abe Lincoln--were
enlightened, selfless leaders. America was, as
Ronald Reagan once said, the shining city on a hill.

But Hussain's teachers made him delve
deeper into America's past, into the dark corners
of her history, to the hidden areas Americans
didn't want to face or even acknowledge.

America, Hussain was told, rightly worried

about threats from within, but its attention was always pulled in multiple directions. Hussain knew the American political system was excellent at dispelling tensions. The system was designed to prevent revolutions, and always had with the exception of the civil war. The founding fathers knew factions were the way to keep a democracy alive. Multiple factions would jockey and vie for power. Political coalitions would form and dissolve, making it impossible for any one group to gain ultimate power. However, what was needed to make the system work was a constant state of political combat, an endless list of enemies.

At first, America's enemies had been the European colonial powers, Hussain's teachers showed. America was birthed from these nations. Like a child rejecting its parents, it was only natural that America's first enemies would be the British and the French. In the 1800's America threw in the Spanish for good measure. The Mexicans next felt America's wrath. Later that same century Americans turned upon itself in a civil war. Fifty years later it was the Germans, then the Austrians, the Italians, and Japanese. Soon afterward the Soviets, the North Koreans, Vietnamese, and Chinese took center stage in succession. Throughout this entire history, America did its best to exterminate any native peoples who stood between the country's perceived manifest destiny.

After the defeat of every enemy a new, even more menacing, foe was identified and the battle continued. Yet something changed in 1989, his handlers taught. The collapse of Russian communism threw the American government into disarray. Or more precisely, the organizing effect of an external enemy was thrown into chaos. A new threat was needed to keep its political systems running. "But who?" the handlers asked. "Which nation could take the place of the Soviet Union, a country that possessed the power to physically destroy the United States?"

"The question is flawed," Hussain answered. "It assumes the new threat has to be a nation-state."

The handlers' lessons drove Hussain deeper into American antiquity. At its core, the American government was designed to protect its citizens from external threats. This makes sense, Hussain was told, given its founding in revolution. The country's founding document, the Constitution, established five goals for the federal government, but in its two centuries of existence, protecting its citizens from external threats became the central focus.

Yet, in the last fifty years while an external threat had remained constant, Americans themselves had changed, they taught. Americans' access to information had increased. Their willingness to accept politicians' pronouncements had eroded. Historians point to the Vietnam debacle as forever altering Americans' acceptance of endless villains.

The rise in Soviet power allowed the U.S. political system to brush off its citizens' concerns. The façade would be maintained for several more years. Who in their right mind could deny that a godless country with an army that defeated the Nazis and now, backed by nuclear weapons, was a

threat to America's survival? However, by the end
of the 80's the Soviet system had collapsed under a
tidal wave of corruption and bad decisions.
Historians and political pundits hailed it a
watershed moment, a victory for freedom over
oppression. But as the Soviet system sank, so too
did the American government's ability to focus
Americans' natural tendency to quarrel on an
external threat. American factions which had for
more than two hundred years been fairly
harmonious began to turn upon themselves.
Government leaders realized a new adversary was
needed.

"What happened next, Jamil?" the teachers
had asked.

"September 11th," Hussain answered
matter of fact.

"Correct. Islam would now be cast into
America's bad guy role."

Since the 18th century the United States
ticked off a list of enemies concentrated in the
northern hemisphere. Great Britain, France,
Germany, Russia. This focus was not intentional.
These countries just happened to threaten
America's soul. Not its spiritual soul. America
had never been worried about defending that from
external threats. Rather, these powers threatened
its true soul, commerce. These powers threatened
America's access to raw materials, its ability to
transport those resources to American factories,
and ship finished goods around the world.
America could put up with many things, but if a
country blocked or merely threatened its ability to
make a buck, that would not stand.

Decade after decade, all of America's adversaries were brought to heel, brought to understand the error of their ways. Commerce was king. Trade was good. At least, from the American point of view, there was enough to go around if all played by the rules. America was the new world and a new organizing force would be imposed upon its old world brethren. Don't interfere with the flow of goods, and all will be fine. England, France, Germany, Japan, even Russia, once bitter enemies, were eventually turned into friends. This is the way it should be.

"What's the lesson, Jamil?" his teachers asked.

"Countries that share similar belief systems can eventually work out their differences," he replied to the pride of his teachers.

Islam, or at least the Islamic Libya, had nearly followed this path toward friendship, Hussain was taught next. The Barbary pirates based on the North African coastline had disrupted commerce soon after America's founding. President Jefferson saw these pirates as a grave threat, so grave that he dispatched his infant navy clear across the Atlantic to protect America's growing interests. Diplomats were dispatched as well. Freedom of the seas was at the heart of the conflict. The crisis was only averted after the United States assured Tripoli that the conflict was not between Christianity and Islam. The United States was not a nation founded on the Christian religion, or so its peace offer assured. Problem solved.

The cultures that dot the shores of the

Mediterranean are thousands of years older than
that of America. Their time horizon stretches back
to before that of Christ. Americans are a forgive-
and-forget lot. They had things to build, places to
go, lands to plow, and forests to clear. Ancient
quarrels couldn't be allowed to stand in the way of
progress.

But Islam and its believers were different.
The settling of ancient quarrels wasn't one of many
priorities, it was the only priority. Everything
would be resolved from this effort. Muslims'
memory was better and longer. There would be
no turning of the other cheek. Its jihad with
America wasn't based upon a competition for
resources, although they had that fight with the
west too. No, this war was a spiritual conflict for
the world's soul. Islam saw America as a land of
infidels in need of conversion or death, not a
market of consumers to be opened. These
different world views resulted in different rules for
battle, different goals.

America had never faced a threat like this.
Nazi Germany or Imperial Japan had come close.
They had wanted world domination and to convert
conquered peoples to their twisted world view, but
at their heart the Axis powers' imperial motivations
had been about industry and business. Yes,
Japanese and German armies were wrapped in the
trappings of holy orders. Axis politicians
promoted their armies' conquests as evidence of
the blessing of the higher power. But the religious
trappings were for the masses. A simple way to
convince wavering mothers and fathers to send
their sons off to die for the economic dreams of

the Emperor or the Fuehrer. But religious impulse wasn't the true motivation of these countries' action. Germany's access to Lebensraum, living space, was her true incentive, as it was for Japan. America could understand Germany's and Japan's impulses. It too shared the desire to push its frontiers. The Axis' fatal crime was that they took by force the resources that America identified for itself. Japan's sinking of America's Pacific fleet couldn't go unpunished either.

Islam's threat to America was different. Islam doesn't want America's oil, its land, or even its people. It wants America destroyed. America was the great Satan, for it threatened Allah's plan for the spread of Islam. America must not be allowed to exist. The great Satan cannot be negotiated with. Islamic diplomats would not be sent to meet with the devil's minions. Jihad, righteous war, was needed to deal with the devil. There would be no negotiated truce, no peace treaty. When these two world views collided, only one would survive. The actual conclusion of the war may take countless generations, but Islam's true believers were patient.

America wasn't ready for this type of conflict. Ten years of war was about all the soft American public could stomach. In the coming holy war, Americans' stamina was to be tested as it had never been. And it would be found deficient.

Mohammed, Allah's last prophet, began the fight with the world's infidels more than a millennium before. What was another thousand years of warfare to Allah's warriors? Hussain and al Qaeda knew the rules of war and its time horizons had changed. America apparently did not.

Like most al Qaeda foot soldiers, Hussain also received basic training--learning to fly, build bombs, and engage in hand to hand combat. But after he was pulled from the Middle Eastern battlefield, Hussain's training was augmented. He was taken to the historic site of Ulmar at the foot of the Alborz Mountains on the Caspian Sea. There his training included non-traditional subjects such as psychology, geology, and Islamic history. He also received drill instruction in other countries including Yemen, Colombia and North Korea. It was at Ulmar, however, where Hussain was inducted into the sect of the Nazerites, a Muslim cult dating back to the 11th century.

The Nazerites were skilled assassins. Their history was full of daring political killings, including the murder of Raymond II in 1152, the great-grandson of the leader of the First Crusade. Raymond was slain by infiltrators disguised as Catholic monks.

"When your force was small, deception was the key to victory," Hussain was told. And deception would be critical to Hussain's current mission.

Hussain's devotion to Islam would also be key to success. He was a devout Muslim without question, but he held non-conventional beliefs. Hussain didn't believe in commonly held miracles. He was a man of science. He knew Allah didn't part seas, turn water into wine, or even carry the prophet to heaven on a white horse. Science revealed that Allah didn't bend the natural laws.

Traditional miracle stories were the mullah's way of illustrating the Lord's power over the masses. These miracles were simple parlor tricks, easily repeatable by any good magician today. The stories were not to be taken literally.

Allah did perform miracles of a sort, however, through the faithful. The first step was for the pious to accept that deep faith was the vessel for the Almighty's action. Hussain had learned that with Allah the faithful could do things that others believed impossible. Combining these traits with a recent revelation, Hussain now had the ability to take down the Great Satan. A true miracle. He credited his Islamic teachers with opening his eyes to the latest piece of the puzzle.

In particular, it was the example of the 13th century Sultan, Al Kamil, that had been the source of Hussain's first flash of insight. Al Kamil, he remembered, on August 29, 1221 defeated the Christian Crusaders' fifth effort to push the Muslims from the Holy Land. Al Kamil had opened his mind to Allah's wisdom, calling upon the force of the almighty to destroy an enemy.

Allah delivered.

The previous crusades had attacked Jerusalem from the north. The Christian armies traveled predominately the overland route across Europe--through Constantinople, across the Byzantine Empire (modern day Turkey), assembling at Antioch and moving on to Jerusalem. None of the crusades had achieved a permanent hold on the Holy Land. The Fifth Crusade had the same goal, but employed different tactics. Christian leaders set their sights on capturing the heart of the Egyptian Fatimid Kingdom. The Fatimids had supplied the Muslim occupiers, and Christian kings believed permanent victory in Jerusalem lay in denying the Muslim armies their supplies. At least that was the theory.

In 1221, the armies of the Fifth Crusade pitched camp at Damietta along a branch of the Nile delta. They were outsiders, invaders, infidels who didn't have the backing of Allah. More importantly, they didn't know Egypt's mighty river, the Nile. Allah and Al Kamil did. The Nile's floodgates were opened, inundating the invading army's camp, forcing their surrender. Expand your mind, look to Allah for the means of our enemy's destruction was the lesson Hussain took away from Al Kamil's example.

Armed with all his new training, Hussain was ordered to the United States. This he expected, but it was what he was told to do next that he didn't expect. Deepen his faith, take no hostile action, blend in, but above all, observe. His handlers commanded him to compile America's strengths and especially her weaknesses. Once educated, and only then, was he to determine the means to exploit this information, and, if possible, develop a plan of attack that with limited resources could inflict a truly devastating blow.

Yet, al Qaeda wanted to take the war an additional step. Their Islamic ancestors could repel invaders but were incapable of actually waging war. The Christian crusaders always enjoyed strategic military advantages over the Islamic forces. The Islamic armies lacked the ability to reverse the table and take the fight to the

invaders' homeland, putting the infidels on the
defensive. The attacks of September 11th changed
all that. Hussain believed al Qaeda was now
capable of preventing them from ever returning.

This was revolutionary. Past attacks on the
United States had been carried out for effect, for
propaganda. In the end those attacks had no
lasting impact upon the United States' ability to
project its power around the globe and especially
within the Middle East. Even the highly successful
destruction of the World Trade Towers and
damage to the Pentagon had failed to shatter the
hated Great Satan. Like all previous attacks, al
Qaeda gained significant press and pushed
hysterical conservative U.S. lawmakers to clamp
down on American freedoms. Yet in the end the
damage was unable to take down the beast.

This failure infuriated Hussain. Countless
loyal and pious Muslims had been asked to lay
down their lives, but there had been little real
impact upon the United States' action. America
was still the world's superpower, her obscene
culture continued to poison the Muslim world and,
most vile, U.S. troops continued their occupation
of sacred lands of the Middle East. Hussain was
tasked with finding a way to end all this. With
Allah's help he would be successful.

For several years Hussain was frustrated in
his effort to turn up something that could inflict
the amount of damage desired. But his handlers
urged him to remain patient, not to lose faith.
Allah acts on his own schedule. When the time is
right, he would reveal the way.

Then it happened. During a Discovery

Channel documentary on plate tectonics and the earth's hot spots, such as the Hawaiian Islands, he got the second piece of the puzzle. The key to America's demise lay within her own continental heart. He cried for joy at the perfection of what had to be an idea inspired by Allah. He called his handlers with his plan. At first they were skeptical, but as he explained the benefits and risks, they became more convinced of its worthiness. They authorized his further investigation, which he did immediately.

That was roughly ten years ago. For years Hussain blended into the corruption that was American culture. During that time he remained pure in his support of Islam and his hatred of America only grew.

The death of Osama had hit Hussain hard. He had been close with the leader. He vowed to make America pay for its actions. On Bin Laden's death he vowed their celebration would turn to despair. However tragic the loss of the leader might be, it wouldn't change Hussain's plans. Contingencies were in place in the event of the death of high level leaders. Hussain continued his operation.

With the death of Osama, however, Hussain did worry that his cover might be blown. Hussain assumed FBI agents would break down his door at any moment. He had prepared himself for going out in a firefight. But, the FBI never came.

Hussain's communication lines with his handlers fell silent as well. This he expected. His trainers stressed that security required long periods

between communications. Yet, it was a shock
when his handler finally reconnected with him a
few years ago. The plan, his plan, was being
implemented.

His cell phone rang, jolting him out of his
trance. "Jamil," he answered.

"You in position?" came the response.

"Yes."

Hussain recognized the voice. It was his
handler, his mentor, his adopted father. Because
Hussain had come to Islam late in life, his mind's
hold of false teachings and beliefs was formidable.
But through countless beatings and harsh
discipline, Hussain accepted the one true path. He
both loved and hated his *father*, but his methods
had led to Hussain's finding Allah, to finding
salvation. The choice had been clear, Allah or the
Devil. Life or Death.

America had the same choice. Accept
Allah, or die. She had rejected the former. Like
Hussain's mind before its conversion to Islam,
America's conscience was clouded with lies, false
Gods, and wicked beliefs. She would be punished.
She would get death. Hussain felt no remorse for
what had to be done. Allah's enemies must be
eliminated. Hussain's soul swelled with pride
knowing he would be the sword that cut out the
devil's heart.

"Good, tonight it's time to take the next
step in your plan. Is your team assembled?"

"Yes."

Team? It was hardly a team. More like a
collection of people whose efforts are used to
achieve a goal. A team implies common

66

understanding of their goal. His collection of personnel did not share a common understanding. Even better, some members didn't even know they were on the team.

Hussain had also learned this lesson from the attacks of September 11th. Hussain's operation called for coordinated action among multiple conspirators. It also called for complete compartmentalization. Only a select few knew the operation's actual aim. This was done for security, the fewer in the know, the smaller the chance of being discovered or, even worse, betrayed.

Yet, this compartmentalization was needed for effectiveness as well.

Hussain remembered the World Trade Tower attacks as if they happened yesterday. How television pundits and clueless politicians, almost before the towers had collapsed, were left scratching their heads as to how al Qaeda could convince nineteen seemingly healthy, well-educated young men to conduct a suicide mission, killing thousands of people in the process.

A slight smile crept across Hussain's face, for he was one of a very few who knew Mohamed Atta, the leader of the day's assault, and the three other pilots. Their convictions to the cause were responsible for its success. The fifteen remaining so-called terrorists were just average people of modest means. Several weren't even devout Muslims.

The question remained then, how to convince the others to lay down their lives? The answer was simple, al Qaeda didn't. These fifteen conspirators had been told they were on a totally different mission, one of hijack, hostage ransom and exchange. The details didn't really matter, did they? What mattered was these fifteen assisted in the hijack of the planes. None of them knew they would die that day. Obscuring the mission's goal made it much easier to recruit volunteers. The same strategy would be used for this next attack. Except in this case, Hussain's "team" would know even less than the September 11th soldiers.

This was due to Hussain's circumstances. He was conducting his operation deep within the United States. He would have to select co-conspirators from the population at hand. There simply weren't enough pious Muslims, or, more importantly, Muslims in positions of power or authority who could help with his mission. Once again Allah would have to provide.

"Any questions?"

"No," Hussain responded.

"Then go! Allah Akbar." The line went dead.

Hussain exited the car. A late spring snow dusted the parking lot. It crunched under Hussain's feet. It would be gone in the morning sun. Curious, Hussain thought. Like the melting snow, America would soon dissolve under the righteous and blinding light of Islam. A warm wind blew across the parking lot. Hussain took it as a sign from Allah. He pulled back his hood and headed to the hotel lobby. The hotel reader board read:

Spokane Tea Party
8:00pm in Roosevelt Lounge

In Hussain's opinion, it was a meeting of some of the most conservative, prejudiced people in the Northwest. In other words, the last spot the police would suspect an al Qaeda solider had found recruits for his mission. Again, a slight smile crept across Hussain's face. He was in the right place.

Chapter 5
Yellowstone Backcountry, June 1, Early Morning

Ranger Cole could tell something wasn't right. Through his high powered night vision binoculars he could see two men dressed in camouflage. They each carried a sidearm. The larger of the two had a rifle over his shoulder. One appeared to be entering data into a handheld GPS system. Cole handed the binoculars to Jennifer Chin, his partner. "What do you think?" he asked. Cole and Chin had been patrolling the backcountry for the past several days, checking camping permits. They were headed back to the trailhead when they spotted the suspicious pair.

Chin put the binoculars to her eyes. She adjusted the focus. The skin on her forehead wrinkled, indicating her confusion. "They look like poachers," Chin answered.

This produced an audible grunt of agreement from Cole. More than just about any other criminal operating in national parks, Grayson Cole hated poachers. They stole from the American public for personal profit.

Poaching had been a problem since the creation of the first parks. Wildlife, such as deer, elk, and fish, were the predominate resources stolen from the parks. However, poachers also took plants, such as mushrooms and berries. In recent years the Park Service had seen a rise in the killing of bears to harvest their gallbladders. Bear gall bladders could fetch $3,000 in Asia where it was believed to cure all kinds of ailments. Cole didn't know if gall bladder remedies helped *any* human medical conditions. He seriously doubted it. However, he did know it didn't help the bears. His bears.

"However. . ." Chin trailed off.

"Go on," Cole urged. He knew what she was about to say.

"I don't see any kill. The two are wearing body armor, and one has a high powered rifle." Chin used the binoculars' zoom to get a better look at the firearm. "It appears to be an automatic assault rifle. I'd guess five-fifty six mm M27 IAR." IAR stood for infantry automatic rifle. "A little too much fire power for killing deer or even elk," Chin deduced.

"What about grizzlies?" Cole pushed.

"Possible. However, that rifle would tear the animal apart. It wouldn't leave much of a trophy."

The suspects didn't fit the typical MO of a poacher. They appeared to be looking for something and Cole bet it was not an animal. "The flak jackets are also troubling," Cole added. "They appear military." Cole knew they weren't attached to any nearby unit. As soon as Chin and Cole had spotted the pair of weekend warriors, Cole had asked HQ to contact the local military base to see if the Army was doing any training in the park. Normally, the military would alert the Park Service when it was conducting operations in the park, and those were usually limited to orienteering operations. Never had the military come to Yellowstone this heavily armed. No, this wasn't an authorized military op.

Cole raised the binoculars again to his eyes.

The two men were obviously looking for
something. Cole had seen this type of behavior
before. Souvenir hunters plagued civil war sites
like Gettysburg. They were nothing more than
thieves and grave robbers looking to steal a
memento. Often the artifacts were sold to private
collectors who, because the item was stolen, hid
them away, lost to the public forever. He disliked
grave robbers nearly as much as he hated poachers.

Cole's gut told him the heavily armed men
weren't souvenir hunters, they didn't have metal
detectors. Besides, Yellowstone was mostly devoid
of cultural artifacts. Native peoples historically had
tended to stay away from the area, while non-
natives only became aware of the place a little
more than a century ago.

No, they weren't grave robbers.

Geocaching was his next thought. But he
quickly dismissed it. Geocaching was a new sport,
a game really, where participants used GPS systems
to find specific sites where small 'treasures' had
been hidden. Geocaching was frowned upon in
the national parks because it often required
tramping cross country through fragile
environments and unsafe locations. This could be
particularly dangerous in Yellowstone where one
wrong step could cast one into a boiling hot pool,
down a bottomless canyon, or face to face with a
fearsome grizzly or cougar. In addition, the
geocaching often required leaving or taking
something to prove one's presence at the site.
One of the National Park Service's guiding
mantras to the visiting public was, take only
pictures, leave only footprints. As harmless as

geocaching seemed, it conflicted with this philosophy and normally wasn't tolerated.

Cole removed his hat and ran his hand through his hair, collecting his thoughts. "Chin, call HQ and update them on the situation. Tell them we need a SWAT team in here. We will continue to monitor the suspects."

"Will do," Chin responded, pulling out her Motorola walkie-talkie.

Cole pushed the binoculars to their maximum zoom. The two men were brought clearly into view, although it was difficult to make out their faces. One man was punching information into his GPS, while the other appeared to take down information in a notebook.

Ranger Chin returned from making her radio call and crouched near Cole. "I've alerted HQ. They say a SWAT team is being flown by helicopter from Bozeman. The team should arrive in thirty minutes and will check in when they are ten minutes out."

"Great, we'll hold here and continue to watch the men," Cole explained. Rule one of law enforcement, bring sufficient backup to any engagement.

Cole and Chin had just finished setting up of their stakeout, when Chin spotted movement on the far horizon. "What's that?" she asked, pointing at some moving dots on the far horizon.

Cole swung the binoculars around and focused on where Chin was pointing. "Shit. They're campers. The kids we checked on yesterday." Cole dropped the binoculars from his eyes. The hikers could now be made out with the naked eye.

"I don't think they see each other."

"That will change in about ten minutes," Cole grumbled. He dropped his pack, pulled out additional ammunition and OC pepper spray from one of the compartments. Chin did the same. Cole slung his shotgun over his shoulder. Turning to Chin he ordered, "Tell HQ the situation has changed. We've got civilians entering harm's way and you will be cutting off the hikers."

"What about you?" Chin asked.

"I'm going to introduce myself to our suspects," Cole said, striding off into the morning murk.

Chapter 6
Yellowstone Backcountry, June 1, Early Morning

Akmed Sadr furiously entered data into his GPS. Hussain wanted this information to be correct. "Come on you idiot," Akmed barked at Abu Akbar, his companion on this outing. "Hussain will have our heads if we don't get this right." Akmed and Abu both knew Hussain. They knew Hussain would only accept success. Failure was unacceptable, failure meant death.

The two men had been surveying the Yellowstone backcountry off and on for days, mapping and identifying sites where the earth's crust was weak and thin. Akmed had no idea why their chief wanted this information. It seemed like a waste of time. But he'd learned long ago not to question. Besides, the sooner he finished the surveying, the sooner he could get out of this Godforsaken hell hole.

Akmed was tired. Abu was tired too. The climate was getting to them both. The high altitude, thin air, cold nights and drifts of snow were new and unwelcome to two boys from Saudi Arabia. Akmed had never been more than ten miles from the Persian Gulf before he met Hussain. Now he was in the western United States thousands of miles from home in the Yellowstone backcountry mapping stinking geysers and hot springs. If he didn't have such strong devotion to Allah, Akmed would have told Hussain to fuck off, or at least that's what he told himself.

Akmed put down his rifle. He needed a drink of water. Amazing how much water a person went through here. It was nearly as much as he drank back home. He also felt just as sluggish as he did on some of Saudi Arabia's hottest days. Like Hussain, Akmed had gone through terrorist basic training, but primarily at Saudi Arabia's low elevations. He had spent most of his life at sea level. Akmed had been standing in Jeddah, the largest seaport in Saudi Arabia, when he had received an urgent call from Hussain demanding he fly to Wyoming immediately. Akmed, like Hussain, was Al Qaeda. There was no questioning an order from a superior.

So, here he was, standing in the high altitude lodgepole pine forest of Wyoming at more than 7,700 ft. above sea level. There hadn't been time to acclimate to the new environment. He hadn't even had time to pull together a complete crew. Akmed knew this was his team's weakness. However, what he didn't have in manpower he made up for with firepower. No one in his right mind would mess with two heavily armed men. If they did, Akmed was prepared to send them straight to Allah. The Almighty would deal with them.

Akmed sat, drinking from his canteen. The water quenched his thirst and for the moment revived his strength. "Come on you lazy son of a bitch. We've got to get this information before sunup," Akmed barked at Abu. He knew the sun would be up in less than an hour and with the sun came park visitors. Like a vampire, Akmed's dirty work must be complete before the first ray of sunshine.

Abu shot Akmed a dirty look, mumbled a curse, and headed into the woods.

Abu was a short, wiry man. Akmed knew he was weak. The man constantly complained of stuffed sinuses and runny nose. His head pounded. The blooming Yellowstone wildflowers with their flowers poking through the snow banks weren't helping his allergies. The man was continually digging into his pockets, downing Claritin pills as if they were candy.

Akmed couldn't relate. In Saudi Arabia allergies weren't a problem. Here in Wyoming it was another story. The affliction obviously sapped Abu's energy. Both al Qaeda foot soldiers missed the sand and heat of home. Mountains and forests were as foreign as the moon.

Akmed watched Abu shrink into the forest thinking if there was a stereotypical al Qaeda soldier, Abu was the exact opposite. The man wasn't even a Muslim. Rather, Abu's father, one of Saudi Arabia's wealthiest businessmen, pushed his son to join the organization. The father had contacted Hussain directly begging him to take his son. He obviously believed joining al Qaeda would turn his son into a Muslim and a man. As far as Akmed could see, it had only turned him into a sniffing, complaining weakling. It was obvious all Abu wanted to do was go home.

Akmed knew they'd have to finish quickly. The sun was almost up now. He put the lid back on his water bottle when a scream cut through the forest.

"Aaaaa."

It could only have come from Abu. That idiot must have fallen into a hole or something. Akmed got up from the downed tree he had been resting on and set out to find his partner. He crossed into a wooded glen, stepping over several downed trees, finally coming upon his downed and moaning comrade. A puzzled look crossed Akmed's face. Abu appeared to be barely conscious, but hadn't fallen into a hole or stepped in a hot spring as expected. Rather, even in the low light of early morning, Akmed could see Abu's normal tan face had a bright red streak across it. Blood flooded from one nostril. Perhaps he had been stung by something. He had no idea what type of stinging insects or poisonous snakes might live in these woods. Akmed took a quick look around. Nothing.

Abu continued to moan on the ground, his arms tucked behind his back. "Abu, what the hell happened? Get up," Akmed urged. "We need to get the hell out of here." He bent down, placed his hand on Abu's shoulder in an effort to roust the downed man.

Light reflected off something around Abu's wrist. What was this? Was he wearing bracelets? Akmed took a knee and rolled the still moaning Abu on his stomach. He grabbed one of Abu's arms to examine his wrists? Hand cuffs. Spinning around, he jerked his head back and forth in a panicked search. Akmed drew his weapon, knelt down next to Abu picking up his GPS system.

"Drop the weapon. Get on the ground," a voice yelled from in front of Akmed. A tall, uniform-wearing man stepped out from behind a tree. He pointed a shotgun directly at Akmed. To his shock, Akmed saw a man in a ridiculous flat hat standing a few feet away. He had no idea who he was, but the badge on his chest told him all he needed to know.

"Drop the weapon," the police officer repeated.

Akmed knew he was caught. He was not going to complete his mission. Hussain would certainly kill him and Abu. They had failed.

The ranger continued to bark his commands. Akmed didn't hear him. Allah was speaking to him, telling him what to do. A calm determined look came across his face.

He raised his revolver.

The ranger again yelled, "Drop it!"

Akmed fired.

The ranger fired his shotgun nearly simultaneously. The shotgun's slug hit Akmed square in the chest, knocking him back several yards. His weapon flew from his hand out of reach. Akmed crumpled to the ground, flat on his back. The ranger pumped his shotgun, chambering another round.

"Get on your stomach," the officer yelled at Akmed.

Akmed ignored him. He was at peace. His revolver was out of reach. He was defenseless, the fight was over. He had one last card to play. He fumbled through his pockets.

"On your stomach! Get your hands out of your pockets," the officer repeated, closing the distance between himself and Akmed.

Akmed raised his left hand, palm open. He

pulled his right hand from his pocket. A small object was clenched in his fist.

"Drop what's in your hand," the officer shouted.

"Certainly," Akmed replied. He opened his fist. The small object fell onto his chest. "God is great!"

Grenade!

Cole dove for the bushes. The grenade went off with a deafening roar, sending a cloud of dirt and rocks rocketing into the air.

He pulled himself from the bushes and dusted off the dust and rock that landed on him from the blast.

The explosion had killed both suspects and blown them to kingdom come.

Hearing the explosion, Ranger Chin ran down the trail to assist her partner.

"Cole! Cole! You okay?" Chin screamed.

Chin came upon Cole holding his head trying to silence the ringing in his ears.

"What the hell happened?" Chin asked.

"Not sure." Cole replied. "I thought I'd seen it all." Plenty of idiots visited the parks and came with all kinds of stupid ideas. Fishing with dynamite, letting their dogs run off leash, putting their kids on the backs of bison. But my God, this was crazy. Killing yourself with a grenade."

Violence like this was rare in the national parks. That didn't mean it didn't exist. Desperate people took vacations like everyone else and brought their problems with them. Minor traffic stops could turn into a firefight. A few years back a ranger at Mount Rainier was gunned down by a paramilitary survivalist who had just shot four people at a New Year's Eve party. But he was a soldier suffering from PTSD. He had acted alone, obviously fighting demons that followed him home from Iraq. He was running from the police and happened to take a turn into a national park. It was a terrible tragedy, but unlikely to be part of a larger plot.

The two men lying blown to bits in front of Cole were different. They were part of a team, armed with high powered rifles and grenades. They had come to Yellowstone for a purpose.

Cole bent down to examine the GPS the taller man had been holding. It was destroyed. The grenade blast had turned the sophisticated and obviously expensive piece of equipment into a clump of twisted and burnt junk. Turning it over in his hand, Cole examined the device closely. It wasn't a run of the mill GPS, something picked up at REI. No, this was military issue with satellite telemetry data transmission. These guys were sending park coordinates to someone. But who? And why?

Cole placed the GPS in his pocket. He doubted the forensics team would be able to recover any data from it, but he would bag it for evidence all the same.

He returned his attention to the two dead camouflaged-wearing men. A murder-suicide? This was new.

Chin could see her partner was troubled. "What's the matter, Cole?"

Cole sighed, wiped the last bit of dirt from his

face, and straightened his tie. "What am I going to tell the paramedics this time?"

Chapter 7
South America, Colombian Coast, May 26, Early Morning

The North Korean sea trawler, Blazing Sun, slipped into the Colombian seaport. The trawler looked like it had been through hell. And it had, crossing the Pacific to reach this tiny fishing village.

The port stunk of fish and diesel fuel. A light sea fog hung in the air, obscuring visibility to a few feet. The boat's captain didn't like the fog, but who he was going to meet did.

A light breeze blew through the port kicking up light waves. Small two-person fishing vessels tied to the docks bobbed with the harbor chop. A boat bell rang in the background. It was a little after two in the morning. The sun wouldn't be up for several more hours. But sunlight wasn't important for this operation, stealth was. Local fishermen wouldn't be tending their nets for a while, so no locals were there to notice the Blazing Sun slip into the harbor. Even if there had been, most residents wouldn't give the ship a second glance. Its cargo wasn't fish, but a far more important bounty from the sea.

The trawler pulled up to a dock far removed from the main fishing piers. A small yet serious group of men met it at the docks. The small artifact that had been pulled out of the North Pacific weeks before was now encased in what looked like a locked watertight casket. It was quickly unloaded and transferred to a covered truck. The truck pulled away as the trawler headed back to sea. The whole operation took under five minutes.

Chapter 8
Spokane Red Lion Conference Center, May 26, Evening

Tea Party leader Charles Sinclair III was growing impatient. Captain Joseph Hansen was late. Sinclair was spending a pretty penny on this Tea Party convention, and his keynote speaker was nowhere to be seen.

Charles Sinclair was nearly 75 years old, yet still carried a strong jaw line. His grey eyes could be intimidating when directed in one's direction. He was in excellent health, but realizing he had limited time left on the planet he would use the time remaining to serve God's plan.

Sinclair had grown up in the northeast, attending Yale where he studied geology and business. At Yale, Sinclair joined the Skull and Bones club, a social fraternity where he made powerful relationships. In the years that followed graduation, Sinclair combined these relationships with his drive and knowledge to build a multi-billion dollar commercial empire. The empire started in high tech earthquake monitoring systems and expanded to include hotel, restaurant, and other hospitality establishments. This combination of interests struck some outside the Sinclair circle as odd, but Charles had always been interested in rocks. This love led him to Yellowstone and the lucrative park monitoring program. At Yellowstone, he was disgusted at the state of accommodations. They were too few, rustic, and in Sinclair's opinion run-down. It didn't matter that the public seemed to love the service of the concessionaire. Charles was determined to get the hotel contract.

Sinclair had been cozy with the previous administration, a huge campaign donor raising millions for a successful presidential re-election. As it would turn out, Sinclair also had Bones brothers in the previous administration. So, when the concessions contract for the Yellowstone hotel, restaurant, and gift shop contract came up a few years back, his rainmaking ability plus his political connections had made the public request for bids a mere formality.

Sinclair was used to getting what he wanted and if that meant a few rules got bent, so be it. The carrot often went to the fastest and smartest rabbit. But it also didn't hurt if the rabbit was well connected.

Sinclair's empire was built on control. Control centered on people doing his will without question. He had a plan, a mission. Sinclair was convinced that God had chosen him for a special purpose. A duty fated by the Almighty. No one would stand in his way, certainly not his enemies, but neither would his friends. The execution of Sinclair's plan meant everlasting salvation, not only for himself but for millions, if not billions, of Christians as well. Nothing could be more important than its successful completion.

Sinclair's revelation had come while on a group tour to the Holy Land as a young adult. Ever since that trip, everything he did was designed to fulfill God's blueprint. Unfortunately, Captain Joseph Hansen followed his own course. This drove Sinclair crazy, throwing uncertainty into his most important effort.

Sinclair looked at his watch again. The Rolex Submariner timepiece had been a gift from his wife for his 65th birthday. It read 8:23 pm. Every tick of the watch reminded Sinclair that Hansen was running late. "Damn him," Sinclair said. Tonight was the latest of many instances where Hansen deviated from design. Former Alaska Governor Sarah Palin was wrapping up her remarks. Hansen was next. "Joe better get here soon," Sinclair fumed to no one in particular. "It's so like him to be late." If he wasn't the best damned motivational speaker the Tea Party had Sinclair would've cut ties with him long ago. But Hansen was the best. He could turn a phrase, sum up thoughts, and project messages which deeply connected with the masses. Hansen's southern California good looks, charm, and oratory skills made him the Tea Party's best recruiter.

His personal story didn't hurt either.

Captain Hansen had served as a Marine sniper and fought against al Qaeda in Afghanistan. He was the best sniper the service had seen since Vietnam. He held several marksmanship records including the longest kill shot with a rifle. Captain Hansen's typical mission was to provide cover for Army patrols. In the summer of 2002 Captain Hansen and his spotter held off an insurgent ambush, taking out more than three dozen attackers from a distance of more than 750 yards. By the end Hansen had spent approximately twenty four hours in battle, never once taking his eye off the scope. The crosshair had been burned into his retina. The image remained there for several days.

Hansen received medals for valor and bravery including the Silver Star. Yet, Captain Hansen prized his Prisoner of War Medal most. He was captured by al Qaeda after a particularly hard fought battle. Hansen and his spotter held off more than a hundred terrorists, giving Army medics time to airlift dozens of soldiers wounded by an IED. Hansen provided close support until he ran out of ammunition. In the end, Hansen's spotter was dead, he had exhausted his secondary weapon's ammunition, and received gunshot wounds to his right thigh and arm. Yet dozens of American soldiers were saved that day. But it marked the end of Hansen's involvement in the Afghanistan war.

The full power of the United States government was unleashed to secure the captain's release. The State Department, the Army, the CIA and even a few clandestine backdoor channels within al Qaeda were explored. Nothing worked.

In 2006 al Qaeda released Joseph for reasons still undetermined by the Defense Department. Department of Defense records showed that Captain Hansen had spent four years in captivity. While he expressed a desire to return to combat, higher-ups in Washington believed Hansen had done his part and rotated him stateside to a hero's welcome. His transition to non-combat operations proved difficult, though. Like many returning veterans, he had become disillusioned by the Paine administration's execution of the war. He requested and was granted a discharge. Upon his return to civilian life, Hansen became an outspoken critic of the

Paine administration in general and its Middle Eastern policy in particular. Hansen railed against what he deemed the Paine administration's coddling of terrorists. "We are not in a police action," Hansen was quoted in the New York Times. "We are in a war for survival. The quicker we learn this fact the better. Unfortunately for America, President Paine isn't a quick learner." Statements like this made Hansen an immediate darling of the right, dubbing him G.I. Joe.

"We must never end the fight against the godless who struck the first blow in this war of good versus evil," Joseph thundered to the national media.

Looking back now, Sinclair believed Hansen was a gift from heaven. Sinclair remembered the day the captain showed up at Sinclair's Christ Advocate Church. Hansen caught the congregation's attention and Sinclair's in particular.

At that time, Sinclair was the leader of the Spokane Tea Party, but was struggling to find ways to take his message national. Hansen was the answer to his prayers. A bolt from heaven sent directly from God, there could be no doubt.

Sinclair and Hansen became best friends. Sinclair was taken in by Hansen's charisma while the army sniper was intrigued by the billionaire's engineering company, Sinclair Enterprises. Hansen was most interested to learn that Sinclair's company had the contract to provide and maintain Yellowstone National Park's caldera monitoring equipment. While in Afghanistan, Hansen told Sinclair he kept his sanity while in captivity by planning visits to national parks like Yellowstone after the war. Now with Sinclair he had been able to get a behind the scenes tour of the nation's first park.

But it was the combination of Sinclair's resources and Hansen's people skills that took the Spokane Tea Party to the next level. There were now weekly media interviews on Fox, CNN, MSNBC, and even the hated National Public Radio had called. This exposure led to speaking engagements around the country, fetching a pretty penny for both Sinclair and Hansen. They now regularly dined with corporate moguls and congressional leaders.

However, the Tea Party's national agenda, a return to traditional values, minimal government, and reduced taxes, had been stymied by the Paine administration. Any congressional or state effort to rein in the out of control federal government was blocked by the president. The Paine administration was also destroying the customs and culture of rural America, by protecting dangerous predators such as the gray wolf and locking up more land from energy development.

Yet, it was Paine's Middle Eastern policy that had Sinclair most upset. The misguided president was working with the heathen Muslims on a peace treaty. Peace treaty his ass. It was a death sentence for Israel, and an affront to God's plan.

Sinclair was a Christ Advocate. A fundamentalist evangelical church which taught the second coming of Jesus Christ would occur when the Jews regained control of Jerusalem's Temple

Mount. The Paine administration, however, was pushing a two state solution for the Middle East, cementing Muslim control of the temple, preventing the return of the Messiah. Sinclair was a devout conservative Christian, his church's dogma required men of faith to take action to hasten Christ's return. No one man, not even the President of the United States could or would stand in the way of prophecy. Not if Charles Sinclair had anything to do with it.

Sinclair was sickened by all the effort and years wasted fighting President Paine. How many laws had the president vetoed now? Dozens? Sinclair had lost count. At least that many administration lawsuits had been filed blocking needed change. And if re-elected this November all could be lost. Sinclair, with God's help, would not let that happen.

Paine, the last obstacle to heaven's restoration, would be swept away soon. God had sent an angel who would bring wrath upon the unholy. And, better yet, the angel would strike shortly. That is if Hansen could keep to a simple timeline.

Where could he be? Sinclair checked his Rolex again.

Sinclair was about to pull out his Blackberry when he saw Captain Hansen. The Marine captain strode toward the ballroom. He was wearing a pullover hoodie sweatshirt with Norte Dame Football emblazoned on the front. Hansen was not wearing the agreed upon attire. Sinclair would have to let it slide.

"Where the hell have you been?" Sinclair

demanded.

"Sorry," the captain replied. "I got held up."

"Well, get in there. You're on."

Chapter 9
Grant Village, Employee Housing Development, June 2, Late Evening

Ranger Cole had finished his day. He was tired, too tired to go to sleep. Insomnia was occurring more often as he got older. He lay in bed in the back bedroom of his 1950s single wide trailer for hours staring at the ceiling, thinking about the previous day's events with the two camouflage-wearing men. *Who were they?* He had turned over the collected evidence to the FBI, but had heard nothing since. Something wasn't right about the encounter. Cole knew they weren't poachers. They didn't fit the MO. At their hearts poachers were cowards who stole the public's wildlife. Few had the steel to blow themselves up. His mind was racing. He just couldn't sleep. He knew it probably wasn't a physical ailment, but he would nevertheless stop and see Doc Johnson the next time he was in Jackson Hole and get it checked out. Just to be safe.

Cole got up, checked his clock radio. 10:48 p.m. He had received the radio as a gift from someone who had never been to Yellowstone, let alone Grant Village. The clock worked fine, the radio not so much. Grant Village was smack in the middle of nearly thirteen million acres of wilderness, roadless backcountry, and rural pasture land. The closest radio station was in Jackson Hole nearly seventy miles away. If Cole stood on his tiptoes and held the radio up against one corner of his kitchen ceiling he was able to get a single Christian radio station out of Jackson, but that was it. Some nights, if the atmospheric conditions

were just right, he could also pick up San
Francisco's KGO. His tech friends told him some
AM signals like those sent out by the powerful
KGO bounced off the ionosphere and could be
picked up hundreds of miles away. Either way,
Grant Village was about as remote and detached
from civilization as one could get in the
continental United States. This was hard for city
slickers to comprehend. There was actually a place
where radios and, God forbid, cell phones didn't
get a signal. "How can that be?" they would ask,
staring blankly at their useless iPhone or
Blackberry. Cole could have told them about the
remoteness of the park, its size, the difficulty of
maintaining cell towers in the harsh Wyoming
winters, or the fact that there just wasn't enough
demand to justify the development of additional
radio stations. But they didn't want to hear that,
besides Cole didn't care to explain it. He was just
happy that there were a few remaining places
where one could unplug, or nearly so, from the
rest of the world. In the back of his mind, Cole
knew Yellowstone's isolation from civilized
communications was ending as well. A sense of
melancholy about this could overcome him if he
let it. The park had acquired internet access a few
years back, making it a lot easier to file his patrol
reports. In addition, the development of satellite
radio and other similar technology meant it was
only a matter of time until civilization enveloped
the park completely. But not tonight.

Being cut off from the civilized world had
its advantages. The stresses and worries that
gripped those that lived outside Yellowstone's

boundaries didn't seem to penetrate the park. Life moved slower at Grant. There were times when Cole would forget the day of the week. Civilized concepts such as the day of the week often had no meaning in the park where some natural cycles were measured in timescales of thousands of years. The seasons, rather than the day, often had more meaning. If ice was breaking on Yellowstone Lake it was spring. If traffic jams became common it was summer. If bull elk began to bugle their screechy call for a mate it was fall. And if snow began to fall it was . . . well, it could be any season.

Pop culture and its associated drama also often failed to pierce the park. Cole remembered the time they had learned O.J. Simpson had been arrested for murder. He had just come out of the wilderness after a week-long backpacking trip. Cut off from any television, radio, or newspapers, Cole had been stunned to learn the football great was accused of brutally cutting down his ex-wife and her male friend. He had been probably one of only a handful of people on the planet at the time blissfully unaware of the spectacle gripping the country. He later joked that if he had lived in Los Angeles he might have even made an excellent juror as he had no knowledge of the crime.

But living in the Wyoming wilds could have its downsides as well. Cole, like many rangers, didn't own a home. Rather, he lived in government provided housing, and as such wasn't building equity like others. Although, the housing crash this past decade convinced him that not owning may have been good fortune. Yet, it was a lack of anonymity that Cole missed the most. The people that lived and worked in Yellowstone in general and Grant Village in particular were a tight and small community. There were only so many people to play, work or sleep with. If a ranger spent enough time in the service chances were good one would do all three. As a result, one couldn't take a piss without the neighbors knowing about it. Everyone's marital troubles, sexual habits, and work performance were common knowledge. People talked, it was human nature and the park service grapevine disseminated information faster than any viral email. Ironic that in a park of more than two million acres, a ranger could feel claustrophobic. But it happened.

When this feeling overtook him, Cole would sometimes escape to the bright lights of the big city of Jackson Hole to lose himself among the masses. The city buzz never failed to restore the feeling, if only for a few hours, that no one knew the color of his underwear.

Cole stared at the alarm clock again. 10:57 p.m. Throwing the covers off, merely a couple of sheets and a cold weather sleeping bag, Cole got up and put on his clothes. His mind was racing too much to sleep. He couldn't get the armed men out of his head and the sense that they represented something bigger than a mere poaching threat.

Staring at the ceiling wasn't going to make him fall asleep any faster.

No, tonight he would head down to Colter's Hell Hole, the local bar. Cole didn't drink much. He was smart enough to know that self-medicating was not a good long term solution to physical or mental problems. Insomnia in most cases was both. But there was also a professional reason for moderating his drinking. Cole had a certain relationship he had to keep with his rangers. He was their boss, they were his employees and while they could be friendly off duty, Cole never felt comfortable with developing deep friendships with those under his command. There were times when he would have to order them to do something dangerous, yet necessary, and he didn't want his feelings for them to get in the way of making the necessary call. More importantly, though, there often wasn't the time. Like in the military, working one's way up in the park service required rangers to move. The average stay at any one park could be quite short. Cole had found on several occasions that just as he was building a close friendship or relationship, someone would have to move. He didn't resent this. It was the nature of the Park Service. It just made it hard to get close, really intimate, with people. Sure, he was friendly with all his colleagues, and they with him, but those relationships had a surface feel to them. Maybe that's the way it was in all human relationships. He wasn't a psychologist, but it felt hollow all the same.

He had tried building relationships outside his work, in the nearby communities that dotted the borders of the park. But this had proved difficult as well.

The park gateway communities, Cole learned, had a love-hate relationship with the park service. They loved Yellowstone's tourists, or more accurately their dollars, but had no tolerance for the rules that the NPS put in place. How dare the National Park Service prevent visitors from feeding the deer or racing snowmobiles hither and yon? These were the people's parks, right? Why can't they do what they want? They really weren't hurting anything or anyone. The all too frequent questions never changed. Whether it was snowmobile management, wolf reintroduction, or firearm use, a few loud mouths in these towns always seemed to be upset. It struck Cole as odd that they never seemed able to make the connection that the visitors were coming to the park because they weren't overwhelmed by snowmobile fumes, or they could hear wolf howls, or they didn't fear getting shot.

This love-hate dynamic created a passive discrimination in some businesses toward park employees. Cole had been refused service at a couple restaurants and bars. And while he couldn't prove it, he knew it was because he worked for the park service. No, there wasn't much hope in making friends outside the park either. So Cole tended to stick to himself. It worked better that way, and besides he had come to like the solitude.

Cole went to his dresser and pulled out a cotton t-shirt. He grabbed a pair a Levi's from his closet and got dressed. Heading out the door he grabbed his REI fleece jacket. It was a little cold tonight, but he decided to walk the short distance to the Hell Hole.

Entering the dimly lit bar, he made his way to the back. It was surprisingly full for a weeknight. The Hell Hole was a ranger hang out, but there were also a few Sinclair employees, park employee spouses and friends, as well as a few locals here tonight. Cole saw a couple of his law enforcement rangers in a corner booth. He waved, but wouldn't be sitting with them.

He also saw a number of non-park people he knew, but he wouldn't be sitting with them either. Most people felt uncomfortable drinking with a police officer, even an off-duty one.

Cole grabbed a booth in the back. His usual table. He could survey the entire bar from here. Without needing to be asked, the bartender, an attractive young blonde, brought him a Strider microbrew and a bowl of orange slices. It was a local Belgian wheat beer. The waitress was one of many faceless kids who blew into the park each spring and would just as quickly blow out in the fall for school or other jobs.

The beer name was an inside joke. In the book, *The Lord of the Rings*, Frodo, the book's central character, first meets Lord Aragorn, King of Gondor, at the Inn of the Prancing Pony. The innkeeper introduced the king as *Strider, one of them there rangers*. A park ranger thought it funny and made a beer especially for *them there rangers*.

The bar's atmosphere was lively. Couples could be seen playing pool or darts. A juke box played *Blame it on the Tequila* in the background. People were having a good time. Cole knew he couldn't fully engage in the fun, but it helped sometimes just to be around people who were.

Life as a ranger, especially at a remote park like Yellowstone, could be lonely. Cole's only true companion was a malamute husky named Jake. He'd had the dog since he was a puppy and Jake

had been by his side at every one of his park
assignments. It was tricky having a dog in the
park. Yellowstone being part of the park system
had strict regulations, regulations he was bound to
enforce on where dogs could and could not go.
He understood the reasons behind these rules.
National parks, despite common perception,
weren't amusement parks. They weren't places
where people could do anything they wanted.
Rather, Congress had set up the park system to
protect the most special, the most sacred, sites for
preservation and enjoyment of not only present
generations but future unborn Americans as well.
Some called Congress' charge the dual mandate of
the park system. A mandate that required the NPS
to balance use and preservation equally.

Cole hated this misunderstanding. This
mandated balance clearly wasn't the case. It was a
public relations chant. Something to keep
Congress and critics off the park service's back.
But this magical balance had no basis in legislation
or case law. Rather, the courts and even Congress
had made clear over the years that when in doubt
the Park Service was to place preservation above
use. This only made sense. How could the Park
Service preserve something if it allowed it to be
destroyed or damaged by use? It couldn't.
Therefore, the Park Service could only allow those
activities that didn't lead to permanent impairment
of parks' natural and cultural resources.
Unfortunately, off-leash dog walking was one of
those activities prohibited in Yellowstone.

Cole took an orange slice from a bowl on
the table and pushed one into the bottle and took a

drink. He continued to take in the bar's comings and goings. He drank his beer thinking about the bar's patrons. A large group of summer seasonal rangers came through the door. They were laughing, carrying on, and obviously having a great time. A summer assignment in Yellowstone was a great way to spend the months of April thru September. A seasonal ranger was one of the best possible jobs--little responsibility, few bills, and lots of adventure. Cole finished off his beer, fondly remembering his days as a seasonal ranger. It didn't seem that long ago when he had first walked through the Hell Hole's door. However, a lot of water had gone under the bridge since then.

The group found a table and signaled the bartender for a pitcher. Cole continued to watch the group. Without being asked, the cute bartender dropped another Strider on his table. Before he could thank her, she sashayed off for the seasonals' table, a large pitcher of an amber beer gripped in her left hand.

He tried not to stare at the group, a mix of men and women, but he was drawn to their enthusiasm. They were generally having fun. But there was something else about them, something he couldn't quite place. As the bartender asked to see their ID's, it struck him how young they actually were. Every year it seemed the seasonals got younger, yet it was actually he who was getting older. A slight wave of melancholy came over him, but only for a second. He reminded himself that he was a park ranger in Yellowstone, the flagship park of America's park system. This was the assignment he had dreamed of when he had joined the system. He had achieved many of his professional goals.

It was getting late, he finally felt sleep coming. He finished his beer, paid his bar bill and headed out the door. The night was cold. Millions of stars glowed in the night sky. Cole pulled his coat around him against the chill. He was heading home alone, again. The insomnia was passing, at least for tonight. But his inability to sleep was merely a symptom of a larger problem. As much as he had achieved his professional goals, he had achieved few of his personal ones. When he was honest with himself, he wanted a wife. He would like kids. But he was no closer to these than when he first put on the Park Service uniform. He lived in a trailer with a dog. Life was good. But it could be better.

Chapter 10
White House, Presidential Bedroom.
May 27, Early Morning

The phone rang, pulling the president out of a deep sleep. He sat up and reached for his glasses. He looked at the clock radio on the bedside stand. 4:15 a.m. What now? It couldn't be good news, not at this hour. The president had learned early in his term that calls in the middle of the night always carried bad news. Just once he would like to get a call in the wee hours of the morning alerting the president that peace and prosperity had broken out across the world, world hunger eliminated, poverty defeated, and disease eradicated. But that call never came. A man could dream, though.

The phone continued to ring. Another thing the president learned in his more than three years in the White House was that whoever called the presidential bedroom in the middle of the night knew he was there. The phone would ring until he picked up. Failure to answer the phone resulted in a visit from the burly Secret Service agent standing just outside his bedroom door. He couldn't ignore the call.

His wife was still sleeping. She had learned a few things these past couple years as well--how to smile when you didn't feel like it, how to give a ten minute speech while saying nothing, and, most important, how to sleep through early morning phone calls.

The president sighed, bracing himself for the bad news that was about to come as he picked up the receiver and placed it to his ear. "Paine here," he said half asleep.

"Mr. President?" a young but professional voice said on the other end.

The president imagined the voice belonging to a twenty-something intern who'd been given the night shift. *Twenty-something* intern? Unknown to much of the American public, many of the most powerful and important jobs were filled by kids. Okay, technically not children, but still kids to him. They were often young adults just out of college in their first jobs. Paine still remembered his first day in the Senate. His first walk to his new Senate office was something akin to a busy high school between class periods. The halls were crowded and overrun with kids. Kids were running the country. They were drafting policy papers, attending budget meetings, attending to constituents and voters. Paine had never suspected as much before entering the Senate. He had always believed adults were making the decisions. Recently he had begun to doubt if the country wasn't even being run by the twenty-somethings. Kids were doing the research on countless policy and legal matters every day. The type and amount of information, as well as how it was presented to government leaders, could determine the decision to be made. The president was the most connected person in the world, or more accurately the office of the president was the most connected. The office had access to information civilians couldn't imagine, yet Paine was entirely dependent upon his staff for that information. It required a level of trust not found in many other professions. If the president's staff told him the sky was falling, the leader of the free world wouldn't have the capacity or the time to confirm the fact himself, he would have to trust their information.

"Mr. President?" the young voice on the other end of the line asked again.

The president didn't recognize the man's voice. His staff turned over quite regularly, at least at the junior levels. Many saw a White House job as their ticket to a big payday. Thus the constant carousel of new voices waking the president in the middle of the night. The only person who couldn't quit the White House was the president. The most powerful man in the world was trapped in the Oval Office. How ironic.

But despite the turnover, there was a long line of eager, young go-getters willing to fill these often thankless, long day jobs. This was in large part because government jobs in the White House or Capitol Hill didn't fit a typical job description or follow a predictable pattern. One day an intern could be making the coffee, next prepping the Secretary of Defense for a press conference, or calling the president in the middle of the night with likely earth shaking bad news. It could be very exciting and intoxicating to be plugged in and in some cases be pulling the levers of power.

Odd that he had asked if it was the president on the other end. Who else would answer this phone?

The voice went on. "Sorry to bother you this early in the morning, but I have some news about the Vice President."

The president was fully awake now. "Go ahead."

"Vice President Winfield has been taken to the Bethesda Naval Hospital," the voice continued. "It appears the Vice President's cancer has returned."

Paine was struck how matter of fact the information was delivered. He and Vice President Stuart Winfield had been friends since they both served in the Senate more than twenty five years ago.

When Paine first decided to run for the White House, he sought out Winfield's advice first. Winfield was straightforward and would certainly tell Paine his chances. Not surprising Winfield was highly supportive. He couldn't think of a more qualified candidate. Paine appreciated the endorsement and returned the compliment, by picking his friend for his running mate.

Now he had received news that his old friend was sick. His cancer had returned. Paine knew Winfield's prognosis wasn't good. Liver cancer was a bitch, seldom giving second chances.

"The Veep is stable, but it's uncertain when he'll return home," the voice stated.

If he'll return, the president thought.

"Thanks," the president finally muttered. "Alert the Cabinet and Chief of Staff Beardsley that I want a meeting first thing this morning to discuss the Vice President's health. Also, notify the House and Senate leadership about the Vice President's condition."

Hanging up the phone, as he lay back down staring at the ceiling, the president realized his upcoming reelection had just gotten a lot more difficult.

Chapter 11
Spokane Red Lion Hotel, Presidential
Suite, May 27, Early Morning

The night's event was over. Hansen and
Sinclair returned to the Red Lion's presidential
suite. The room filled most of the hotel's 23rd
floor and was expansive, containing a living room,
kitchen, two full bedrooms, and a bath with
Jacuzzi tub and shower. Floor to ceiling windows
gave a view of the Spokane River in the distance.
Being early spring, the river was boiling with
snowmelt over the cascade known as the Spokane
Falls. The falls were a fifteen story drop over
volcanic basalt. The basalt was laid down millions
of years before, during a cataclysmic eruption that
covered nearly all of present day Washington in a
sheet of lava tens of hundreds of feet thick. To
the average person the basalt seemed solid as any
other rock. Lasting, unchanging. But as Sinclair
stared out the windows he knew otherwise. He
had studied geology, crawled over rocks and
mountains around the world. He had tapped on
countless boulders with his hammer, studied their
chemical make-ups, and broke them down to the
molecular level. He knew the solid nature of rocks
was an illusion, the result of humans' limited sense
of time. Human thoughts focused on minute
segments of time, seconds, minutes, hours, and
even years. On the rare occasion a person would
think about decades or even centuries, but hardly
more than that. These timescales meant nothing
to a rock. They existed on geologic timescales,
millions and billions of years. But even this was

too limiting. Charles was focused on eternity.

The Spokane River, a constant movement of energy and power, was wearing down and eventually destroying the apparently permanent rock. In a million years' time perhaps there would be no Spokane Falls for the then Chamber of Commerce to promote. This constant movement, constant change, was everywhere in the world, be it glaciers grinding down entire mountains or ocean surf eroding coastlines. Nature, God's creation, had shown Sinclair that an unstoppable force would beat an immovable object every time. Sinclair took the revelation as a sign from the Almighty. It was clear the Lord used earthly forces, such as wind and water, to wear down obstacles. A river, despite the strongest obstacles, would eventually make it to the sea. This was never clearer than at the Grand Canyon, one of Sinclair's favorite places. The Colorado River over millions of years of patient, constant pressure had carved a canyon a mile deep, two hundred seventy miles long, and seventeen miles wide.

Some creationists believed God carved the Grand Canyon in a matter of days during the great flood. Despite his fundamentalist Christian Advocate beliefs, Sinclair rejected this naïve belief. It missed God's higher message trapped within the rock. Christ Advocates' biblical interpretation required holy men to take action against the wicked. Even to kill the unworthy if necessary. Psalms taught that a plague on the Israelites ended when a Phineas priest killed the sinners among the afflicted. God clearly condoned violence against the unholy. The Ten Commandments' prohibition on killing did not apply to devoted followers wiping out evil. Pious men of the Christ Advocate flock, just like the river, were to be God's instruments for wiping away obstacles, such as the unholy.

The Colorado River's Grand Canyon wasn't a parlor trick, as fundamentalists believed. It was the fingerprint of God, a how-to on bringing forth God's plan for earth.

Sinclair took this understanding to heart. He had received the call to be one of Christ's Advocates during his thirties. He had committed himself ever since on becoming God's earthly, unstoppable force. The Paine administration was the immovable object. The Paine administration *would* move. Better yet it would be destroyed.

Hansen followed Sinclair into the room ignoring the drama unfolding out on the river below and collapsed into the suite's recliner chair. He was exhausted, yet energized by the evening. Nearly a thousand had turned out to hear Hansen present the Tea Party's' vision for America. Hundreds had joined the cause, signed pledges to get involved, and, most important, opened their wallets. Sinclair headed to the bar and poured himself a drink. "Sure I can't make you something, Captain?"

"No thanks," Hansen replied. "You know I don't drink. Dulls the senses. Not good for someone in my present line of work."

"Suit yourself." Sinclair poured himself a double bourbon. Sinclair always thought it peculiar how strict Hansen was with his diet and health. He never smoked, drank or ate meat.

Illegal drugs were clearly out of the question. He worked out constantly. And Sinclair had never seen Hansen in the company of a woman.

The man was almost a monk. Sinclair admired devotion to a cause. Hansen was obviously committed to his health and wellbeing.

Sinclair assumed Hansen liked women, but had never asked. He had considered whether Hansen could be into guys. Again, he had never asked. The thought that Hansen might be gay did trouble Sinclair, though. The Bible was clear on homosexuality being a sin. But what had conservative icon Barry Goldwater once said, "It didn't matter if a soldier was straight, just whether he could shoot straight." Sinclair needed Hansen to shoot straight, not be straight. Goldwater had also said, "Extremism in the defense of liberty is no vice." Sinclair liked both of these quotes, although he believed Goldwater should have added, "and God," to the second.

Sinclair had asked Hansen about his non-relationship habits (or lack thereof) once. Hansen had credited it to his captivity at the hands of al Qaeda. "Not much opportunity to drink, smoke or carouse during my stay with the ragheads. Once I returned to the states I had lost all desire to engage in these behaviors. I've submitted to the will of a higher power, which requires my capacities to be continually sharp."

Sinclair crossed the room and sat on the couch across from Hansen, placing his drink on the marble coffee table. The room was a little too polished for Sinclair's tastes. He preferred a more rustic, masculine room. This was too corporate, too stale. But it was the best suite in Spokane and he also liked the best.

"Leading a political movement is harder than combat." Hansen said. "It's a lot of smoke and mirrors, perception and public opinion. Hard to tell when we are making any progress or when the ultimate prize will be reached.

"On the battlefield it's always much easier, more clear," Hansen continued. "Back in the Middle East there was no question of who was good or evil, who stood with God and who with the devil. Friends saved, enemies killed. Simple."

Sinclair picked up his drink and took a long swig. Downing the rest of his bourbon, he placed the empty glass back on the coffee table. He leaned toward Hansen, smelling the hint of alcohol on his breath. "Then it's time to talk about the more *simple* aspects of our plan."

Chapter 12
Colombia, Deserted Seashore, May 29, Early Morning

Several days had passed since the casket had been unloaded from the Blazing Sun. During that time it had been transferred into what appeared to be a normal shipping crate, but this one had been lead-lined and could withstand a fairly large explosion. As such it weighed a ton and required a small army of men to move.

The same covered truck and its group of men, plus a few more that met the trawler earlier in the week, bounced down a dusty Colombian back road to the sea. There was no port this time. Rather, the destination was a deserted part of the Pacific coast. They knew they had arrived at their location as the road simply ended at the beach. There were no buildings, no boat ramp, not even a street sign marking their destination. The sand stretched on for miles in both directions and looked like any other deserted stretch of beach on the Colombian coast. The truck driver could be forgiven if he had gotten lost searching for the right spot. This was exactly as the handlers wanted it. No one in their right mind would be at this spot, this part of the Colombian coast, at this time, unless they were part of this operation. Or extremely unlucky.

However, the driver knew immediately he was in the right place. Pulling the truck out onto the packed sand, the truck's headlights lit upon a small futuristic submarine pulled up on the shore. It looked like something out of the movies. The craft had a low draft, resembling a stretched

football cut in half end to end. Its skin was
smooth and painted black with the exception of a
few slit windows. It was called the *Porsche*. South
American drug smugglers had adopted the habit of
naming their subs after automobiles for reasons no
one could remember. For its size, the *Porsche* did
have an impressive cargo space, holding up to a
ton of materials, usually cocaine. The casket filled
only a small part of the sub's hold. Nothing else
would make this trip though. The current cargo
was too important.

The *Porsche* was the latest development in
the drug smuggling business. In the '70s, South
American drug cartels used small planes to
transport their contraband. Unfortunately, the
U.S. Coast Guard became quite adept at
intercepting these illegal flights. In response,
smugglers turned to dropping drugs from planes.
This prevented the capture of smuggling pilots and
their planes, but the drops were imprecise and
spread the drugs over wide areas, often making it
hard for those on the ground to find. Smugglers
next turned to speed boats made famous in
television shows like *Miami Vice*. The journey
from South America to the United States was hard
on the boats. Nearly half sank making the trip.
Those that didn't were often picked up by
American law enforcement. Profits shrank. The
cartels needed another way to get their goods to
market. If the air and water were denied them,
going beneath the waves was the obvious solution.

By standards of traditional navies, the
Porsche was a joke. Its keel was made up of a
stripped down speed boat. The top was enclosed

with fiberglass reinforced with armor plating, then coated with light, radar absorbing material. It had two salvaged Cummings 250 engines each turning an independent propeller. It was capable of limited dives of a day's duration. With its ample smoke stack the vessel could travel partially submerged for indefinite periods. However, for this mission its ability to completely plunge beneath the waves was the crucial factor. The *Porsche* wouldn't win any beauty, speed or durability contests, but it would get the job done. That's all that mattered

The vessel's captain was Gustov Olfsen, an experienced submariner who had worked for the Swedish Navy. As a sub captain he had tracked Russian submarines for a living. This took him out under the Arctic Ocean, often gliding under the polar ice cap for weeks at a time. However, it had been his experience after the military, as a cruise ship captain, that landed him this job. It was a simple ferrying operation that, if successful, would allow him to retire comfortably to some warm Caribbean island.

After seeing the casket secured and locked away in the hold, Olfsen and his first mate cast off. The men who had loaded the casket were already long gone.

"Dive to submersion depth and set course for Cabo San Lucas," Olfsen bellowed. With that, the *Porsche* began to sink beneath the surface and headed north toward Mexico.

Chapter 13
White House, Washington D.C., June 2, Late Afternoon

Scott Beardsley stood in the cabinet room running a Power Point projector. Scott was the president's Chief of Staff and had been with Paine since his time in Montana.

Scott's business attire, if one could call it that, was a rumpled mess. His coat was off, his collar undone, and his slacks wrinkled. His shoes were scuffed and often untied. Scott hadn't worn a tie in years. A three-day's beard was on his chin. The president's Chief of Staff didn't care about the message his clothes or grooming sent, and the Commander in Chief didn't either.

If it had been anyone but Scott, the president would have fired that person years ago. Yet, Scott was the best White House political operative in a generation. The president's Chief of Staff didn't care about appearances, his attire made this obvious. However, many of his political opponents assumed Scott's apparel meant he didn't care about results either. This couldn't be further from the truth, and many of the Chief of Staff's political opponents held this belief at their own peril.

Scott was a political junky and had cut his teeth on presidential campaigns including those of Clinton and Gore. He had learned the ins and outs of presidential politics, the cutthroat nature of running a campaign, what was needed for success and an ability to size up who had what it took to get across the finish line. His work with the Clinton and Gore campaigns had taught him two

valuable lessons. First, his time with Clinton, the
masterful politician, had taught him what was
needed not to lose. President Clinton had been
the underdog for most of his campaign and
presidency, yet won more battles than he lost.
Clinton had called it politics with a strategic
offense and tactical defense. Through maneuvers,
political calculations, a sharp political intellect, and
on occasion tactical retreat or redirection, Clinton
had been able to confuse and beguile his
opponents. This had been a valuable time for
Scott. He learned much and was forever thankful
to Clinton for his first stint in the White House.
However, it was his time with the Gore campaign
that taught him a more important lesson. What
was necessary to win.

Even to this day, Scott could not forgive
Gore for his failure to push the Florida recount.
Yes, he had lost a Supreme Court case, but Gore's
capitulation at this turn of events merely showed
he didn't have the stomach to do whatever it took
to be president. George W. Bush, to his credit,
would and did do what it took to win. W pulled
strings, used his family and political influence, took
contradictory positions that only made sense when
analyzed from a winner-take-all perspective.

If asked by a reporter on election day what
his hope for the day was, Gore would have likely
responded it was to receive the most votes. At the
end of the day, Vice President Gore got his wish
when nearly 51 million cast their ballot for the
former Vice President. This was more votes than
anyone had received for president up to that time
in U.S. history. But Gore, as well as the country,

quickly learned that getting the most votes didn't
assure victory. The Gore campaign, Scott , and the
rest of the country had learned that day that Gore
had tragically focused on the wrong goal. This
would never happen to one of Scott's candidates
again.

Getting the most votes certainly hadn't
been the objective of the Bush effort. The Bush
campaign would have enjoyed winning the popular
vote, sure, but the Texas governor and company
knew it wasn't necessary in order to achieve
victory. Rather, Bush's central focus was winning
the presidency. He would do whatever it took to
achieve that goal. As it turned out, this didn't
require winning the popular vote or, as some
would argue, even the Electoral College tally.
Rather, it required getting support of one more
Justice than Gore on the U.S. Supreme Court.
That was what it took to achieve victory. Scott
had learned that becoming clear on the goal made
it possible to identify the tactics necessary to
achieve that goal. Choosing the wrong goal
inevitably led to failure. Scott now worked for
President Paine. Scott's goal and therefore the
campaign's goal was to see John Paine sworn in for
a second term the following January. Nothing else
mattered.

On the opposite wall from Scott's desk
were posted two oversized calendars, November
and January. Two days were circled in bright red
sharpie: Election Day and Inauguration day.
Remain focused on the goal was written across the
bottom. This was a daily reminder of what was
needed to be done and how much time remained

in the campaign.

Clinton had won in large part due to the country's fatigue with the Reagan-Bush agenda. It was a well-known secret that in 1992, with Ross Perot in the race, just about any Democratic candidate would beat George Bush. He merely needed to show up. However, the 2000 election revealed to Scott that it took more than the fundamentals of getting out the vote, raising money, building a strong state network, or even getting the most votes to win the White House, or even securing two hundred seventy electoral votes. No, the White House was won by doing anything and everything to secure the presidency. A candidate must be all in, if he wanted to be president. To focus on anything else was folly or worse, delusion--both deadly to a presidential campaign, pure and simple. Scott's job was to make certain the president's willingness, his spine, was strong enough to take the campaign to the end.

Four years earlier, Scott had made clear he would only run Paine's campaign if Paine had the strength and willingness to play rough in order to win the White House. Scott explained he would prefer to run a lofty campaign, but he expected any candidate he managed to *vigorously* defend the values and programs he believed in. The public wanted a fighter, he had told Paine. And a true fighter shouldn't be above employing the tools artfully wielded by the opposition. People talked about their desire for a more civilized political discussion, but it was hot air in Scott's opinion. The electorate rewarded candidates who could not only take a punch, but give one as well.

It wasn't like Scott didn't hope for a more civil discussion. God knows the country would benefit from everyone at least getting on the same political page. Yet, again this wasn't the goal. To achieve the country's agenda, one needed political power. And to achieve political power one must sometimes call a spade a spade.

Political pundits and talking heads crowded the Sunday morning talk shows chattering about how the country wanted leaders who were problem solvers. Scott always had to laugh when he heard this. Where was the evidence? Scott hadn't seen it, moreover his experience told him otherwise. The country, deep down, wanted fighters. Men and women who took strong political stands and were willing to fight like hell for those positions. Fighters, at least from Scott's experience, were rewarded with election success.

A central aspect of Scott's campaign philosophy focused on identifying where his candidate's comfort level was regarding purely political maneuvers, or what some called dirty tricks. Those could include awarding military contracts to swing states or launching IRS investigations of an opponent's political donors. Scott knew liberals got queasy and weak kneed when confronted with such bare-knuckled political moves. But conservatives figured out long ago that doing the unseemly was the path to power and had abandoned any qualms about making such moves. Scott had lost his reservations as well.

Scott admired the conservatives for having the clear grasp of what was needed to win. They understood that to have a vision for the country and no power was the worst possible outcome. To implement one's vision, political power was needed. To achieve political power, doing the unbecoming was sometimes necessary. No, always necessary.

Political campaigns were rough business, Scott knew. But it had always been so. Take Thomas Jefferson's campaign in 1800. It had been an extremely bitter affair, his opponent calling into question Jefferson's allegiance to the United States. While the election of 1884 centered on the rumored illegitimacy of Grover Cleveland's son.

No one was going to hand President Paine a second term. He would have to fight for it. But Scott thought this was good. History showed that the best candidates were forged in a heated campaign. Protracted, difficult political battles required candidates, at least the good ones, to identify their core beliefs and fight like hell for them. Often unknown to the candidates, the fighting infused a deeply felt ownership of these values and the public policy needed to achieve these values. A candidate who believed in what he was saying was a better communicator. Like a good preacher, a heartfelt message resonated with the audience. Deeply felt messages produced an authenticity in the candidate's speech, in his mannerism, in his public appearances. An authentic candidate would win nearly every single time. An authentic candidate was better than a smart candidate, better than a candidate with experience, even better than a candidate with connections. Thankfully, Paine had all these qualities, which should make him unbeatable in the fall.

But, Scott believed fighting, at least political fighting, shouldn't be limited to campaigns. A failure to fight for policy was the second flaw of candidates and the first flaw of a politician. Often once a candidate achieved election victory, they put aside their fighting ways and began to search for the elusive political consensus. Yet, like the mythic unicorn or mermaid, consensus didn't exist.

It may have at one time, but no longer. Consensus required at least two sides acting in good faith to achieve a political goal. But that good faith evaporated years ago. Politics was a dirty business of determining who gets what. The fight, the struggle, produced strong, well-crafted plans. Sadly, many, mostly in his party, were either ignorant of this fact or, worse, choose to ignore it. Thankfully Scott was fully aware that the rules had changed.

Nothing was achieved by consensus. In fact, in Scott's view it produced the worst possible candidates and public policy. His political experience had shown the American voter craved and rewarded leaders who fought for what they believed.

Winning elections was only half the battle. In many cases, that was the easy part of governing. Make promises, meet voters, state your case and repeat. Oh yeah, and the candidate needs to raise a few dollars as well. It wasn't rocket science. It wasn't even as complicated as sausage making. But through all the baby kissing, TV debates, county fairs, fundraisers, there was an end to the race, a clear goal.

Passing legislation, drafting public policy, moving public opinion was different. There was no end to the debate, no end of the line. Discussion, investigations, and hearings went on and on and on. Many times these discussions led to nothing, no resolution. Even when a vote was taken, a bill signed, or a court order handed down, there was always opportunity for another vote, a legal appeal, or new investigation to reopen the argument. This endless battle often took many new politicians by surprise. It certainly frustrated the public. Many couldn't understand or didn't care to appreciate how the American government actually worked. Why did Washington have so much trouble getting things done? Had the federal government lost the ability to deal with the truly important problems?

Scott knew these weren't the right questions. The U.S. political system worked nearly perfectly. Yes, a few adjustments could be made to the process, such as reining in the flow of corporate money, but all in all it was working as the founders had envisioned.

The founding fathers had set up a government where decisions were never final. There was always a way to appeal any decision. If one wanted definitive results, final answers, they should move to China or North Korea, the world's last few dictatorships. What had George W. Bush once said, governing would be easier if he were dictator. True. But that wasn't the American way.

Many politicians, especially presidents,

failed to grasp this. They expected a political battle to be a sprint with a clear finish line. But it was a marathon. No, actually a never ending treadmill that only seemed to get faster and faster. The finish line continually moved like a mirage just beyond one's grasp. Many politicians bemoaned this fact. They called it partisan politics. Scott called it reality.

Scott knew the only way to truly win, to achieve a permanent political victory, was to get one's opponent to surrender. They would have to become so exasperated, so frustrated, so exhausted that they would take their political marbles and leave the game. Scott had seen many countless opponents quit the game in disgust.

But the flip was true as well. One could never really lose a political fight if one never quit. Always appealing, always calling for another vote, always filing another legal challenge insured that any defeat was temporary. A good politician never admitted defeat. Why would he? Rather, a good politician was always fighting for a future victory, even if that victory never really came.

President Paine, if Scott had anything to do with it, would fight hard for his beliefs. In fact, Scott expected this campaign to be an even nastier, harder slog than the one four years before. In part because Paine now had a record to defend.

In less than four years, President Paine had righted the ship of state. He had shored up the economy, stabilized employment, improved its defenses, and even added a few new parks. But it wasn't enough to secure victory. It hadn't been fast enough, it hadn't been broad enough, it hadn't been you-name-it enough, or so went the opposition mantra. What was the old saying, if President Paine walked on water his detractors would say he couldn't swim.

At its core, President Paine's, and really Scott Beardsley's, philosophy on government was that the federal government not only could improve people's lives, but it *should*. The bumper sticker theme of his opposition had been that it was the role of the individual to determine his or her fate. Each person was responsible for pulling themselves up by their own bootstraps. How many times had Scott heard Senator Michael Healy talk about his father's humble beginnings, that he had never received one ounce of government assistance. Of course, the truth was ignored, that the good senator's beginnings weren't humble, that he had inherited much of his wealth and position.

Scott didn't besmirch Senator Healy his good fortune. Scott wanted all Americans to have an equal shot at the pursuit of happiness. But it was how men like Senator Healy saw the government's role in insuring that happiness that Scott took issue with.

Senator Healy's view, as best as Scott could understand it, was that the federal government should do as little as possible for its citizens. Little more than protecting people's access to guns, deporting illegals, and building the military. Government wasn't in the business of making American citizens' lives better. That was each person's responsibility, the good Senator from Virginia bellowed every time a microphone was put before him.

Scott knew the opposition's words revealed their true thinking. Government wasn't in the business of making lives better. Scott would agree, the federal administration wasn't in business at all, it was into governing. It was a very real and significant difference in world views.

Running a country was different than running a business. A business' goal above all was to make a profit. Good businessmen cut expenses and raised revenues to maximize profits. Good businessmen, according to the opposition, were allowed to, in fact required to, do anything legal to maximize their profits. Closing a plant or laying off hundreds of American workers and moving those jobs overseas are completely rational decisions. Yet, the United States wasn't a business. Its goal wasn't to turn a profit. Its primary responsibility was to protect its citizens. The president and his detractors agreed on this point. However, they starkly disagreed on how and what constituted this protection. Improving their health, cleaning their water and air, providing basic and consistent education, protecting public lands, regulating drugs and food quality, setting market rules were all part of protecting U.S. citizens, just as important in Scott's view as deploying the military.

But where in the Constitution was this *expanded* authority the opposition chided? The founding fathers never envisioned regulating the environment. Therefore federal agencies like the EPA were a big government overreach, obviously unconstitutional they would maintain. If it was so obvious then why haven't the agency's detractors ever filed a lawsuit challenging the EPA's constitutional underpinnings?

Rather they would bloviate on and on about if a power wasn't explicitly mentioned in the Constitution then the federal government was barred from exercising it. Almost as if repeating the mantra over and over would make it true. It didn't matter to these zealots that the founding fathers hadn't envisioned the airplane either, but this didn't stop senators like Healy from singing the praises of the federal government's Air Force. Scott always had to chuckle at this hypocrisy. It clearly revealed their lack of constitutional understanding. More importantly, it revealed they hadn't likely read it either.

Like most Americans, Scott knew the Constitution was the central blueprint for how the federal government was supposed to operate, what powers the government's three branches were to have, how that authority could be exercised, and by what means the branches check the other's authority. However, Scott also knew the Constitution's preamble laid out the *why* of the federal government.

At the time of the Constitution's drafting, the country had completed a successful rebellion against the British Empire. The Articles of Confederation which governed the colonies' association during the war had been found too weak and cumbersome. If the colonies were to sustain their victory a new political compact was needed, one which would allow for the central collection of revenues, the raising of an army, and the regulation of trade. But the founders went

further than to ask the *how* and the *what* questions
of government, they also asked the *why*. Why was
the new government needed and what would be
the overriding goals?

The misguided or historically ignorant
believed the federal government had been set up
with the single goal of providing security, mainly
through the military. While this was one of the
government's goals, the founders also laid out in
the preamble the federal government's
responsibility to establishing justice, securing
domestic tranquility, supporting the general
welfare, and securing liberty.

The preamble then is where Scott, and in
turn President Paine, believed the administration's
authority sprang to follow its domestic and foreign
policy. Scott would call it a strict interpretation of
all of the Constitution's mandates. One of Scott's
first official acts as presidential Chief of Staff was
to convince the president to seek a Department of
Justice analysis of Scott's constitutional
interpretation. Not surprisingly the D.O.J. agreed
with Scott.

Yet despite the president's aggressive and
successful record it clearly had not made everyone
happy, especially the country's conservative
Christians. His position on abortion, school
prayer, and tax policy had particularly set them off.
Though the president's work with the Israelis and
Palestinians on Middle East peace had been the
last straw. These groups believed the president
was the antichrist. When pressed, though, they
would back away from this charge. Maybe
President Paine wasn't the antichrist himself, they

would admit, but under their breath they would
accuse him of at least being one of his minions.
And right-wing blogs and media outlets did all they
could to feed this perception. Political fallout,
splatter as Scott called it, from these efforts
inevitably hit the Chief of Staff. In fact, Scott did
all he could to encourage conservative ire and draw
their fire. It was his way to better protect the
president and in turn the president's policy agenda.

Scott adjusted the PowerPoint projector,
bringing the presentation, the re-election strategy
slide, into better focus. He advanced the
PowerPoint to the next graph. It showed
numerous opinion polls from around the country.
The information was sliced and diced countless
ways, probably by some Ph.D. student intern from
Harvard. Numerous graphs and multi-colored pie
charts made the information more appealing to
look at, but no less easy to understand. Fifteen
percent of 35 to 45 year olds supported this, while
forty seven percent of 18 to 25 year olds opposed
that. The numerous slides made murky what was
obvious. The public was with the president on all
the major issues, be it abortion, tax policy, or
defense spending. That support wasn't always
solid, but they supported him. Why the graphs
couldn't merely say that, Scott would never
understand. He decided to dump the PowerPoint.

Making things more difficult was a sickness
shared by many in Washington D.C., especially
liberals. Scott had learned long ago that having the
ability to make problems more not less
complicated was a prerequisite for working in the
nation's capital. No problem, no challenge, no

matter how small could be simple. Every problem had to be nuanced, analyzed from every angle, studied to death.

On its surface this made sense. Problems should be studied. They should be understood and analyzed, a decision could always benefit from more information. At a gut level the public understood this need. This need to make problems harder also came from liberals' fear of making a mistake, a fear Scott knew conservatives did not share. But it was opponents of progress who also understood this process and manipulated it to their advantage. If a policy change or legislative action, especially one you thought might go against your interests, was about to come down, the surest way to stall or even kill its implementation was to call for more study. This made the person calling for additional analysis seem reasonable and those opposing it irrational. Never mind that additional study seldom turned up new information, it merely wasted scarce dollars and irreplaceable time.

An entire industry of consultants sprouted up in Washington over the past century to provide the decision makers with every possible approach for exploring a problem. The high-priced, well-dressed analysts wouldn't be necessary if problems were easy. Therefore it was in their best interest to make problems hard, difficult, intractable, and not the least of all incomprehensible. It was mind-numbing and caused many lesser political minds to run out of Washington screaming, often dumber than when they arrived.

But not Scott. He thrived on cutting

through the political bull-shit. He had the uncanny
ability to see through the spin, identify its
weaknesses, and ask the pointed, yet necessary
questions. Those on the receiving end of Scott's
interrogations often reacted as one would at
witnessing someone shitting in church. Scott
didn't care. This wasn't church, besides it wasn't
he who was shitting. It was those he was
questioning. He was merely calling them out on it.
And it seemed like there was a lot more floor-
shitting these days.

The Washington inner circle, the elite,
called him an ass at their carefully controlled gala
dinners and cocktail parties. They whispered *puppet
master* as he walked by, referring to his undue
influence over the president and his advisors.
Scott let that perception continue. In fact, he
encouraged the elite's use of the term. A puppet
master meant someone pulling the leader's strings.
Someone with real power to make people bend to
his will. It was a simple and understandable
assumption, yet it couldn't be further from the
truth.

Scott wasn't a puppet master, hell, he
wasn't even an orchestra conductor. At least a
conductor knew the tune and like a musical traffic
cop made sure everyone played the same song. He
didn't even have that much power.

No, Scott was more like a magician. His
job, pure and simple was to pull rabbits out of
hats, guess people's cards, and make pretty ladies
disappear. In other words, make the public and,
better yet, his opponents believe and see things
that may not be true. Make the president appear

to have more support than he really did, show overwhelming public opposition for a particular piece of legislation, build a media firestorm over a proposed congressional action--these were all mastered illusions. Making the voting public believe in the inevitability of the president's re-election was his next trick.

Al Gore had been outmaneuvered, outhustled, and outfought in the 2000 election. Scott would never let that happen to another one of his candidates. He called this meeting to discuss next steps in the campaign. The president would likely win re-election, but no one would take a November victory for granted. In fact, Scott wanted to crush Senator Healy, destroy him if possible, providing the president an undeniable mandate for his second term. If Scott could also insure the party's presidential victory in the next election all the better. Scott knew anything short of total domination this fall would be spun by pundits and congressional backbiters as a sure sign of the presidential weakness. The media talking heads would interpret the so called weak results as a sure sign of blood in the water. That was the way politics worked. Any event could be spun either positively or negatively. Whoever got to the microphone first and the loudest often controlled the conversation and thus the debate.

Scott never forgot a lesson he had learned in college regarding the art of political spin. The Soviets had been masters of bending reality toward their socialist view of reality. Scott remembered the joke regarding the two person speed skating race between an American and a Soviet. The

American had won the race quite handily. The Russian, if Scott remembered correctly, had fallen and would end up losing to the American by a lap. How had the Soviets interpreted the result? The Soviet speed skater finished second. The American finished second to last. It was a true statement, and accurately described the turn of events from the Soviet point of view. Any event, any result, could be spun, turned to an advantage. He spent his career learning this skill until the point he had become a master at spin. One political cartoonist had drawn Scott as a circus performer entertaining lady liberty by spinning numerous plates on long poles. There were dozens of poles spinning countless plates. Simply more than his two hands and legs could hold. A member of the circus audience asked a fellow crowd member how did Scott do it? The hinted answer was that Scott would bring out an additional appendage, implying that his spin was screwing the country.

He had the cartoon framed and hung on his wall.

Scott sat opposite the president who in turn sat at the head of the cabinet room's table. The president wore his custom hand-made Italian business suit. It fit perfectly, but was too expensive for Scott's tastes. It had been a gift from the Italian Prime Minister so the president didn't feel quite as bad wearing it. The blue business suit with contrasting red tie made Paine look even more presidential. Scott knew the president liked looking the part.

A stack of documents, reports, and books were spread out across the Cabinet room table.

They contained the opinions of well-paid lobbyists, economists and lawyers. All the same information that was contained in Scott's report in paper form. Scott wondered how much paper the White House generated every day. It seemed like a waste.

The president picked up a sheet of paper, the latest CNN/New York Times poll printed on it. The numbers were troubling. The president could tell that just from the look on everyone's face. Yet, the funny thing about polls was that they only gave the reader a view of the past. Polls could not tell the future. This was the error many a politician made reading the latest poll. The public's opinion from three days past was no indication of what or where it would be three days future, let alone an election in six months' time.

The Cabinet room was smaller than most expected. Built during the Taft administration, the room could barely accommodate the fifteen Cabinet officials. When the press and presidential aides crowded in the room it became unbearable. Thankfully, it wasn't crowded today. No press, no aides, no interns.

Around the White House Cabinet room's large conference table was the president's re-election team, including party leaders from battleground states.

The president took in Scott's report. The president had heard the information numerous times before. Paine ran his hand over his head, ruffling his previously well coifed hair. Thankfully the press wasn't present to snap a shot of the most powerful man in the world in a less than regal state. While Scott was droning on, the president,

Scott could see, had trouble maintaining his focus. He stared off into space. The Commander in Chief leaned back in the chair and took in the room's paintings.

On the walls were presidential portraits. It was tradition for every president to select portraits of his four favorite chief executives. The paintings came from the Smithsonian's National Portrait Gallery and were to symbolize past administrations and their influences on the current one. Scott knew they were really Paine's heroes. During the transition, President-elect Paine had chosen Lincoln's portrait first. Although a Republican, this man's portrait was easy. Paine had always admired Lincoln's steadfast unwillingness to compromise on the preservation of the Union. It was good for a president to know and hold onto at least one steadfast value.

Next, Paine had chosen Teddy Roosevelt. Roosevelt had been the first modern president who truly loved the job. Roosevelt believed in a can-do approach to governing. He hadn't wanted to hear why he couldn't do something. Rather, he wanted his advisors to tell him how he could do what he believed was necessary for the good of the country. Roosevelt was also clear on what he opposed. Scott knew Paine respected that too. Most politicians could tell the public what they were for, democracy, freedom, etc., but few candidates, especially, a liberal one, could state with conviction what they stood against. Liberals always balked when it came to stating their opposition to something. Roosevelt stood against the private accumulation of power and the wanton

135

destruction of natural resources. For a president
to know what he was against was as important as
knowing what he was for. It made it easier to
decide where to lead.

President Paine had next chosen Harry
Truman. Paine was struck by President Truman's
ability to keep things in perspective. No president
before or since had on day one in the job been
thrown into more hot water than *Give 'em hell
Harry*. Yet, despite his trial by fire he had
successfully led the country through the end of
World War II, contained the growing threat of the
Soviet Union, and transitioned the country to a
peace time economy. Through all of this Truman
remained an everyman. While president, the man
had loved to take strolls down Pennsylvania
Avenue and even took trips to the bank to deposit
his own checks.

The president's final pick, Scott
understood, had been the most difficult. The
president had thought long and hard about the
fourth choice. In the end, Paine had selected a
president who shared a trait with the other three,
the love of politics. In other words, the
understanding that at its heart politics was a game
of picking winners and losers. Viewing it as a
game made achieving administrative goals easier.
Bill Clinton was the consummate politician,
consistently beating his political enemies. The man
had been impeached and still finished his second
term with sixty percent approval ratings.

Scott went over the final polling data.
President Paine continued to stare at the paintings,
asking himself what these previous presidents

would do in his situation. The Chief of Staff had nearly completed his thirty minute presentation, but the point could have been summed up in a single sentence: the president had a fight on his hands.

The president sat at the far end of the table, now listening intently. "So, if I have this straight, the election at this point is a dead heat."

"Correct," Scott answered.

"And to win we are going to need to carry at least one state we lost in the last election."

"Correct again."

"And," turning to address the entire team, "we've identified North Carolina, Wyoming, and Oklahoma as possible pickup states."

"Yes, sir. Although, your campaign team has settled on Wyoming as our best bet," Scott said. "You are currently up by five percentage points in the Cowboy state. We've also got Wyoming Governor Ted Carson out campaigning hard for your re-election. His approval ratings are in the high 60s and he appears to be pulling your state numbers up. It also doesn't hurt that there's a rumor going around that he may be added to the ticket as Vice President."

"Gee, I wonder who started that bit of gossip?" President Paine stated, shooting a crooked glance toward his Chief of Staff.

Vice President Winfield had been discharged from Bethesda just two days prior and already rumors were circulating about his future in the administration. Political pundits were burning up hours of airtime speculating on the Veep's condition. Unknown to these talking heads was that the Vice President's prognosis wasn't good. The Army doctors at Bethesda had determined Winfield's cancer was back and it had metastasized throughout his body, including his lungs and brain. He had nine months, a year at most, to live.

President Paine returned to the discussion at hand. "What else do we have planned for the state?"

"I'm glad you asked. The political team would like approval to schedule an August campaign appearance in the state. In particular, we'd like you to give a major speech at Yellowstone on your vision for the National Park Service. The NPS is celebrating its anniversary that month. A celebration of the park system's future will receive significant play across the country and most importantly in Wyoming."

"Good. It's mom, apple pie, and national parks wrapped up in one."

"We'd like to make an announcement of the trip in the next couple of days."

"Do it," the president ordered.

Chapter 14
Cabo San Lucas, Mexico, June 3, Early Afternoon

"Up scope," Olfsen ordered. The hiss of hydraulics filled the bridge as the rudimentary periscope went up. With an audible click the periscope locked in place.

The tub was so loud Olfsen half expected patrols flying overhead would hear their arrival in Cabo. Olfsen had been assured that the *Porsche* wouldn't be detected by the Mexican Navy. Of this, Olfsen had no doubt. The Mexican Navy wasn't known for its ability to track, let alone stop, drug subs. But just to make sure the Mexican sailors wouldn't be a problem, Olfsen was assured the local commanders had been taken care of. He assumed this meant the commanders had been paid off, but with this client he couldn't be entirely sure a more violent fate hadn't befallen the officers.

Olfsen removed his glasses and peered into the periscope's eyepiece. The scope wasn't even as sophisticated as the most antiquated devices he'd had in the Swedish Navy, but it was sufficient for this mission, that of spotting, tracking and determining the range of surface vessels. The *Porsche* had no weapons. So this information wasn't used for sinking ships, but rather for avoiding them. Tonight, however, such information would be used for getting in close, very close.

Olfsen spun the scope through its circle looking for their contact vessel. Where was it? Spinning through the 360 degree arc, he first spotted a Mexican Navy vessel. A quick dose of adrenaline shot through his body in reflex to the days in the Swedish Navy. A good captain always received a jolt when an enemy warship filled his view screen. The rush passed as quickly as it came. Nothing to worry about. Since the bloody Mexican drug war had broken out these ships were out and visible to give tourists a sense of security. But the naval vessel, although top of the line for Mexico, lacked the ability to find or track the *Porsche*. The *Porsche* was virtually invisible to both Mexican military and law enforcement ships. Besides, hadn't the local commander been taken care of?

Continuing his periscope search, Olfsen finally found his target.

The Carnival *Brilliance* Cruise ship came into his view screen. The Brilliance was the next generation massive cruise ship, holding more than five thousand passengers and crew. The *Brilliance* had been chosen for this mission because of its massive size, acoustic signature, its speed, and its itinerary. The *Porsche* would hide under the *Brilliance*. The prospect of riding under a massive cruise ship was not something Olfsen envied. However, the U.S. military and its tracking satellites were quite sophisticated. The Navy couldn't find the *Porsche* with conventional surface radar or sonar, however, satellite technology had advanced far enough that it could spot sub wakes even while submerged. Consequently, satellites had their electronic eyes glued to the ocean straddling the U.S./Mexican border looking for telltale unattributed wake patterns. The clear

indication of a sub. Drug smugglers had
discovered that hiding under other vessels,
especially legitimate vessels like cruise ships, were
the best way to avoid satellite detection.

"Dive to submersion depth," Olfsen said.
"Start the clock." The *Porsche* would have roughly
twenty four hours of breathable air from that point
forward. That shouldn't be a problem as they
would be on the surface in U.S. waters long before
then.

The *Porsche* slowly sank beneath the waves
like a shark with quiet purpose. "Ahead slow,"
Olfsen called to his first mate. The *Porsche*
dropped to only fifty feet below the surface,
roughly its maximum dive depth. The sub wasn't
built for deep dives, rather for stealth. At this
depth there was still enough sunlight for the crew
to navigate by sight. "Pull us up under the ship."

The *Porsche* glided under the massive cruise
ship. "Full stop, cut engines," Olfsen ordered.
The *Porsche* went deathly quiet, as if sinking to its
watery grave. Hopefully that wouldn't be the case.

"Extend grapples, slow surface." Olfsen
had only performed the grapple maneuver in
simulations. This was the first field application.
And although his employers assured him it would
work, the grapple was an untested device.
Moreover, it was he, not his employers that was
afloat fifty feet beneath one of the largest cruise
ships on the seas inside a fiberglass coffin.

Two large hybrid magnet suction cups
extended out of the top of the *Porsche*. These cups
would create a bond between the submarine and
cruise ship, a bond strong enough to withstand

even the shearing forces the *Brilliance* created once at its return voyage cruise speed. Or that was the theory anyway.

The *Porsche* rose to a scant twenty feet beneath the cruise liner. All surface sunlight had vanished, immersing the sub in a near jet-black void. But it didn't matter. An indicator probe extended from the top of the sub would tell the captain when they were ten feet from contact. A few seconds later he got confirmation of this fact.

"Contact light, Captain," the first mate whispered.

"Surface to slow," Olfsen said. He was sweating. Countless things could go wrong at this stage, not the least of which was hitting the cruise ship too hard and damaging the sub. That would quickly end their trip and likely both of their lives. The final seconds before contact was achieved seemed to drag indefinitely. Olfsen let out a breath in relief with the small thud from above that indicated the magnets had locked onto the hull.

"We have magnetic contact and hold," the first mate confirmed, looking up from his control panel with a sheen of sweat on his forehead.

"Excellent. Create vacuum seal," Olfsen directed.

A slight hiss filled the sub as the suction cups created a vacuum seal between the sub and ship. The first mate's control screen flashed a green all clear signal.

"Cut power," Olfsen said. Now they would wait.

Chapter 15
Yellowstone National Park, Pelican Cone, June 4, Late Afternoon.

The climb up Pelican Cone, a nearly 10,000-foot mountain on the east side of the park, had been a long one. Jessica Drummond and Tom Reynolds huffed up the last few yards to the summit. The trail up the mountain was not marked and was poorly maintained. It didn't appear on any park map. This was on purpose, as it was a trail used to access caldera monitoring equipment rather than for hiking. The public wasn't barred from hiking up Pelican. Drummond and Reynolds had passed a few hardy hikers earlier in the day, in fact. But they just weren't encouraged to do so. Park Rangers were advised to urge visitors toward more maintained trails.

The Park Service, Drummond knew, used this passive form of management to their advantage. Visitors were curious about the park. They wanted to know where they could see wolves, where they could dip their body in a hot pool. The Park Service within reason had to accommodate these requests, but nothing said they had to promote these activities. So, unless someone asked for directions to a specific wolf viewing spot or where the hot spring swimming area was, the Park Service wasn't going to go out of their way to tell anyone. The same went for this trail. It wasn't closed, but it wasn't promoted or highlighted either. This kept would-be vandals from damaging the expensive volcano monitoring equipment at the end of the trail.

Drummond and Reynolds crested the last

little rise on the mountain. The monitoring equipment came into view. The two park scientists walked the remaining hundred yards to the site and dropped their packs. The monitoring station was an inverted steel culvert, roughly a yard in length. The culvert top was enclosed with a locked cover. Drummond opened the lock revealing the GPS, gas monitoring, and seismograph equipment safeguarded within. Reynolds retrieved his laptop computer and hooked it up to each of the three devices. Twenty minutes later the data had been downloaded for analysis.

"What do you think?" Dr. Drummond asked.

"This data confirms what we've been seeing at our other locations," Reynolds responded.

Drummond and Reynolds had spent the last two weeks personally visiting a select number of the park's volcano monitors. They wanted to double check the telemetry they'd received at Mammoth headquarters.

"Like the other sites, earthquake activity is up and the GPS data shows this site has moved several feet to the east since last year," Reynolds went on.

"That data agrees with the other GPS sites, and is a pretty good indication that the land under Shoshone Lake is moving upward," Drummond said.

Dr. Drummond had seen ground displacement like this in Iceland. The Eyjafjallajökull eruption, a volcano in southern

Iceland, had been one of the first times where GPS monitoring was used to predict an eruption. Weeks before the volcano's 2010 blast, the ground around the mountain's peak had been pushed up and out in all directions. It was later determined that molten rock had been moving up through the volcano, inflating and expanding its central peak. Something similar was happening here, at Yellowstone. Although on a scale that dwarfed any previous example.

"What about volcanic emissions?" she asked.

Reynolds tapped a few keys on his computer bringing up a new screen. On it were spreadsheets, charts and pie graphs. "Those are up as well," Reynolds replied staring at the data.

"Where is it highest?" Drummond asked.

"Just over that ridge," Reynolds stated, pointing at a nearby hill.

"Well, let's go check it out," Drummond replied.

The two scientists closed the lid on the equipment culvert and set out for the source of the emissions. It was a short walk.

Cresting the ridge, Drummond gasped at the site before her. A small forest of trees, the entire mountainside, all dead.

"Could a fire have done this?" Reynolds asked.

"Not likely. Look, none of the bark is burnt. Neither is the forest floor," Drummond pointed out.

Walking deeper into the forest, the two scientists saw the ground was littered with dead

animals, squirrels, raccoons, birds, and even an
entire herd of bison. One large male buffalo was
still barely alive, gasping for breath. Panic gripped
Drummond. "Get your respirator on, now!"

They both dropped their packs and
fumbled for their emergency gasmasks. They
hurriedly adjusted the devices to their faces.

"What the hell is going on?" Reynolds
asked, his voice muffled through the mask.

"I've seen this once before," Drummond
yelled through her mask. "Back in 2003,
Yellowstone's Norris Geyser basin spewed out
high levels of volcanic gases, hydrogen sulphide
and carbon dioxide. Ground temperatures went to
near the boiling point. Five bison were killed."

Drummond pulled two small devices from
her pack. The first appeared to be a fancy cell
phone with a small probe extending from the top.
The other was a ground thermometer. "But I have
never seen anything of this magnitude."

Dr. Drummond walked out into the forest
until she found a relatively clear patch of ground.
Kneeling down, she shoved the ground
thermometer into the dirt. Getting back up, she
extended her arm with the cell phone-like device
clutched tightly in her hand. After a few moments
of walking she came to a stop. Still extending the
device, she made a slow circle. The device beeped.
"Just as I thought," she said. "What is it?"
Reynolds replied. "The atmosphere is saturated
with carbon dioxide and hydrogen sulphide."
"Hydrogen sulphide and carbon dioxide are gases
found in magma," Reynolds said. "I know,"
Drummond agreed.

Returning to the thermometer, Dr. Drummond pulled it from the ground. Reynolds peaked over her shoulder as they both read the ground temperature. Ninety eight degrees Celsius. Drummond converted the temperature to Fahrenheit. The screen read two hundred eight degrees.

"We need to get off this mountain and report these developments to headquarters," Dr. Drummond said, trying to keep the panic out of her voice.

Chapter 16
Pacific Ocean, Off Northwestern
Mexican Coast, June 4, Early Morning

The Carnival *Brilliance* had pulled out of Cabo at precisely 3:00 p.m., rounded the Baja peninsula and pushed its engines to maximum. The *Brilliance* was scheduled to be in Long Beach, California the next morning at 5:00 a.m. to begin unloading passengers before setting off on the next cruise. Unknown to the *Brilliance* captain, his ship had a stowaway, and not the normal drunk tourist, but something far more deadly.

Below the surface, Olfsen was cursing under his breath. His client hadn't warned him about the noise. It was damn deafening in the cramped sub with no way to block out the roar. The *Porsche* also shook like a hypothermic shipwreck survivor. So much so that Olfsen began to worry his sub might break apart.

"Captain," the first mate shouted. "We've thrown a propeller."

"Which one?" Olfsen asked.

"It's engine number two."

"How bad is it?" Olfsen asked fearing the worst.

"We can likely make it to our destination. But not back to Colombia."

148

Chapter 17
US Coast Guard Station, San Diego,
June 4, Early Morning

"We've got a ping, Commander," Chief Petty Officer Sandra Fulson stated, turning from her computer screen.

Another ping? Commander Arthur Sanford put down his Coke and got up from his desk. It was five in the morning and he was already on his third soda. What could it be this time? Kitty litter, Chinese toilet seats? The damn nuclear detectors were too sensitive, constantly producing false positives. "Report," Sanford said through a yawn.

"We've got a detection ping tracking north just outside Long Beach, California," Fulson replied.

"A ship?" Sanford asked.

"Not sure. At first I thought it was. I ran the satellite confirmation program. The detectors pinged a cruise ship."

"A what?" Sanford found that odd. Previous pings had come from Navy vessels, cargo ships and even a garbage vessel that had inadvertently picked up spent nuclear materials meant for Hanford, Washington. But never a cruise ship.

"Are you sure?" Sanford requested.

"Yes. I've run the confirmation twice. It's the Carnival *Brilliance* based in Long Beach." Fulson brought up the satellite image of the ship. A red blinking cursor sat like a bull's-eye on the *Brilliance*.

"Do we have a computer analysis on potential material?"

"Well, that's the odd part, sir" Fulson stated. "Both the outer and inner harbor detectors were triggered."

To provide an early warning of any potential threat the harbor's outer detectors were set extremely loose. To eliminate false positives, though, the inner detectors were calibrated more tightly. A hit by both typically meant they weren't chasing a ghost.

"The ship is now coming back clean. Inner harbor sensors on second pass report nothing." Fulson indicated to the red blinking cursor that was now green.

"That is weird," Sanford said. That had never happened before. "I guess it's another false alarm." He rubbed his face, trying to shake the sleepiness. "But let's call NEST just to make sure." The Nuclear Emergency Support Team could field the liability on this one.

Chapter 18
Long Beach, California, June5, Early Morning

The dawn broke as the Carnival *Brilliance* pulled into Long Beach, California a little after 5:00 a.m., ten minutes behind schedule. Not that the passengers would notice. Most were still fast asleep in their berths. Yet, the ship's captain was aware of the delay and even worse the ship's inability to achieve top speed. Surprising given the *Brilliance* was less than a year old and top of the line. It should be able to maintain and surpass its top speed. He would have his engineer check out the engines during the turnaround here in the States.

Standing on the ship's bridge, the captain watched as passengers began to disembark the *Brilliance*. Gangplanks had been extended, allowing passengers and crew to move back and forth from the dock. Meanwhile, dockworkers were already transporting crates of luggage, garbage and other materials from the huge ship. Forklifts raced back and forth along the dock retrieving the crates and transporting them to their new destinations. They returned with new crates, loaded with food, champagne, towels, beach balls, bingo cards. Everything necessary to run a week-long cruise. The forklifts deposited their new cargo near the ship to have it lifted by multistory cranes and placed within the hold of the *Brilliance*. The process would go on for hours. It was almost like a ballet the way the machines moved back and forth, ferrying the goods and supplies on and off the ship. The captain was mesmerized by the efficiency of the process. It all went like clockwork. The dance on the dock made it all the more annoying that the ship, his ship, was ten minutes late into port. That was unacceptable. The captain picked up the bridge phone and dialed his chief engineer. He wanted the engine diagnostic started now.

Chapter 19
NEST Headquarters, Washington
D.C., June 5, Afternoon

"What is this?" Special Agent Dianne Harris demanded, slamming her assignment sheet on Director Tonya Donaldson's desk.

"Come on in, Harris," Donaldson said calmly. She had anticipated Harris's reaction to the announced assignments. She was prepared.

"You're sending Thompson and Goodwin to investigate the cruise ship?" Harris went on without taking a breath. "This decision doesn't make any sense. I'm the best agent you've got. Quite frankly, you need me out in the field not stuck here in Washington."

Director Donaldson had dealt with agents like Harris before. Hot-tempered, eager, to the point. She knew she would have to let the rookie agent vent until she had exhausted her anger, which Harris did in short order. Just to make certain, Donaldson asked if she was done. At that Harris nodded. "Take a seat then, agent," Donaldson ordered, emphasizing the last word. The sooner Harris learned who was the boss the better.

Harris felt drained and spent, but sat on the edge of her seat, tensely.

"Look I know you're disappointed at not getting assigned to the cruise ship investigation," Donaldson explained. "But we have procedures, policy, and law to follow."

Harris began to rise from her chair, about

to launch her rebuttal.

"Sit!" the Director commanded.

Harris sank back in the chair, the full force of the director's reprimand quieting her tongue.

"Dianne," Donaldson now referred to Harris by her first name to lighten the mood and build rapport between them. "I've watched your development for quite awhile. You're smart, motivated, and aggressive. Everyone agrees you're the best graduate to come out of Quantico in nearly three decades. I was happy when I read you'd requested a NEST assignment."

Harris again opened her mouth to speak. Donaldson quieted her with a raise of her hand. "I'm still not done.

"We have more than six hundred employees in this department. They come with backgrounds in nuclear physics, engineering, computer science, mathematics, biology, psychology, and countless other disciplines. They have extensive training in firearms, investigation, bomb disposal, and self-defense. Nearly every one of them is at the top of their field."

Donaldson paused and went on. "However, do you know their most important ability?"

Harris stared at Donaldson, no answer coming to her mind.

Without really waiting for Harris' response Donaldson answered. "Teamwork." Donaldson could see that Harris wasn't getting the point. "Our mission is one of the most important undertaken by the federal government. We have to be perfect. Missing just once could mean the death of millions." She let that sink in for a minute. "To achieve one hundred percent success takes hundreds of people working together as one. Every NEST agent must check his or her ego at the door."

She looked Harris directly in the eye and said, "Agents with a cowboy, go-it-alone mentality aren't going to make it here. This isn't the movies."

Harris shifted in her chair. She now wanted to be anywhere but the director's office.

"Harris, can I give you a little advice?" Donaldson said with a soft, calm tone, which had been developed with years of practice.

Harris nodded, knowing she really didn't have a choice.

"After teamwork, trust is the most important quality for a NEST employee." Donaldson sat back in her chair, crossed her legs and reached for her cup of coffee on her desk. "When I say trust, I mean trust in your teammates, trust in your partner, but most importantly trust in NEST's decision making process. Seldom do we have perfect knowledge about an assignment. Shoot, in my twenty years of doing this job, I've never had perfect knowledge regarding any assignment. We are always in the dark about some aspect of our work."

Donaldson took a drink from her cup, and as she began to speak again she slowed and lowered her voice. She had studied child psychology in college and knew hushed tones required a listener to pay more attention. She needed Harris' full attention. The advice she was providing could mean the difference between a successful or disastrous career.

"Sometimes we are in the dark because the intel is incomplete while at other times we are purposely cut out of the loop due to the professional judgment of our superiors. It's called need to know."

Donaldson placed the mug back on her desk. "Regardless of the reason for a lack of knowledge, we have to trust the decisions of our superiors. Do you understand?"

Harris understood what the director was telling her. She didn't like it, but she understood it. She wouldn't get the cruise ship assignment. She nodded again.

"Good. The sooner we accept this fact and trust that our higher-ups have a clearer picture the better."

Donaldson was nearly finished and about to dismiss her agent. "Look, Dianne, I know you don't like it but I need my best agent here. If it makes you feel any better, you are scheduled for the next assignment."

As Harris walked out her office door, Donaldson thought about the third most important facet of NEST work: diplomacy. Donaldson had developed diplomatic skill as a grandmother to six wonderful grandkids. Grandma Tonya had made certain that *each* of her wonderful grandchildren knew they were grandma's favorite.

Donaldson watched Harris close the door. The director had been telling the truth when she told Harris she was the best. What the director didn't say to her raw agent was that she considered every one of her agents the best. That was something Harris would have to figure out on her own.

Chapter 20
Spokane, WA, June 5, Morning

Jamil Hussain drove west on Interstate 90. He passed countless restaurant, hotel and gas station signs. A few modest twenty-story office buildings could be seen in the distance. Traffic was light this morning, but would pick up shortly as rush hour began. Police patrols looking for speeders wouldn't likely begin for a while longer, but just to be certain Hussain drove his nondescript white sedan rental car at three miles per hour below the speed limit. No need to draw unnecessary police attention to himself and his mission. Hussain was certain he could talk his way out of any police encounter, and would certainly shoot his way out if he had too. But why take the risk. Hussain was continually amazed at how many of his brethren's plots were foiled by routine traffic stops. It was often a failure of discipline or a lack of attention to detail that attracted police interest. Speeding, illegal lane changes or non-working tail lights were not going to keep Hussain from achieving Allah's will.

Hussain tuned the car radio to a local talk radio news program. Mindless news items that had no value to the people listening droned on in the background. What was it called? Infotainment? Neither information nor entertainment were ever present in his opinion.

He was pulling into his workplace as the newscaster reported an update. "The president announced today a campaign trip to Wyoming. Specifically, the president will deliver a speech in

Yellowstone in August in celebration of the
National Park Service's centennial birthday."

Hussain turned up the volume as the
report was picked up by a White House reporter.
"That's right, Charlie. The White House
announced that the president would be unveiling a
new vision to take the national park system into its
next century. While we get the impression that the
details of this vision are still being worked out, it
appears its goals are to make national parks, such
as Yellowstone, Yosemite and the Grand Canyon,
more attractive to diverse audiences, establish new
parks that more fully reflect the broad story of
America, better protect the system's natural
wonders and wildlife, and update visitor facilities."

The reporter droned on about the park
system, that Yellowstone had been the first park,
and on and on. But Hussain was no longer paying
attention. His mind was racing. It was too perfect
to not be a gift from Allah. The president himself
would be in Yellowstone. Now he would be able
to take down both the head *and* body of the snake.
He would even be able to settle the score with the
park ranger who had killed his men a few days ago.
Hussain had read the news reports about Park
Ranger Grayson Cole who had so bravely taken
down the supposed poachers.

Poachers? What a joke. Hussain thought.
The Americans don't have a clue regarding what's
about to hit them. Hussain was livid his men had
been foiled by what appeared to be a gloried boy
scout. But at least his men had delivered the park
data needed for his operation. He would deal with
Cole soon enough.

Hussain pulled into the parking lot of the 7-11.

Time to check in again with his handler.

Chapter 21
Sinclair Ranch, Jackson Hole
Wyoming, June 5, Morning

Charles Sinclair was in his kitchen. He poured himself a cup of coffee as he reviewed his hotels' latest sales figures. Fox News droned on in the background from a flat screen on the wall. Despite the tough economic conditions, serving national park visitors had been highly profitable the past several years. Park visitation was in fact hitting record levels. Charles' team of economists believed many Americans saw national parks as an affordable vacation destination, even in hard times. Whatever the reason, Charles liked his company's numbers.

Putting down the sales report, Sinclair noticed a breaking report flash on the screen. He took another sip of his coffee while turning up the volume. A Fox News White House correspondent was recounting the president's upcoming Yellowstone trip.

Sinclair immediately grabbed the kitchen phone, hitting the speed dial button for Hansen. The moment had finally come and the plan, his plan, could now be finalized.

Sinclair was half listening to the TV reporter as Hansen's voice mail system picked up. Not only was the boy always late, but he never picked up either. For the first time he realized that he had *never* gotten hold of Hansen. When they spoke on the phone it was always Hansen calling him.

When the voice mail greeting ended with the familiar beep, Sinclair left a short message demanding Hansen call him immediately. He clicked off his cell phone and returned his attention to the TV.

What had the reporter said? The president would be here in August. That didn't leave much time.

Chapter 22
Oregon Coast, June 8, Evening

The *Porsche* broke the surface of the Pacific Ocean just beyond the Oregon coast's surf line. Its special black paint made it nearly impossible to see. Even thermal imagers would have difficulty detecting its minimal heat signature. This fact also made it hard for Olfsen's contacts to find the *Porsche*. He was on deck scanning a black section of the coast. He leaned over and whispered down the hatch, "Turn on the transponder." To a casual observer nothing noticeable had changed, however, Olfsen knew to anyone tuned into the correct radio frequency his craft now stood out like a beacon. He just hoped his friends were the only ones listening. This could be the most dangerous part of the mission.

"Nothing, sir." The first mate whispered up through the hatch.

"Keep transmitting," the captain growled. They were in the right place, he knew. He double-checked the GPS just to confirm. Yes, they were at the right beach at the arranged time. He was transmitting on the correct frequency. Had something gone wrong?

Several minutes passed and still nothing. The *Porsche* bobbed in the water, a real sitting duck.

Small ocean waves lapped the side of the sub, providing an odd hypnotic feel that would ordinarily put him at ease. Olfsen, though, was anything but at ease. Had something happened to the pick-up team? Had the mission been called off? Olfsen couldn't help but wonder if he and his first mate had been set up, perhaps some part of an FBI sting. The FBI a few years back had frustrated an apparent attack on the Pentagon by duping an al-Qaeda wanna-be by setting him up with a phony gun and a fake bomb. The would-be terrorist was arrested just as he was trying to implement his plan. Could Olfsen be facing the same set-up?

Olfsen spun around wildly, scanning the horizons for any sign of a Coast Guard vessel. Nothing. The faint scent of oil filled his nostrils. Just as he had thought. A slight, but visible, oil sheen could be seen trailing behind the *Porsche*, its black, inky mass spreading off into the horizon. The *Porsche* must have developed a leak after throwing its second propeller while attached to the *Brilliance*.

Well, it was just a matter of time now, Olfsen knew, until the Coast Guard did show up. The oil sheen would be spotted and reported by another vessel. The Coast Guard would merely follow the slick to this very spot. For all Olfsen knew, the Coast Guard could be bearing down on him right now. He would have to scuttle the ship, by himself no less. He cursed under his breath that he hadn't demanded better life boat and emergency supplies. How was he to get back to shore?

Olfsen's mind was racing. He was about to order a dive when the first mate spoke.

"Return signal sir," the first mate reported. "Dead ahead."

Excellent. He would be happy to be done with this trip. The lost propeller and oil sheen meant the *Porsche* wouldn't return under its own power. He didn't care. His primary goal had been to get the casket into the United States. He had achieved the goal. His employers would have to understand.

He dropped down into the sub's main compartment, sitting down in his captain's chair. "Take us in," he ordered.

The *Porsche's* single remaining engine fired up with a chug, chug. The drug sub pushed its way through the Oregon surf toward the shore.

The sub broke into the surf line, riding a wave onto the rocky coast. The incoming tide helped push the sub well up on shore. Olfsen gunned the single engine and drove the *Porsche* up the beach where it skidded to a screeching halt so loud he was certain all of Oregon had heard their landing.

"Cut the engines," Olfsen ordered. A deathly quiet returned, leaving the sound of the wind and the waves as all that disturbed the silence. This beach would be the final resting place for the *Porsche* and he couldn't care less. Olfsen was done with the ship. God willing he would get off this God forsaken stretch of the American coast and be on some Caribbean beach within the week to live out the rest of his days.

Four men, one of which was Jamil Hussain, stepped out of a rented Ryder truck and approached the sub. Olfsen opened the hatch, crawled out of the ship and jumped down to the beach. He landed in the surf with a slight splash.

One figure separated himself from the other three and stepped clear of the shadows.

Olfsen was surprised. If this was Hussain he wasn't what Olfsen had expected. He didn't fit the mold of an al Qaeda operative for sure. Olfsen felt his guard come up. This could still be a trap. He had never met Hussain. Perhaps this man was with the FBI. Olfsen shoved his hand into his coat pocket and felt for his pistol. The cold grip slipped into his palm.

"Good to see you, captain," Hussain began. His English was perfect, with no hint of an accent. "I'm Jamil Hussain, here to pick up your cargo. But I'm sure you already know this. I trust your trip was uneventful."

"We had a few problems."

"Really? Such as?"

"The left engine lost a propeller. We've also got an internal gas and oil leak. The cabin is coated. The pummeling we experienced while attached to the *Brilliance* was more than expected. The ship is still seaworthy, but with a single engine and the loss of fuel it's impossible to return to Colombia."

"And the cargo?" Hussain asked.

"It's fine."

"Good. Then let's get it on the truck."

At that the three men approached the *Porsche*. The front of the ship lowered, allowing access to the casket. It was strapped and appeared unmolested from where it had been loaded several days before.

Olfsen noticed Hussain intently watching the entire process. Hussain's men completed the transfer and signaled their readiness to depart. The tide was coming in. Under the original plan, the

Porsche would be lifted by the rising water, enabling its escape south.

Olfsen noticed the four men were about to depart. "What about us? The *Porsche* is filled with oil and gas and is no shape to return to South America. How are we to get back?" he asked, pointing to himself and his first mate.

"Allah thanks you for your service," Hussain replied.

That was the signal. Hussain's men, who had moved closer to the *Porsche*, drew their pistols and put three bullets into the first mate. He was dead before he hit the ground. With the shots still ringing in his ears, Olfsen took cover, diving behind the *Porsche*. He pulled his pistol and fired two shots in the attackers' general direction. They darted behind the doors of the truck, knocking maps, cups and other material from the cabin.

The attackers holstered their pistols and withdrew AR15 assault rifles from the truck cabin. They proceeded to unload their clips in Olfsen's direction. Phosphorus tracer bullets lit up the night, giving the gunfight an odd dance-floor like light show.

Olfsen was in an untenable position. Open beach in front of him, the ocean behind. And he was not a strong swimmer. He had nowhere to go.

"Olfsen?" Hussain called out. "Please don't prolong the inevitable. You cannot escape and are only delaying your fate."

Olfsen let out a, "Fuck you," while firing in the direction of Hussain's voice. Olfsen had to think fast, he knew Hussain was right. He only had a few bullets left and couldn't shoot his way out of this fight. If only he could get into the *Porsche* he might have a chance to escape. The front hatch was still open but would require his leaving his cover behind the sub. Did he have a choice?

Olfsen checked his clip, twelve bullets left. He would have to make them count. Drawing a deep breath, Olfsen grabbed a rock and threw it a distance to his left. It landed with a crack, immediately drawing gunfire from his assailants. At that Olfsen jumped up firing toward the source of the tracers. His shots caught his attackers by surprise, striking the closest in the head.

Olfsen dove through the open hatch at the front of the *Porsche*. Sliding across the oil soaked floor, he reached for the door handle.

Pulling down hard, the latch stopped with a clunk. The sub's cargo door began to close.

"He's in the ship, you fools," Hussain screamed at his two remaining men.

Turning they began to spray the *Porsche* with bullets.

Inside the sub, Olfsen heard the shots ring against its hull. Almost musical, he thought. The machine gun fire would do little damage to the *Porsche*. It was built to withstand attack from Coast Guard and drug interdiction police boats.

The door continued to rise. Only a few short seconds before it slammed shut.

"Damn it," Hussain shouted, snatching the rifle from the nearest gunman, knocking him over in the process.

Clank, clank, clank. The door continued to close. Just a few more inches and it would be sealed.

Hussain lined up the rifle sites on the rapidly closing door. He aimed for the vanishing space between the hatch and sub. He pulled the trigger, firing a burst of regular and tracer bullets into the crack.

The door slammed shut. The attackers could hear the bullets bouncing around inside the sub. At least one ricocheting tracer bullet should ignite the gas and oil soaking the sub's interior.

Nothing happened. The engines didn't fire up. Their appeared to be no motion inside the sub at all.

Several moments passed and then . . . KABOOM! The *Porsche* exploded, blowing the small conning tower completely off the main vessel. The front hatch blew out as well.

Hussain and his men were knocked off their feet and the intense heat lit Hussain's jacket aflame.

Flames shot out twenty feet from the hole where the main bridge had been.

Hussain scrambled to his feet swatting out the flames on his jacket sleeve. No one could survive that blast.

His men were slowly staggering to their feet as well. "Get in the truck," Hussain barked.

"What about Hakim?" one of them asked, pointing at their dead comrade.

"Leave him." Hussain commanded. He hoped the police would conclude that the carnage on this deserted Oregon beach was a drug drop gone bad. Before they had time to suspect otherwise *everything* would be over.

Chapter 23
West Thumb Ranger Station,
Yellowstone National Park, June 9, Morning

Grayson Cole sat at his desk answering email. He had just finished reading the Park Service's morning report, a daily synopsis of the major happenings and law enforcement issues in all the national parks. Rescues, storm preparations, firefighting, it was all in there. There was a slight knock at his door. Looking up he saw an attractive woman standing in the doorway. She was smartly dressed, her raven hair pulled back into a ponytail, penetrating green eyes framed by business style glasses. She looked professional—a rare sight in the parks.

"Ah, can I help you?" he stammered.

"Special Agent Dianne Harris with the FBI's domestic terrorism task force."

"Nice to meet you. Ranger Grayson Cole with the National Park Service." The ranger rose to shake Agent Harris' hand. "Please take a seat," Cole said, pointing at an available office chair.

Cole watched as Agent Harris made herself comfortable in the chair, or as comfortable as one could on government issued office furniture.

"Can I get you anything?" Cole asked.

"No. I'm not here on a social call," Harris answered. Actually, if she had her way she wouldn't be here at all. Agent Harris was newly out of the FBI academy at Quantico, finishing first in her class. She held undergraduate degrees in criminal justice and physics and an advanced degree in quantum theory. At Quantico she excelled in domestic terrorism courses. Harris' class rank qualified her for any assignment, and she took one with the Nuclear Emergency Support Team (NEST). NEST was created by President Ford to investigate the illegal use of radiological materials in the United States. What could be a better use of her skills than preventing a nuclear attack on America?

Yellowstone, however, was not what she had expected as her first assignment. Her idea of the big outdoors was Disneyworld's Thunder Mountain rollercoaster. Besides, when she joined NEST it was assumed she would investigate potential attacks on cities, military sites, power plants, or other high value targets. She knew the terrorist MO. Terrorist attacks were about creating confusion and fear and that's why they targeted major cities, not the outback of Wyoming.

Yet, it wasn't her skill, her desire, or even her gender that got her assigned to this goose chase. No, it was her age, or more precisely her lack of experience. NEST, like any other federal agency, was a slave to seniority. It didn't matter how capable or qualified someone was. Assignments were doled out based on rank. The newest member goes to Yellowstone, while, dare she say, less competent colleagues went to the real action.

So, here was Agent Harris sitting on an uncomfortable chair in a park ranger's office, about as far from civilization as one could be.

"Ranger... Cole, is it?" Harris asked.

Cole nodded.

"I'm here because the FBI believes a terrorist attack on the United States may be

171

imminent."

Chapter 24

Yellowstone Visitor Protection Briefing: Mammoth Hot Springs, June 9, Morning

"All right, all right, everyone settle down." Grayson Cole barked, entering the visitor protection briefing room at Yellowstone's Mammoth Hot Springs headquarters. Agent Harris followed close behind.

The rangers snapped to attention, facing the front of the room. Cole walked to a small table and podium, his ranger flat hat under one arm, a stack of papers in his hand. Cole placed his briefing materials upon the room's podium with the National Park Service's arrowhead affixed to its front. "Take your seats, ladies and gentlemen."

Cole looked out over the two dozen or so rangers in the briefing room. They were young. Roughly twenty seven years old on average. They were also relatively inexperienced, with only a few years of law enforcement among them. For a couple rangers, this was their first law enforcement job.

Agent Harris surveyed the room as well and couldn't believe what she saw. Cole could tell what she was thinking. These were the men and women expected to stop a terrorist attack? He had heard it before. Rangers were little more than a glorified co-ed Scout troop.

Unknown to Harris, the ranger corps was spread thin. Yellowstone National Park was more than two million acres, the size of Rhode Island and Delaware combined or about one law enforcement ranger for every ninety thousand acres. And ninety thousand acres was approximately four times the size of San Francisco.

Yellowstone's overall ranger corps numbered more than two hundred. Yet most park rangers were not responsible for law enforcement. Rather, they focused on managing wildlife, leading hikes, or collecting the trash. In addition, several of Cole's rangers were on fire fighting detail on Idaho state forest land.

The Park Service, however, did enjoy at least one major advantage over potential criminals. Unlike city police forces or sheriff offices, National Park rangers often knew the area they patrolled much better than the criminal. The rangers lived, worked, and played in the parks. Most park criminals were visitors, transients, and had limited understanding of the surroundings. The parks also often possessed limited entry and exit sites. This made it easier to set up road blocks and interdiction sites.

The two dozen rangers took their seats, readying themselves for the briefing.

"This is FBI Agent Dianne Harris," Cole said, pointing to Dianne standing on the side of the room. "Agent Harris will be working with us for a while."

Cole adjusted his papers on the podium before going on. He and Harris had discussed what to say next, or more importantly what not to say. Since the FBI had no firm evidence of an attack, at least not yet, there would be no public mention of the potential threat. Rather, Cole was to put his men on alert. The FBI was merely here to observe. "I'm sure all of you have heard about the submarine found yesterday on one of Oregon's beaches. The Bureau," Cole, said, looking toward Harris, "believes it was a drug delivery gone bad."

"Chief, if that's so, then what's that got to do with us?" a young ranger asked.

"It probably doesn't," Cole continued. "However, the FBI found three dead bodies, numerous high caliber shell casings and a number of maps and papers. One of those maps was of Yellowstone."

A murmur went through the crowd of rangers, followed by a wise crack. "Perhaps they were vacationing drug smugglers."

"Doubtful," Cole stated, ignoring the sarcasm. "I shouldn't need to remind you that one of the first terrorists captured prior to nine-eleven was in North Cascades National Park." Cole noticed Harris sit forward in her seat. "We all know that National Parks make ideal targets because of their remoteness, high public value, difficulty to defend and large visitation. As of right now we don't know if this incident in Oregon represents any threat to Yellowstone, but we have to assume as much. The president has raised the threat level and thus our protection duties will increase."

A groan went through the ranger corps. Threat prevention would take them away from their normal duties. They would now be required to conduct show of force operations designed to protect infrastructure like park headquarters and public attractions such as Old Faithful. Some would spend an entire day scanning the crowd at the Old Faithful amphitheater while others patrolled the HQ parking lot looking for bombs.

None of which was why they had become rangers.

Cole went on for another twenty minutes detailing the new patrol plans. Rangers would be reassigned to the park's front country areas, its hotels, restaurants, and visitor centers. These were obvious targets. Attractions like Old Faithful, Fishing Bridge, and West Thumb Geyser Basin would also have to be searched. He knew there simply weren't enough rangers to secure every possible target. He would have to prioritize.

"That's all, ladies and gentleman. Be safe," Cole ordered. "Dismissed."

On the way out the door, Cole handed each ranger a sheet of paper with their new duty assignment. He hated pulling the rangers out of their normal routines. He hoped his decision about development and coverage would be enough. More importantly he prayed it wouldn't be needed.

Chapter 25
Prayer Breakfast: Cattle Ranch outside Jackson Hole WY, June 11, Early Morning

A select group of men entered Charles Sinclair's home office. They were there for their weekly prayer breakfast. However, this week's agenda was different. These men and women had been plotting for years and today they would finalize their plans.

The men wore white tunics with a large red cross emblazoned across the chest. They called themselves the 1307 Defenders, or the Templar Knights of 1307.

The original Templar Knights had been founded to guard Christian pilgrims on the journey to the Holy Land. Over the decades, the Templars had branched out from protection to banking and commerce. They became incredibly powerful and wealthy. Their power grew to rival many of Europe's monarchs.

At the end of the final crusade in 1272, the Templars lost their purpose and their support among kings of Western Europe. A powerful but purposeless army was a direct threat to Europe's stability. Some historians believe that in 1307 France's King Philip IV took action, framing the knights as enemies of the state. He rounded up the order's leaders and tortured most of them to death. The pogrom happened on Friday, October 13th. Thus the beginning of the curse.

Sinclair founded his order of Templar Knights roughly twenty five years ago and slowly built up the membership to roughly a dozen. He had traced his ancestry and discovered he was a descendant of King Richard, the leader of the Third Crusade. Sinclair believed this was a sign that his Defenders were the inheritors of the Crusaders' mission and that they alone would prevent the destruction of the Christian faith.

The Crusades had begun as an effort to drive the invading Muslim hordes from Jerusalem in roughly 1100 AD. However, the Crusades eventually morphed into driving out the heretics from not only the Holy Land but the Near East and Europe as well. The Crusaders had enemies both near and far.

Sinclair sat at the head of a large round table, an empty chair to his right. Three other men filled the table's remaining seats. A large crusader cross was inlayed in the center of the table. The crusader cross was actually five crosses. A large central cross surrounded by four smaller ones. One cross for every wound Christ suffered at his crucifixion. He had bought it from a Middle Eastern trader who claimed it was crafted in 11th century Jerusalem. On the wall hung framed images of Jesus holding a sword along with photos of Ronald Reagan and John Wayne. Marble busts of Crusader nobles, such as Raymond of Toulouse, filled backlit sculpture nooks. A copy of the Declaration of Independence, an American flag and other tokens of Americana covered the remaining wall space. The office was something out of Disney's American adventure, part northeastern colonial, part western, and part Middle Ages. Sinclair's friends called the office Martha Stewart's nightmare. He liked that.

The people around the table were

respected members of the community, leaders of
local law enforcement, the chamber of commerce,
the clergy, and right-wing paramilitary
organizations, such as the revered Huttaree.

They were chosen by Sinclair and Hansen
because they provided necessary monetary,
intelligence, law enforcement and military
resources needed for the operation. But most of
all they were men of God, all members of his
Christ Advocate church. All trusted the others
with their lives.

Sinclair took his seat, the others followed
suit. A single empty seat remained--the one for
Hansen. "Thanks for coming ladies and gentlemen.
I'm sure I don't need to stress that what we are
going to discuss today is sensitive and not to leave
this room. Is that clear?" he started. All heads
nodded affirmative. "Excellent. It's now time to
implement the final phase of our plan. The past
several years have been spent loading the weapon.
We are now ready to pull the trigger."

A chuckle went through the group.

"For the past four years President Paine
has led this country toward destruction." Sinclair
nearly choked uttering the president's name. "His
conservation philosophy, tax policies and stand on
social issues such as abortion are reason enough to
remove him from office. However, it's his turning
the country from God that sealed his fate. In
particular, his decision to ratify a two-state solution
for the Palestinian Israeli conflict was the last
straw.

"So, let's begin this morning as we always
do, with a prayer. Reverend, will you please make

our offer to the Holy Father?"

"Certainly," Reverend Calvin Thomas replied.

Reverend Thomas, a small mouse-like man, was the leader of the local Christ Advocate congregation. Christ Advocate's theology was based on a belief that the messiah, Jesus Christ, would return only after the establishment of a thousand year reign of a Christian world government based in Jerusalem. A thousand years was roughly the time elapsed since the previous Crusades. And while the Christian world government had not been established, in Charles' mind President Paine's Middle East peace plan would all but doom the Messiah's return.

"Holy Father," Reverend Thomas began, "A dark cloud is enveloping the world. Once again enemies of your plan are on the rise. These dark forces have taken many forms in the past. With your guidance and strength, righteous followers had taken up the cause and held the dark powers at bay.

"Today evil builds again. It is taking a different form, but the goal is the same. Prevent your Son's return forever. We beseech you, Lord, in this critical hour. Give us your strength, give us your protection, and guide our hand so we may bring heaven to earth."

"Duce Volte," Reverend Thomas said.

"Duce Volte," the group repeated.

"Duce Volte," Thomas continued. "God wills it. Amen."

The prayer concluded. Sinclair turned to the man on his left when Hansen burst into the room, pulling his robe over his head as he moved to his seat.

"Sorry I'm late," Hansen began. "I got held up."

As Hansen sat, Sinclair noticed he appeared tan, if not sun burned, and smelled of smoke. Odd, he thought, but paid no further notice. He knew Hansen spent time in the woods in deep meditation. He knew these vision quests required long hours of sitting in the open and included large bonfires fueled by many offerings. But he could at least use some sun screen.

With Hansen settled in his seat, Sinclair turned to Don Fielder. Don, a burly man, was Wyoming's Park County sheriff. He had held the position for fifteen years. He was also a leader in the local VFW, a member of the ultra-conservative John Birch society, and a deacon at the Christ Advocate Church. Don gained notoriety by calling for Wyoming to adopt Arizona's immigration laws, except Fielder took the position a step further. He wanted Wyoming to extend the list of suspects to include liberals, greenies and union members. Don had solid Tea Party credentials.

But Fielder wasn't at the table for any of those reasons. Fielder was here because as county sheriff he would be responsible for part of the presidential security. Security for the president's Wyoming trip would be handled by the Secret Service and the National Park Service. However, because the speech would take place in Park County, the sheriff's office was consulted on the president's safety.

"While I'm not privy to all the security

details, here is what I do know," Don said. "The president will travel to Yellowstone from Bozeman aboard Marine One, landing at Old Faithful around 9 a.m. After a tour of the geyser basin and a meet-and-greet with local officials, the president will fly to the West Thumb Geyser Basin for a speech. He is expected to leave West Thumb around 2 p.m. and head to Jackson Hole for a fund raising dinner.

"The overall security zone at Old Faithful will be roughly two miles." Don placed a map of Old Faithful on the table. Circling the area with his finger, he continued. "It will include the entire developed area and will be closed to traffic beginning around seven in the morning. The president will first stop at the new visitor center, then receive a private tour by the park superintendent. Secret Service will set up a perimeter in the Old Faithful parking lot as well as atop several of the nearby mountains.

"At the West Thumb Geyser Basin, similar security measures to those at Old Faithful will be employed. Secret Service, local law enforcement and park rangers will patrol the perimeter. However, at this location, since the president's podium backs up against the lake, security personnel including my sheriff boat will patrol the water. All in all, the entire west thumb of Yellowstone Lake will be closed to private vessels. Meanwhile, the roads on the lake shore will be closed here and here to private vehicles." Fielder pointed to two points on the West Thumb map.

"Security closures will be put into effect at both Old Faithful and West Thumb roughly one hour prior to the president's arrival. This is being done to reduce disruption for the roughly forty thousand visitors expected to be in the park that day."

"Please continue, Sheriff," Sinclair urged, pouring himself a glass of water.

"At the completion of his speech, the president will board the Marine One helicopter and head to Jackson Hole. The county's security responsibilities will end at that point. As such, I'm not privy to any additional security information."

"Excellent, Don," Sinclair stated. "What you've provided is extremely helpful. Let's now hear from Wayne Stouffer."

Wayne Stouffer sat at the far end of the table. At his side was an extremely large, overstretched briefcase. Stouffer was the president of the local chamber of commerce, but more importantly he was the local representative of the National Rifle Association. Stouffer had access to a wide array of firearms, including some military issued rifles like the McMillan Tac-50. The Tac-50 was a large-caliber sniper rifle capable of hitting a target from more than a mile and half way. "It wasn't easy, but I've secured the needed firearms as well as ten rounds of U.S. Marine issue ammunition," Wayne stated.

"That's great, Wayne," Captain Hansen said. "But I really only need one bullet." *Nor would there be time for a second shot,* Hansen thought.

Stouffer placed the case on the table and opened the lid. He turned it to face Hansen and Sinclair, sliding it across the table. "The American ammunition packs more powder than comparable ammunition, so it will carry further. However, I can't guarantee it will travel the distance you require."

"That's all right, Wayne," Hansen said. "I know a few sniper tricks that should send the bullet further than manufacturer's specifications."

"How will you get around the government's SWATS system?" Wayne asked. SWATS stood for Soldier Wearable Targeting Systems. These were wallet-sized sensors worn by soldiers in the field that could pinpoint enemy sniper positions. The SWATS had been in use in Iraq and Afghanistan for years. The Secret Service would likely use this technology as well to ID sniper locations.

There had been a splash of Army generated press a few years back when the technology was introduced in the Middle East. This always struck Captain Hansen as odd. Why would the Army announce the use of a device that could help neutralize enemy snipers? Surely al Qaida, the Taliban, and Iraqi insurgents would read the press regarding these wonder devices and alter their tactics accordingly.

Then it hit him. Of course the enemy would see the press reports. That's exactly what the Army wanted. An enemy sniper would have serious doubts about firing if he knew the army had the means to easily locate him. But why let news of the technology leak? Why not say that the U.S. armed forces now had the ability to locate and kill enemy snipers? A vague statement would seed more doubt. The enemy wouldn't know if the Army's new capability came from improved satellites, a traitor, or some other advance. Not knowing the source of the threat would prevent the enemy from adopting appropriate countermeasures. There had to be a reason for the specific leak.

It could be Army incompetence, which was always possible. However, another press target was the Army itself. U.S. forces had been getting slaughtered for years by enemy snipers. Planting the story would tell soldiers there was a miracle technology that would save their lives, making it a little easier for them to do their jobs. But again Hansen was left with the question: why not just deploy the system with no fanfare?

There seemed to be only two reasons. First, to maximize the system's deterrent effects on the bad guys and psychological benefits for the good guys, the news of its deployment had to be spread far and wide. No one would know how many of the sensors were in use. Rather, they would only know they could be in use. This told Hansen there were actually few of the devices. If the Army had few of the devices, it was unlikely the Secret Service had many either.

Next, the effectiveness of the devices was seldom reported. Why? If the goal of the media reports had been to change enemy behavior, reports on kill rates of enemy snipers would be highly effective propaganda. But the stories didn't come. This told Joseph the technology was less effective than hoped. Again, good news for their current operation.

"The SWATS devices don't prevent a sniper from taking a shot, they merely help identify his location and direction," said Hansen.

"But won't that impact yours and Charles' escape?" Stouffer asked.

Sinclair, obviously interested in the answer, turned toward Hansen.

"I wouldn't worry too much about our escape," Hansen said with a sinister look. "By the time the Secret Service knows what hit them we will be long gone."

Chapter 26
Montana State Highway 191, June 12, Early Morning

For more than a decade Sinclair Enterprises had the volcanic monitoring contract at Yellowstone. They were responsible for staffing, maintaining, and inspecting the more than one hundred park monitoring stations. This initial entry into Yellowstone allowed Sinclair to branch into other services. Along with keeping the public safe, Sinclair Enterprises was responsible for managing all the hotels, restaurants, and gift shops. Millions of park visitors were served every year and because Yellowstone was so remote, that meant daily deliveries of nearly every type of item from laundry detergent to Jack Daniels whiskey. All those items required lots of trucks going in and out of the park on a regular basis. Seldom were they stopped, never had they been searched. Hussain was counting on the record continuing.

He had spent the last several years infiltrating Sinclair Enterprises, learning the company's operations, delivery schedules, staff activities. This information told him how to get the casket into the park.

Hussain had also penetrated the Sinclair volcano monitoring program, uncovering the location of the park's many geyser sensors and monitors. Hacking into the system's mainframe, he easily downloaded the needed sensor's schematics and technical information. This told him where to place the casket.

Although he risked exposure, Hussain maintained his covert contact with Sinclair

Enterprises. The nature of Yellowstone required
Sinclair to continually adapt, alter its business
habits. Roads would wash out or, worse, massive
wildfires could burn huge acres, closing Sinclair
hotels, restaurants and stores to the public. This
meant things such as delivery schedules or
computer codes were changed continually and
without warning. Hussain was too close to his
final destination to be foiled by a simple change in
company operations.

Hussain pulled his Ryder Van over to the
side of the road, just to the north of Yellowstone's
west entrance. He had been driving for what
seemed like days, more than a thousand miles from
the rendezvous with the submarine at Oregon.
The team spent the previous day in Jackson Hole
before heading out for the next engagement.

During the drive, Hussain was glued to the
radio, especially conservative radio. He sought out
stations that carried Rush Limbaugh, Sean Hannity
and Glenn Beck. His thought was that
conservative media would more likely speculate
that a destroyed submarine might be part of a
potential terrorist plot. Every thirty minutes, as
the local stations recapped the news coming from
FOX, he expected the announcement of a national
manhunt for his cell. It never came. Rather, the
press was reporting the burned out sub as a drug
delivery gone badly. Perfect.

His heart did skip a beat at one point on
the trip when Glenn Beck announced before a
commercial break that the Paine administration
was likely covering up the real threat behind the
submarine. Hussain sweated through three

minutes of gold, exercise, and voice data commercials only to learn that Glenn believed the sub was actually the newest method for smuggling illegals into the country. The Arab and Colombians found dead on the Oregon beach were evidence of this, Beck bellowed. Hussain guessed, at least to Beck, the Swede found at the crime scene didn't count as an illegal. Idiot. Once again America's racist assumptions blinded it to the real threats. It would be their downfall.

Hussain was exhausted, but he was on a tight timeline. He would soon rest in paradise.

The night was black. The moon had recently set, casting the road in complete darkness. Countless stars painted the night sky, providing the scene with a heavenly glow. Hussain had never seen so many stars. The heart of the Milky Way seemed to hover just overhead. He saw the face of Allah in its celestial grandeur. If paradise looked half as glorious as the night sky, he would be happy indeed.

Hussain knew he was in the right place, at the right time, with the right weapon. A meteor streaked across the sky, painting the night sky like a boat on water. He smiled, taking the shooting star as a good omen.

Exiting the cab of the rented truck, he walked to the front of the vehicle and popped the hood. Now that the hook had been baited they would wait for the prey.

It didn't take long before the Sinclair delivery truck was spotted. "Here it comes," whispered one of Hussain's men.

"Excellent, make yourselves invisible,"

Hussain ordered. Hussain turned on the truck's
four-way flashers and walked out into the deserted
highway, waving his arms to flag down the
approaching truck.

Park visitors weren't like people in cities or
even rural areas. They were generally friendlier,
more willing to help a stranger. Hussain was
counting on this. He returned to the truck's
engine and flipped a switch on a small black box
attached just under the air filter cowling. Smoke
started billowing from the device.

Hussain stepped back into the street and
began to wave down the already slowing Sinclair
truck. It was a large eighteen wheel semi with
Sinclair Enterprises painted in large red letters
across the trailer. It pulled over to the shoulder
and came to a stop behind the disabled Ryder
truck. Setting the parking brake, and turning on
the emergency flashers, the driver climbed down
from the cab. He approached Hussain.

"Looks like you've got some trouble.
Anything I can help you with?" the driver asked.

"Thank you so much for stopping,"
Hussain answered. "Yours is the first vehicle I've
seen in nearly an hour. I was beginning to wonder
if I'd see anyone before daybreak."

"That's possible. There aren't many people
on the park roads at this time of night. That's a lot
of smoke coming from your engine. What seems
to be the problem?"

"Not really sure, but the truck has been
having difficulty all night. I think the altitude has
made the engine overheat. Here, please take a
look."

The truck driver thought this strange.
"You said you've been here more than an hour?"

"Correct."

"That's odd given the amount of smoke coming out of your engine. One would think it would have cooled off by now."

The driver moved to the front of the vehicle looking under the hood. "What's this?" the driver asked, pointing at a black box.

At that Hussain pulled a small hand held Taser from his pocket, shoving it into the driver's neck. A slight gasp escaped his mouth. His body went stiff, eventually slumping to the ground.

"Get out here and take this man to the truck," Hussain barked to his comrades.

They jumped from the truck and hustled to pick up the unconscious driver, dragging him into the rider truck.

"Give me his uniform. Bind and gag him," Hussain said. The men did as they were told, giving the Sinclair uniform to Hussain. "Excellent. Now transfer the casket to the delivery truck. Move."

Hussain knew Allah was on their side. They had gotten this far without trouble. Yet there was always a chance of discovery. The longer they stayed on the side of the road the higher that chance.

It took only about a minute to transfer the casket. It was now securely stowed, the rear door of the Sinclair truck closed and latched. Hussain finished buttoning the driver's shirt and placed the Sinclair hat on his head. He checked his appearance in the mirror. *Not bad*, he thought.

This will work.

"Now get in the rental truck and return it to the agency in Spokane," Hussain stated.

"What about the driver? What should we do with him?" one of his men asked.

"Dump him in a ravine somewhere. Just make sure he isn't found for a while. We are too close and can't risk discovery now." Hussain climbed up into the cab of the semi and started up the engine. Rolling down the window he gave his men their final orders. "I'll see you at the rendezvous point. Allah be with you both."

Their rendezvous wouldn't be on earth.

Hussain eased the semi off the shoulder and onto the road. He glanced in the rearview mirror and watched the Ryder truck execute a U-turn. It would take his associates the better part of a day to drive to Spokane. They would never make it. The bomb Hussain planted in the truck would detonate in roughly six hours.

No loose ends. Not this close to the end.

Chapter 27
Yellowstone's Bechler Road, June 12, Late Night

The Sinclair truck's lights cut through the dark. Beyond the reach of the headlights Hussain could see nothing. While he drove the vehicle as fast as he dared, not knowing the park roads prevented him from pushing it too fast. He was close to his delivery and he didn't want it to be foiled by a speeding ticket, or worse, hitting a bison.

The road conditions added to Hussain's difficulty. It was cratered with holes like the surface of the moon. It obviously had not seen maintenance in many years. Everything was falling into place. The road had not seen a vehicle in sometime, and, more importantly, he hoped it wouldn't for some time to come.

The truck jerked and bounced down the road, smashing against the underbrush and trees growing on the shoulders. Branches and leaves were left in the truck's wake. A sign ahead came into view: BECHLER TRAILHEAD NEXT LEFT.

"Praise Allah." He wasn't sure how much more bouncing the truck could take. Hussain's heart began to race. The prize was near. Stay calm, he told himself. Yet, he couldn't help but feel a wave of conflicting emotions. Excitement that he was so near the end of his quest, and joy that he would soon be with Allah in paradise. At the back of his mind, however, lurked depression. All his many years of service to Allah were coming to a close. Much of his adult life had been spent taking down America and he was entering the final phase of his work. He couldn't help but feel sorrow that it was nearly over.

Pulling into the Bechler trailhead parking lot he found it deserted. National Parks, unlike National Forests or even some state parks, forbade dispersed camping. Hussain knew overnight guests stayed in designated campgrounds, hotels, or backcountry cabins. This meant front country sites like trailheads should be deserted soon after sundown. Better yet, it would remain so until just before sunup, several hours from now.

As Hussain was shutting down the truck, two groggy hikers, a man and a woman, came out of the woods. They held up a sign with Jackson Hole printed on it in black magic marker.

Hitchhikers looking for a ride south. He had to think fast. He could leave them. It was unlikely the two would see anyone before he completed his mission. But he couldn't take the chance.

Climbing down the cab, Hussain reached for his 9mm Beretta stashed under the seat. He checked that he had a full clip and walked over to the smiling hikers.

Chapter 28
Yellowstone Backcountry, near Riddle Lake, June 13, Late Afternoon

"What the hell are we doing out here?" Harris yelled.

Agent Harris and Ranger Cole were seven miles in the backcountry, patrolling the Riddle Lake area. It was late afternoon, but still hot and somewhat muggy. Harris was not enjoying the hike. She hadn't walked this much in the woods since she was a child. She liked it now about as much as she did then, which was not much.

"Agent Harris, while you are tasked to Yellowstone, some normal operations and law enforcement must continue," Cole explained. "As I understand your mission, you are here to learn more about the park and potential weaknesses. Patrolling the backcountry is one of the best ways to understand the park."

Harris knew Cole was correct. Normal operations needed to continue. On several occasions terrorist attacks were thwarted by routine law enforcement. All counter terrorism agents knew Oklahoma City bomber Timothy McVeigh was apprehended during a normal traffic stop. She wouldn't tell Cole of her agreement, however. She couldn't give him the satisfaction.

Cole and Harris ventured deeper into the backcountry, rounding a bend revealing a large meadow. The trail went off into the distance climbing a slight hill.

From just over the rise came a deathly scream.

It pulled Cole and Harris out of their conversation. Cole jumped into action and ran down the trail. Harris was caught flat footed, but quickly followed the sprinting ranger.

The source of the scream came running over the rise. Cole and Harris stopped cold. A young woman, roughly in her 20s, shot past the two officers. She appeared to be running for her life. And she was. In short order the source of her fear soon came charging over the rise.

"Jesus Christ!" Harris said.

"A bear, actually," Cole responded. "Ursa horribilis, or more commonly known as a grizzly bear." He could see the bear was pretty typical, approximately three hundred pounds, though a little small for a Yellowstone bear. This was to be expected, given the bear had likely just come out of its winter den. It was probably cranky and had one goal, find food to put on weight for next winter's hibernation.

Cole quickly summed up the reason for the chase. The woman had been hiking alone and startled a mother grizzly. Her cubs could be seen in the tops of a nearby tree.

Instinctively, Harris drew her service pistol and got a bead on the charging bear.

"Put that away," Cole barked, startling Harris. "That pistol will only piss her off." Further, Cole didn't have time to explain that female grizzlies were extremely valuable. The Yellowstone grizzly population was slowly returning from near extinction. Approximately three hundred to four hundred grizzlies roamed the park's interior. Just a few decades earlier, the bear population had been down to less than one hundred. Park scientists quickly learned that female bears were the key to restoring the population. Male bears could mate with multiple partners, while females were limited to a single partner about every two years. Further complicating the matter was the low success rate of grizzly bear reproduction. More than half of all cubs didn't survive their first year. The NPS' calculation was simple. The more female grizzlies, the more cubs, and the more cubs, the greater number surviving into adulthood. Therefore, the NPS would do all it could to protect female bears. In other words, Cole would only shoot this bear as a last resort.

The grizzly stopped roughly fifty yards away. She was still agitated, snorting and growling. Cole pulled a canister from his belt, handing it to Harris. "Here take this and point it at the bear."

Harris inspected the canister. It looked like a can of hair mousse. "What am I supposed to do with this? Throw it at the bear?" she demanded. She was shaking. Quantico hadn't prepared her for a charging bear.

"Just point it at the bear. But don't fire until I say," Cole responded, pulling something from his coat pocket. Sarah Palin had been right about one thing, Cole thought. One didn't want to get between a mamma grizzly and her cubs. The bear continued to move toward them, snorting and growling as she approached.

Cole motioned to Harris to back down the trail. "Lower your shoulders, bend at the waist, and don't stare into the bear's eyes," he whispered.

"Why?" Harris asked.

"That grizzly thinks we are bears too and that we threaten her cubs. We need to make ourselves as non-hostile as possible and reassure her we mean no harm."

"Are you kidding me?"

"Do it," Cole hissed through clenched teeth. He didn't have time for a clinic on backcountry survival measures.

Turning toward the bear, but avoiding eye contact, Cole stated in a low, calm voice, "We're sorry mamma. We didn't mean to disturb you and your cubs. We're leaving now."

The bear didn't seem reassured. She had stopped about twenty five yards away, but continued to snort. She bounced on her two front paws, an obvious sign of agitation that even Harris could understand. "I don't think she's buying it," Harris observed.

"Get ready with the canister."

Harris brought the canister up, pointing it at the bear, finger on the trigger. She was shaking.

The bear charged.

Harris could now see what Cole was holding in his hand, a cigarette lighter. This was insane. Cole was holding something else in his other hand. He lit it, starting a shower of sparks and snaps. He held the snapping item for a second longer as the bear continued to charge.

"God it's fast," Harris gasped.

The bear was almost on top of them. Cole tossed the item a few yards in front of the beast.

BANG! BANG! BANG! BANGTY, BANGTY, BANG!

The popping firecrackers startled both Harris and the charging bear. The bear skidded to a halt mere yards from the two law enforcement officers. She was confused, but wouldn't stay that way for long.

"Now!" Cole ordered.

"Huh?" Harris mumbled still focused on the bear.

"Fire now!" Cole repeated.

Harris was in a daze, time seemed to have slowed. She had forgotten her hold on the canister. The bear had taken all her attention. "Oh. . . right."

Pointing the canister directly at the bear, she pulled the trigger. A cloud of high pressure, red gas erupted from its nozzle, enveloping the bear's head. The pepper spray burned the bear's eyes, mouth, and nose. The grizzly let out a yelp of obvious pain, turned and hightailed it back to her tree-clinging cubs.

Only after the bear crossed the far rise and dropped out of sight did both Harris and Cole breathe a sigh of relief. Harris felt weak. All blood had left her head and she collapsed.

It took a few moments for Harris to regain her senses. Cole was kneeling next to her, holding his canteen up to her lips.

She downed a gulp of water. "I'm sorry," Harris apologized.

"What for?" Cole asked, retrieving the canteen taking a drink himself.

"I froze," Harris explained. "I'm not sure what came over me. That's the first time it's ever happened."

"So you've stood down a charging grizzly before?" Cole asked.

"No, it's just . . ." Harris begun.

"Then don't be so hard on yourself. There are very few people who would react much differently than you did," Cole explained.

"You're probably right. But to be totally honest, I thought you were going to get us killed. I wanted to shoot the bear."

"I totally understand. Most park visitors would share your instinct. However, years of experience working with wildlife has shown Park Service rangers that non-lethal tools, such as firecrackers and pepper spray, are effective in repelling bears. Other than burning eyes and nose, the grizzly will be fine."

Harris started to get up. Cole held her by the arm and helped lift the FBI agent to her feet.

"You basically fended off that bear with smoke and mirrors. If I hadn't seen it myself, I wouldn't have believed it," Harris stated.

"Now you know. At least here in Yellowstone, and I'm sure it's true elsewhere, doing something unexpected, causing confusion, is sometimes the best measure. The trick is knowing when to do the unforeseen."

Cole began heading back toward the trailhead. "Here, you'll want to keep these." He handed Harris the pepper spray and a packet of firecrackers. "I think you've earned them."

Chapter 29
Centennial Geyser Basin, June 14, Early Morning

It had taken Hussain several hours to reach the Centennial Geyser Basin. Hiking in the dark was difficult. It was slow going. Like driving the truck, he was cautious. He couldn't risk being injured. Nor could he use his night vision goggles. They had limited battery life and he would need them for later. The slow pace meant he had arrived at his destination by mid-morning when the target was bathed in sunlight. It was too exposed then for him to place his package, so he had waited roughly a mile from this target for nightfall. It was well after the moon set before he set out again.

It was a fifteen minute hike when Hussain crested a final hill and descended into the Centennial Geyser Basin. The basin was new and not fully explored. The NPS hadn't yet established any campgrounds. Again, it was unlikely any campers would be in the area. He double checked the area to make certain all was clear.

Setting down his pack, he pondered how light the package was that he carried. Less than thirty pounds? Strange that such a tiny object could lead to the destruction of Islam's most hated enemy. But Allah worked in fantastic ways. Small didn't mean insignificant.

Hints of first light could just start to be seen in the eastern sky, but the heavy woods surrounding the geyser basin still made it difficult to see. Large shadows played tricks with depth perception. Hussain trusted Allah completely, but only a fool would travel in an active geyser basin without some earthly help. He pulled the pair of night vision goggles from his pack and placed them over his head. He removed the casket from his pack as well. Hussain's night vision goggles had built-in infrared detectors and a GPS navigation system. These aids would be crucial if he was to reach his target successfully.

Hussain switched on the goggles and GPS system. The world was transformed from a voidless place to an eerie pale green moonscape. He scanned the area, getting his bearings. The infrared system kicked in, revealing plumes of searing steam and boiling hot water. The basin truly did look like hell. Only fitting that this site would mark America's destruction. Like Al Kamil destroying the Crusaders on the Nile nearly a millennium before, Allah's army today would be the earth itself.

Taking a deep breath, Hussain headed into the geyser basin. His night vision goggles would help prevent him from stepping into a hot pool or steaming mudpot. The goggles, however, couldn't prevent him from being doused by an unexpected eruption. Nor could they prevent Hussain's inadvertent step into a dormant thermal feature or breaking through the area's thin crust. He would have to be cautious.

Hussain took his time. He had to get this right.

It took him roughly ten minutes to find his target, although the GPS said he had only traveled about one hundred yards from where he stepped off the established trail. The goal of this particular quest lay near the cone of the new Centennial Geyser. When it finally came into view, he was underwhelmed. It was a device that looked like little more than a waterproof Tupperware container with a small laptop computer inside. Protruding out of the computer was a bundle of wires that exited the container through a sealed watertight hole. The wires continued a few yards to a sensor that lay in the splash zone of a nearby geyser. The computer/thermometer set up simply measured the temperature of the geyser's runoff water and the intervals between eruptions. This particular geyser had an average temperature near the boiling point and a three hour eruption interval. To the lay person this information didn't seem all that earth shaking. But Hussain knew minor changes in the water's temperature or eruption interval could indicate major changes in the park's magma chamber. The park was riddled with these simple, low cost, but important devices. They took the pulse of the park and would alert the Park Service of any pending changes.

But that information wasn't extraordinary in itself. Rather it was something more particular to Centennial that led Hussain to this spot. Park Service analysis showed the place Hussain had chosen was where the earth's crust was the thinnest. At least it was the thinnest spot that could be reached from land. There may be spots under Yellowstone Lake where the crust was thinner, but Hussain didn't know for sure and besides he could never reach them. He would have to trust that the spot he had chosen was correct. Hussain thought again how foolish it was of the Park Service to post this critical information so boldly on their website. Their own openness would lead to their downfall.

Hussain knelt to get a better look at the Centennial Geyser computer monitor, examining its power source in particular. The Tupperware system didn't need much power. A small nearby solar panel was all that was necessary. In fact, the system ran on such little power that most of the energy produced by the solar panel was wasted.

Hussain took off the pack he had been carrying and put it on the ground, feeling the finality of this act. He was so close now. He unzipped the top of the pack and pulled out the briefcase within. He placed it next to him. He stared at it. Saying a silent prayer, he flipped the latches and opened the lid.

Again Hussain was underwhelmed by what he saw. Contained in the lower half of the briefcase was a small electronic device about the size of a notebook computer and twice as thick. Several lights and readout displays were blinking yellow. Hussain knew this meant the device was in standby mode. In the lid of the briefcase were a small keyboard and another readout display. On the side of the keyboard were two tiny USB ports. Hussain pulled two USB cables from the front pouch of his backpack. He plugged them into the keyboard's side ports. On the geyser monitor computer were two similar ports. He plugged the other ends of his USB cables into them. Hussain turned to the keyboard and typed, SUBMIT--the English translation of the word Islam. He pressed enter and the yellow indicators turned green. The explosive was now armed.

The device didn't seem big enough to do the job. Hussain's handlers assured him it had the punch necessary to produce a blast equivalent to a magnitude 7 earthquake, at least locally. And that's all that mattered. The Hiroshima bomb, by comparison, produced energy equal to a magnitude 6 quake. This bomb was a fraction of the size and contained more power. Hussain knew the earth had only twenty or so magnitude 7 earthquakes each year. Yellowstone's largest quake in recorded history was in 1959, a massive 7.6 jolt. That earthquake had brought down mountains, changed the course of rivers, and was felt as far away as Spokane. The '59 quake hadn't produced an eruption, but its epicenter was outside the volcano's crater. This quake would not only be within the caldera, but also at its weakest point.

None of Hussain's handlers knew for sure if the bomb's blast would trigger an eruption, but on paper it appeared sufficient. The blast would surely vaporize the surrounding forest and geyser basin, nearby lake shoreline, and any creatures or people unfortunate enough to be in the immediate vicinity. A mushroom cloud hundreds of feet tall would billow into the Wyoming sky. If this had been New York or Los Angeles his bomb's blast would kill millions instantly, hundreds of thousands in the weeks that followed, and grip the nation in fear that other cities could be wiped out at any moment. But Hussain and al Qaeda had only one nuclear device. They had chosen the bomb's placement carefully. They wanted to inflict maximum damage. Unless al Qaeda came into possession of dozens of bombs, a single blast even in a city like New York or Washington D.C. wouldn't end the American menace. Al Qaeda was unlikely to get another chance to inflict monumental damage. It had but one bomb. A single stinger, it had to hit the devil's heart.

The device was small, roughly thirty five pounds. The bomb dropped on Hiroshima had been far heavier, having been carried to its target by a B29 bomber. The bomb Hussain carried today fit easily in his backpack.

His bomb also carried a bigger punch than the Hiroshima device, equivalent to hundreds of tons of TNT. If all went according to plan, Hussain knew, the atomic blast would trigger a volcanic eruption sending ash and smoke tens of thousands of feet into the air, far higher than the flight path of commercial aircraft. It would be glorious. He only wished he could actually see the full destructive sweep. But regrettably, Hussain would be incinerated in the first few seconds, perhaps minutes, in the bomb's detonation. Perhaps he would be at the foot of Allah to witness the end of the great Satan, a thought that gave him great comfort.

Again he turned to his backpack and removed a small iPhone. "Amazing," Hussain whispered. All that remained was to text, TO ALLAH, and righteousness would be delivered to America. He wanted to push the button in that very moment and be united with Allah before the sun rose. But now was not the right time. He would wait. His handlers had been correct. It would be better to detonate the bomb during the president's speech, and thereby insure the destruction of the United States. Only a few more days now.

Hussain zipped the pack closed and hoisted it onto his back. He next closed the lid to the briefcase and hid it out of sight under a small bush. Not that he really needed to. Hussain knew the geyser monitor was so efficient it only needed to be checked every other year, usually on the Fourth of July. The next scheduled maintenance was more than a year from now. The United States Geological Survey scientists picked July 4th because the geysers made them think of natural fireworks. He headed back toward the boardwalk trail. Real fireworks would be coming soon enough.

Chapter 30

Yellowstone, Mammoth Hot Springs, Park Headquarters, June 16, Afternoon

Grayson Cole was back at his desk finishing paperwork. This time a report on Harris and the grizzly encounter.

There was a knock on his door. Cole stopped typing.

"Ranger Cole?" Harris asked. The voice lacked some of the confidence of previous days.

Cole looked up from his computer monitor. "Please come in, and call me Grayson."

Harris took a seat. She appeared to hesitate before speaking. "Are you busy?"

"Not really, just finishing up my report on our encounter with the bear. Hey, you can help me. How do you spell fainted? Or maybe I should use, passed out?"

"Real funny," Harris countered.

"What's up?"

"Look, I've been withholding information from you," Harris started.

"Oh," Cole replied, straightening in his chair.

"My first impression of you and your rangers was of a bunch of bumbling Dudley Do-Rights," Harris sheepishly admitted. "No offense."

"None taken. May I ask your impression now?"

"Several days in the park and yesterday's encounter with the bear has revealed an unexpected level of professionalism and experience. Your team knows what it's doing."

She swallowed and went on. "I really could use your help."

"What can I do to assist?" he offered.

"I'm tasked to Yellowstone because it appears the burned out sub found in Oregon may have been carrying more than drugs or illegals." Agent Harris hesitated for a brief moment then asked, "What's your security clearance level?"

That question took Cole by surprise. In his entire Park Service career he had never been asked the question. "Ah, I'm not sure."

"All right," Harris said, getting up and closing his office door. "I'll probably get in trouble for telling you this, but the sub is more interesting than we first thought."

"Really? How so?"

Harris returned to her seat and continued.

"While we still believe it was either smuggling drugs or, less likely, ferrying illegals, an analysis of the wreckage by the Department of Energy found it to be extremely hot. . . . radioactive hot."

"What does the bureau think it means?"

"Not sure, but we have to assume the sub may have been transporting a nuclear device. And since a map of Yellowstone was found at the site, the FBI is concerned the park may be a target."

"Makes sense."

"There's more." Harris waited as if for dramatic effect. "We just received reports of a Ryder truck explosion outside of Coeur D'Alene, Idaho. Can you guess what we found?"

"It's hot."

"Correct, and. . . ?"

Cole thought for a second and responded with a sigh, "A map of Yellowstone."

"Bingo."

Cole knew finding maps of Yellowstone at both locations didn't necessarily mean anything. The Park Service printed millions of those maps. They could be downloaded for free off the internet.

"We have no evidence the truck was in Yellowstone, but it's an odd coincidence, don't you think?" Harris asked. "A hot sub and now a hot truck having connections to the park."

A cold realization went through his body. "You know the president is scheduled to be here in a few weeks. Will his trip be cancelled?"

"Not sure, those decisions are above my pay grade." Agent Harris went on. "In the meantime, the public story will remain that the sub was carrying illegal drugs. There is to be no mention of the radioactive components of the sub or the truck. Not even to your ranger corps. We also ask you to avoid commenting on the truck explosion until local and federal law enforcement has more information. We don't want to cause a panic."

"Agreed," Cole said. "What would you like the Park Service to do in the meantime?"

"Stay sharp. Be on the lookout for any unusual people or activity. And please contact me if anything strikes you as out of the ordinary."

Unusual people and activity? Does she mean the countless visitors who come to the park every year unprepared for a wilderness experience? Or does she mean the local militia members who refuse to put license plates on their cars and are convinced the U.N. has dug tunnels under the park to hide a blue-helmeted invasion army? "Okay. Anything else?"

"Yes, one more thing. Are you familiar with Sinclair Enterprises?"

"Of course, they run the park's hotels and restaurants."

"Well, the bureau received a report from their HR department that one of the delivery men and his truck has gone missing. Mr. Sinclair has agreed to meet with us to discuss the disappearance."

"Okay." Cole replied.

At that Agent Harris got up from her chair. "I've got to check with maintenance about accommodations. But I'll be seeing you again shortly."

She turned and left his office.

Be on the lookout for unusual activity, he thought. She's got to be kidding. That pretty much summed up a *normal* day in Yellowstone.

Chapter 31
Jackson Hole Wyoming, Charles Sinclair's Ranch, June 18, Afternoon

Cole pulled the Park Service Jeep Cherokee up to Charles Sinclair's driveway. Agent Harris sat in the passenger seat making notes on a small tablet. The Sinclair driveway was more like a road. He wondered how the thing got plowed in the winter. The city probably did it for free.

Prior to coming out to Charles' house, Cole and Harris had done some research, which resulted in Sinclair becoming a person of interest. A quick run of Charles Sinclair's name through the National Criminal Information Center (NCIC) system turned up nothing. Not surprising, a Google search revealed Charles's philanthropy and community service. He was a member of several civic organizations including the local chamber of commerce. He served on numerous corporate boards and even led the local Boy Scout troop. A real Boy Scout, it seemed.

Digging a little deeper revealed Charles' support of conservative politicians and organizations. Some of the groups, like the Conservative Council, bordered on extremism. Again, not that surprising. The Yellowstone region was home to some of the most unconventional people in America. There was something about the remote, off the grid parts of the world that brought out the crazies. Just outside the northwest corner of Yellowstone had been the headquarters of the World Universal Triumphant Church. Cole had driven by the so-called church's sprawling compound several times. The church leader

believed she was the reincarnation of a twenty
thousand year old Mongol warrior named Rada,
Rumie, Runny, or some such nonsense. Cole
couldn't remember. During Sunday services the
church leader summoned Rada through a
combination séance, play, talk show. Rada would
possess the church leader, holding court spewing
nonsense about the fate of the world and the
cosmic imbalance of dark and light. Back in the
80's Rada predicted nuclear war, so the church
congregation built fallout shelters and stocked up
food. The bombs never came. Cole saw the Rada
con as a great money making scheme. The packed
Sunday parking lots revealed a shocking number of
nearby people bought what was being peddled in
the church. The church finally fell on hard times
when it was raided for stockpiling a huge cache of
illegal weapons. So much for peace and love.

It was obvious from Sinclair's associations
and his numerous public statements that he openly
disdained the federal government and the Paine
administration in particular. A news search
revealed a letter to the Jackson Hole newspaper
about federal taxes and the illegality of the federal
income tax. It would appear Charles had drunk
the extreme conservative Kool-Aid.

This brought a chuckle from Cole. It
appeared to the ranger that much of Sinclair's
fortune derived from milking a government tit.
Park and Forest Service assistance, especially wild
land firefighting, protected Sinclair's lavish lifestyle.
What really got under Cole's skin were Charles'
objections to installing wild land fire prevention
measures, such as removing brush around his

house. "No federal bureaucrat is going to tell me what to do on my land," he said.

Subsidized anarchy. Sinclair wanted tax dollars spent to plow his road, fight local fires, and subsidize the water for his ranch, but without any of the safeguards and requirements that come with those expenditures. Not a bad way to make a living.

Ranger Cole stopped the Jeep in front of the garage. It was a large structure capable of holding five cars, clearly bigger than accommodations provided Cole by the Park Service. Sinclair's house itself was more like a lodge, something out of Western Homes & Gardens. Which, actually now that Cole thought about it, it was. Large raw cedar posts created an archway over the front door. Gray and white flag stones provided an entrance walkway.

Cole and Agent Harris walked up the path to the door. He placed his flat hat on his head and adjusted his clip-on tie. He loved wearing these ties. It reminded him of his childhood, when his mother made him wear clip-on neckwear for church or other important family events. But clip-ons weren't just a fond childhood memory. This one was an important safety device, as important as the bullet proof vest he was wearing. Many law enforcement officers had been choked to death with their own ties, spurring the change in neckwear.

He reached the front door and rang the bell. Dixie rang through the hall. But of course, he thought.

A large muscular man opened the door,

214

"Yes," he said. "Can I help the two of you?"

"Grayson Cole, Park Service ranger and FBI Agent Dianne Harris to see Mr. Sinclair."

Agent Harris flashed her FBI badge. Cole realized he didn't have his wallet credentials. They were back in the rig. The flat hat, badge, and the 9mm Sig Sauer pistol on his hip would have to be enough law enforcement identification.

The large man paid little attention to either officer and like an automaton showed Cole and Harris to Charles' office. They walked through the large great hall. A two story, floor to ceiling river rock fireplace was at the far end. A crackling fire was already lit. Large flag stones made up the great hall floor. Several mounted deer, moose and elk trophies hung on the walls. Cole couldn't help but notice near the center of the room the full size stuffed polar bear. A Boone & Crocket plaque designated it the largest polar bear ever bagged.

Just off the main hall was Sinclair's private office. Cole and Harris were asked to remain there. Mr. Sinclair would join them shortly. Cole thanked the burly man and placed his flat hat on the Crusader table. Maps of Yellowstone were spread across it. Large X's marked several spots, including three in the West Thumb area. On the table was also a box of very large caliber ammunition. It had to be for hunting a very large animal, such as an elephant or the polar bear he had just met in the foyer.

They walked around the office, viewing the various photos and artwork. Cole was certain one of the paintings was an original Charlie Russell. If so, it would have cost a pretty penny.

Continuing around the room, Cole stopped
at a picture of King Richard. *Defender of the one true
faith and hero of the third crusade* was inscribed on a
small plaque on the picture's frame.

"He was a man of great faith, backed up
with conviction," Charles Sinclair said, entering the
room. "A very rare combination today."

"Indeed," Cole replied. "Grayson Cole,
Yellowstone National Park Ranger. And this is
Agent Dianne Harris with the FBI."

"Charles Sinclair, but call me Charles."
Sinclair shook hands with the two officers and
returned his attention to the picture of King
Richard.

"The crusades were the first salvo in the
battle between good and evil. Between the forces
of Christ against the forces of Islam. King
Richard," Sinclair said, pointing at the picture, "led
the successful third crusade in 1192, driving the
Muslims from major sections of the Holy Land.
His victories were not sustained and thus the need
for additional crusades to the Middle East,"

"Interesting, although I seem to remember
the following crusades were less successful in
driving the Muslims from the Middle East, and
instead they turned their wrath upon the unfaithful
within Christendom, eventually sacking
Constantinople, the seat of the Catholic faith at
that time," Cole said. "It was the beginning of the
rift that plagues the church to this day."

"Impressive, Ranger Cole. Anything else?"

Cole thought a second and went on. "The
Crusades wedded Christianity and Islam to specific
sites, such as Jerusalem. The problem with having

a faith wedded to a specific place is the place can be taken away. Then the question is what happens to your faith?"

"I see you are a student of church history. Did you study the Crusades in school?" Sinclair asked.

"Some, but more importantly knowing history is part of my job." More than just about any other federal job, a National Park Ranger must be a jack-of-all-trades. They are required to not only protect the public from criminals, but they are also there to fight wildfires, provide first aid, and conduct search and rescue operations. These, however, were the minimum requirements. Rangers were also expected to know the best places to eat, the secret fishing spots, the name of every park plant, flower, bird and animal, the geologic history of the area and the prehistoric and historic past of the humans who lived, worked and played there. A favorite pastime of park visitors was Stump the Ranger. Cole prided himself on having yet to be stumped.

"What lesson did you take away from your Crusade study?" Sinclair asked.

"Holy endeavors can end up with unintended consequences, and can ultimately turn its power against itself," Cole responded.

"Isn't that true of all human action?" Sinclair inquired, his left eye brow rising slightly.

"I suppose, however, the Crusades had impacts lasting for more than a millennium. It's a warning that people should give more weight to uncertainty and be careful in their actions."

"Interesting."

Just then a man entered the room. Apparently surprised to find the office occupied, he began to turn and excuse himself. Sinclair stopped him and introduced Cole and Harris.

"I know you," Harris stated. "You're Captain Hansen, the Marine hero of Afghanistan." Turning to Cole, Harris went on almost giddily. "Hansen is a sniper with the longest recorded kill shot."

Hansen blushed a bit, obviously uncomfortable that he had been recognized. "That was a long time ago," Hansen deflected. He moved to the Crusader table and cleared it of the map and rifle shells.

"Well, I imagine you didn't stop by today to talk history of the Middle Ages and hear Captain Hansen's war stories," Sinclair stated. "To what do we owe the pleasure of today's visit?"

"Correct," Harris said. "We're investigating the disappearance of one of your employees, a Jason Johnston."

"Ah, yes. Quite disturbing. Everyone in the company is concerned about his safety, as you can imagine. I hope you have some good news."

"Actually, no new developments. However, the FBI and Park Service continue the search of the park and nearby area. I was hoping you could provide us more information. Is there anything you've remembered about his behavior prior to the disappearance? Anything out of the ordinary?"

"No, not that I can remember. However, I didn't work closely with Jason. He was in our shipping department. As you can imagine, Sinclair

Enterprises is a multi-billion dollar operation and sadly I don't know every employee, let alone their personal habits."

"Do your vehicles have locater transponders?" Harris continued.

"No, but that's something we will look into shortly," Sinclair responded.

"I understand," Harris replied. "As I said, we will continue the search of the park, including Sinclair's park properties."

That got Sinclair's and Hansen's attention. "What was that?" Sinclair asked.

Cole jumped into the conversation. "We've begun a search of Sinclair properties, nothing intensive. Rather, site visits to all properties, asking questions and searching for additional clues to Mr. Johnston's whereabouts."

"You think he may be hiding in one of the Sinclair facilities?" Hansen asked.

"Not necessarily, but it makes sense to search places he worked in and was familiar with. We still haven't found his truck. It may still be in the park. Finding it could point to Mr. Johnston's location."

"Do you suspect foul play?" Sinclair asked.

"Anytime a normally reliable person goes missing it raises suspicions. Can you tell me anything more about the employee? Had he been acting erratic or depressed recently?"

"No, not that I am aware. Again I didn't really know the man. Do you think he may have hurt himself?"

"It wouldn't be the first time a person killed himself in a national park. Sadly it happens more often than the public would suspect," Cole explained.

"I'm sorry we can't be more helpful," Sinclair said, exchanging a glance with Hansen.

"That's quite all right," Cole said, getting up to leave. "Here are our cards. Give either Agent Harris or me a call if you think of anything that may help the search."

"Certainly," Sinclair replied.

Cole placed his hat back on his head. Sinclair and Hansen walked them to the door.

When the green and white ranger vehicle had driven out of sight, Sinclair turned to Hansen. "We need to advance our deployment."

Chapter 32
White House, Roosevelt Room,
Washington D.C., June 20, Afternoon

The Roosevelt Room was a small conference room named after Presidents Theodore and Franklin Roosevelt. It was part of the executive mansion's West Wing, just across the hall from the Oval Office. On the room's fireplace mantle sat Teddy Roosevelt's Nobel Peace Prize, as well as a dramatic painting of the 26th president as a Roughrider on horseback charging up San Juan Hill. Off to the right of the fireplace was a portrait of FDR.

The small, windowless former office had been named the Roosevelt room under President Nixon when Teddy Roosevelt's Nobel prize had been prominently displayed in the room. Yet to keep future presidents, especially Democratic administrations from changing the room or renaming it after another future chief executive, FDR's picture was hung in the room as well. It was a masterful act of political decision making, one that understood the game at the heart of politics.

Today, the room was the setting for another more substantial political decision. The president's reelection team filled the room.

Scott Beardsley sat on the president's left. The rest of the campaign team took the remaining seats. Scott was going over the latest polling data with the team. It wasn't good. "We're down another three points, Mr. President," he said matter of fact. "We're now in a dead heat with Senator Healy."

Senator Michael Healy was the junior Senator from Virginia. He had been instrumental in leading the minority party's opposition to the president's agenda. Senator Healy had reached the peak of power in his party. It had been a pretty typical path to its top. He was born into one of America's most wealthy families and inherited the highly successful Healy aviation business. His leadership of Healy Aviation and hefty campaign contributions caught the eye of political leaders, landing him the Chinese ambassadorship. From there he was tapped to run the Treasury Department under the previous administration. After the election of President Paine, Michael Healy found himself out of a job. He could have easily returned to Healy Aviation. But he had gotten a taste of politics and liked it. And when Virginia's junior senator died, roughly six months after Healy left the Treasury Department, his path back to politics was open. The Virginia governor tapped Healy to complete the rest of the vacant term.

The fact that Senator Healy had never won an election was not lost on Scott. Nor that Healy had almost no domestic policy experience. In Scott's book, he wasn't qualified for the nation's highest office. This was clearly revealed during a campaign stop in Idaho. A reporter asked what a Healy administration would do about the deteriorating western cattle guard situation. Healy knew nothing of the issue, assuming the term cattle guards referred to real people rather than road barriers. Instead of deflecting the matter, Healy stuck to his party's message and stated that government shouldn't be guarding cattle. He had about as much connection to the people as the Queen of England. Scott would do everything in his power to insure Paine's reelection.

"Damn," the president said.

"It gets worse," Scott continued. "The polling out of the battle ground states has dropped as well. We are now down in North Carolina and Oklahoma, and only up two points in Wyoming. I don't need to remind you we have to win at least one of these states to secure reelection." He hesitated and swallowed before going on. "It's time to seriously consider dumping Vice President Winfield and adding Governor Carson to the ticket."

The president knew the future of Vice President Winfield would come up at this meeting. He expected a spirited debate on the matter. Some of his advisors would argue that dumping the VP would be seen as an act of a desperate campaign. Others would argue the campaign needed to take decisive action and inject energy into its efforts. Frankly, Vice President Winfield's illness had prevented him from campaigning.

Meanwhile, Senator Healy's running mate, Missouri Governor Robert Bowers, was pounding on the president at every campaign stop. It was two against one. Unknown to those in the room, the vice president's future was darker than publicly known. The doctors weren't sure how long the vice president had left. It could be months or years. However, the president had only shared this information with Scott. The president's best friend was dying. Scott knew the president would grant

as much dignity to the vice president as possible.
But politics wasn't about dignity or playing fair. It
was about who gets what and when. It was bare-
knuckled and brutal. The first rule of D.C. politics
was that if you wanted a friend in Washington then
get a dog. There were no friends in Washington.
For all his political adeptness, Scott knew the
president hadn't quite learned or accepted this
lesion entirely.

"Is there no other option?" the party chair
from Illinois asked.

"Unfortunately, no." Scott took the
opportunity to hand the group a piece of paper
with Wyoming polling data, graphs and charts on
it. "Governor Carson remains extremely popular
in Wyoming." Scott stated. "Moreover, we quietly
polled voters in the state and across the country
about the idea of adding the governor to the
ticket." Scott again paused looking Paine directly in
the eye. "You would win Wyoming by ten points,
Mr. President. And be all but assured of victory."

"Won't adding Governor Carson to the
ticket be seen as a desperate move of a losing
campaign?" This question came from the leader of
the Massachusetts delegation.

"We ran those numbers as well. If the
move is made because of the VPs health, the
public is willing to give the president the benefit of
the doubt. I'd recommend making the
announcement that you're adding Carson to the
ticket at your upcoming Yellowstone trip."

Scott reached for a cup of tea, drank and
went on. "We should begin to leak stories about
the VP's ailing health. That will set the table for

the Wyoming statement."

Paine let out a deep breath. The room
went quiet. All eyes were fixed upon him.

Paine had been listening intently, taking a
few notes. It was obvious he was going over the
possibilities in his head. He was about to decide
the political fate of his best friend. It was an
excruciating dilemma. But, Scott knew it had been
Vice President Winfield who had reminded then-
candidate Paine that countless excruciating
decisions would be made every day. Could Paine
do that? Could he see clearly and do what was
best for the country despite his personal feelings to
the contrary?

At that time, the answer had been yes. But
even in Paine's wildest dreams, the president had
never considered that one of those decisions
would include his best friend.

The president stood. Everyone followed.
"Ladies and Gentlemen," he began. "Senator
Healy is unqualified to lead this nation. I shudder
to think what would happen to our great country if
he gains this office. As much as it pains me, I will
do everything I can to win election this
November." He strode toward the Roosevelt
Room door. He stopped in the doorway and
turned to the campaign team that remained in the
conference. "Please begin preparations for adding
Governor Carson to the ticket."

Scott followed the president out of the
conference room toward his private office at the
far end of the hall. He pulled out his cell phone
and began to dial the Park Service director. He
needed to begin coordinating with the Park Service

on what now had become a major political event.

Chapter 33
Yellowstone, Mammoth Hot Spring Headquarters, June 25, Morning

Cole was again at his desk, this time finishing up a poaching report. Some idiot had shot one of the park's bull elk solely for the antlers and left the carcass to rot. He had shot the animal in front of several park visitors, including at least one family with small children. It had definitely ruined their trip.

He had taken down the violator with a blast of pepper spray. The poacher faced multiple violations--poaching, trespassing, illegal discharge of weapon, and reckless endangerment. He would be going away for quite awhile.

The phone on his desk rang. Without much thought, Cole lifted the receiver, placed it to his ear as he continued to type on his computer. "Cole," he stated automatically.

"Ranger Cole, this is Scott Beardsley with the White House," came the response.

Cole stopped typing and sat up in his chair.

"Ranger Cole, I'm calling to inquire about the president's upcoming trip to Yellowstone."

Finally. He was beginning to wonder how long they would wait before calling him. "Mr. Beardsley, it's a pleasure. I'm sorry we won't get to meet in person."

There was a pause on the other end of the line. "What do you mean?"

"You're calling to inform us about a change in the president's plans. I'd been alerted this might be the case. And, quite frankly, given all that's going on in the park right now it's probably the right call to cancel the trip."

There was a longer pause on the other end.

"Ranger Cole, I'm sorry but there seems to be a miscommunication. The president isn't cancelling his Yellowstone trip. He's moving ahead, and even plans on making a major announcement while in the park."

"You've got to be kidding?" Cole said.

"No, sir. In fact, we expect the Governor of Wyoming, the state's senior senator, the Speaker of the House, the Secretary of the Interior, the Director of the Park Service, and dozens of local dignitaries to be in attendance."

Cole couldn't believe what he was hearing. "Mr. Beardsley, is the president aware of the situation here in Yellowstone? We have a suspicious missing person investigation, significant wildfire activity, and FBI inquiries about domestic terrorist operations. On top of that we have increased volcanic activity in the park. This may not be the best time for the president to visit."

"Ranger Cole, I appreciate your concern. However, short of the increased volcanic activity, what you've described is a typical day for the president. There are larger, shall we say, political forces at work here."

Unbelievable, Cole thought.

"I appreciate your concern, Ranger Cole. However, the president is coming to your park. The FBI, Secret Service, and local law enforcement will be at your disposal. If you need additional resources, just call. Short of a volcanic eruption we expect the Park Service to provide for the president's safety."

Cole stuffed an objection. He knew Scott's answer wasn't a statement, but rather an order. "We can do it."

"I know you can. I look forward to meeting you."

The line went dead. Cole hung up his phone, let out a sigh while gazing at the ceiling. Idiots. He would never understand politics. It seemed that decisions were always made in order to gain some sort of partisan advantage. Unfortunately, that partisan advantage didn't always, at least from his point of view, promote the public's welfare.

Coming to Yellowstone seemed like an unreasonable risk. But hadn't he passed along his concern? Hadn't he properly presented his objection? He had, but couldn't shake the feeling that something about the presidential visit was troubling.

Chapter 34
Yellowstone's Bechler Road, June 26, Afternoon

Yellowstone's Bechler region was one of the most remote sections of the park. Few if any park visitors knew about it, let alone visited it. However, Cole's experience told him that desperate people often found these parts of the park, and that made it an excellent place to search for the lost Sinclair truck. Besides, most of the front country sites had been combed.

Cole and Harris drove the only road in this part of the park. It was hardly a road, more like a scratch in the ground. Several large tree branches lay across the road, as if they had been snapped off by a giant. Someone in a large vehicle had recently driven down the road. Turning the Jeep Cherokee around the last bend Cole spotted a large truck. No effort had been made to hide it.

"There it is!" Harris said.

"Get on the radio and let HQ know we've found the missing Sinclair truck," Cole said, parking their SUV a distance away.

Cole turned to Harris. "We'll execute a high risk car stop."

The two officers opened their doors and drew their guns. Harris held a shotgun, placing it in the V between the SUV body and door. He did likewise, holding his 9mm Sig Sauer semi-automatic pistol in the cruck of the driver's door.

Cole turned on the Jeep's PA system. "To anyone in the truck, come out with your hands up." He wasn't sure if there was anyone in the vehicle. In fact, it was likely there wasn't anyone inside. However, standard law enforcement training required a ranger to assume someone was in the truck and, until determined otherwise, that person was assumed to be dangerous.

He waited a few more seconds before returning to the PA system. "If you don't come out with your hands up in the next three seconds I will send in the German Shepherd." Cole wasn't part of a K9 unit and had no dog with him today, yet whoever may or may not be in the vehicle didn't know that. And the mere mention of a dog often got reluctant suspects to show themselves.

Still, nothing moved in the vehicle. Either there was no one inside, at least no one living, the person was deaf, or they were so desperate even the threat of being mauled by a dog didn't motivate them. For now Cole would assume that later.

"Cover me," Cole said to Harris.

Leaving the cover of the SUV door, he approached the parked truck with caution. The rear door of the truck trailer was closed. The door lock was lying on the ground. A box of what appeared to be medical devices were scattered about the ground. Cole quietly placed a large stick in the door clasp, effectively sealing the rear door shut. If there was someone inside the trailer he wanted them to stay put until he searched the truck cabin.

That done, he moved slowly toward the passenger side door. He would have preferred a more protected approach, but had no choice. He advanced to the truck's passenger side door, his service pistol held out in front of him extended at a forty five degree angle toward the ground. Reaching for the door handle with his left hand, he took a deep breath and quickly opened the door.

"Police officer. Hands up," he yelled. But there was no one there.

A quick scan of the truck cabin revealed little. There was no indication of a struggle, all appeared to be in order. On the floor of the cab he found a Sinclair driver's uniform. Probably not a good sign. Climbing down from the cab, he walked cautiously back to the trailer door. If there was someone inside they certainly knew he was here. Standing before the trailer door, Cole decided the prudent thing to do was to wait for backup. He had called in his location, so assistance was on the way. Unfortunately, it would be several hours before anyone arrived. He and Harris could use the time to better search the truck and surrounding area for clues.

Cole reached down to make certain the stick was secure. Glancing at the bottom of the door, he noticed something oozing from beneath it. On closer inspection he realized it was blood. He couldn't be certain it was human. He heard a low moan, a muffled cry for help. It came from inside the trailer. The situation had changed. There was an emergency and someone's life apparently was on the line. Damn it. They couldn't wait for backup now.

Walking back to the SUV, he explained the situation to Harris and his plan of action. Returning to the trailer, he removed the stick and lifted the latch and prepared to throw the door open. Holding his pistol in his right hand, he lifted the door with his left. It was an awkward movement, but the door was counter-weighted and went up easily. Shooting up and reaching the end of its track it locked in place with a loud BANG!

The truck trailer was packed with supplies of every kind. Souvenirs, foodstuffs, office supplies and medical equipment were thrown about. The drive up the Bechler road had obviously been tough on the cargo. One large box was open, its contents strewn about the floor.

Gun still in hand, Cole bent down and picked up a small device. It was a clip-on badge about the size of an oversized postage stamp. On its face was a red cross next to that of a radiation symbol. An apparent warning light was blinking bright red.

This was not good.

Convinced the trailer was empty of any threat, Cole shouted, "Get up here Harris!"

He heard again the low moaning. It was coming from a large crate. Moving over to it, he saw blood oozing from the bottom, spreading across the floor. The crate was large, about six feet long and half as tall, large enough to hold a person. The top had been tampered with. Several of the lid's nails were missing. It was obvious someone had opened the crate and resealed it.

The moan grew loader.

Cole tried to lift the lid off by hand. It wouldn't budge. He looked around for something to open the crate. He found a stash of shovels, axes and Pulaskis. Obviously the firefighting equipment the park had ordered.

"Give me that axe," Cole ordered Harris,

who had just arrived at the open door. She handed over the axe. Cole placed the blade in the crack between the crate and its lid. Grabbing a shovel, he whacked the blunt side of the axe, jamming its blade deep between the two crate pieces. He then pushed down on the axe handle. The crack opened up with a creeeeaaak!

Cole repeated this process several times until the top came lose. He pushed it aside, revealing the source of the moaning. Inside were two people, a man and woman roughly in their twenties. They'd been shot. Grayson reached down and felt for a pulse on the man's neck. Nothing. He did the same for the woman, but got a faint sign of life. He knew pulling her out of the box might inflict more injury, but she was losing blood fast and to save her he had to stop the flow. "Help me."

It took some effort, but Harris and Cole were able to lift the woman and place her on the trailer floor. Her breathing was labored, but continuous. Cole searched for wounds, a difficult task considering she was soaked in blood, likely both hers and that of her partner in the box.

The woman coughed and spit up blood. Opening her eyes, she looked at him. She moved her mouth. A low wheeze came out. Cole leaned in closer and quietly yet firmly said, "Can you tell me who did this to you?"

"Soldier," was all the victim could get out. She wheezed again. More blood oozed from her mouth.

"Can you tell me anything more?" he urged.

234

Nothing. The woman's eyes rolled back into her head as she slipped into unconsciousness.

Cole looked around and found a box labeled medical supplies. He smashed open the top with the axe. He pulled out gauze and ace bandages and set about searching for a wound to close.

He found it. At the back of her head was a single gunshot wound. The entry wound was over the left eye, matted with hair. An exit wound was just behind the left ear. Whoever shot her had obviously assumed she was dead. Cole had seen plenty of gunshot wounds, mostly careless hunters who had shot themselves or their partners, but he could see this shot traveled through only one of the brain's hemispheres. That would have limited the damage to the brain and maybe explained why she was still alive.

He covered the wound with gauze and wrapped the ace bandage around her head to hold it in place. He repeated this process as blood seeped through the bandages. There wasn't much more to do now than wait for the rescue helicopter. It arrived roughly twenty minutes later. Park paramedics stabilized the patient and whisked her off to the local hospital in Jackson Hole.

All was again quiet. Cole sat on the end of the trailer, hanging his legs over the edge. Harris had gone with the victim in case she could provide more information. While exhausted, he knew the hard part of the investigation had just begun.

He now had another mystery on his hands. What the hell was going on? Yellowstone had seen its fair share of visitor deaths. Many people had been gored by bison, mauled by bears, tumbled down cliffs, or fallen into hot springs. But the death of two poachers followed by an attempted double murder was an unprecedented level of violence. In all his years at Yellowstone he had never heard of such a thing. He had ruled out a murder-suicide of the couple. No weapon had been found. Hard to shoot oneself and dispose of the gun. About as difficult as nailing oneself in a box.

Several questions raced through his head. Had the Sinclair driver killed the two park visitors? If so, what was the reason and where was he? Or was this the work of someone else? If so, where were the suspect and the driver? He couldn't help shake the feeling that all three incidents, the poachers, the hikers and the missing driver, were connected. With the president coming he had to assume they were.

Returning his attention to the Sinclair truck, Cole realized it was the only vehicle in the area. So the suspect may have stolen the victims' vehicle or hiked out of the area. Either way Cole had to act quickly.

He got on the radio and called into dispatch, asking that an all-points bulletin be sent out for the truck driver, Jason Johnston.

Cole was mentally exhausted, his mouth dry. He sipped some water from a canteen he had retrieved from his vehicle. He tried to place it down on the trailer floor next to himself, but tipped it over. The canteen spilled water over the trailer floor.

"Damn."

He righted the canteen and noticed something stuck to the floor where he had placed his water bottle.

He picked it up. It was a patch, roughly the size of a credit card. On its back was Velcro, indicating the patch was meant to be taken on and off. Flipping it over, Cole saw that the patch was actually an American flag. Several of the stripes were white. However, the areas of the flag that should be red and blue were tan or sand color.

That was odd. Holding the patch up to his face for a closer look, he couldn't help but wonder what it was doing here. Then he remembered the victim's gasp. What had she said?

Soldier.

Cole jumped down from the truck, dashing toward his vehicle. He had a call to make and feared the time to catch this killer was running out.

Chapter 35
Sinclair Enterprises Outbuilding, Yellowstone Lake's West Thumb, June 30, Afternoon

Sinclair had been right. This was the perfect spot from which to shoot the president.

The sniper den was actually an old, half buried outbuilding used by Sinclair Enterprises to house maintenance equipment for the company's volcanic monitoring program. The room was small, roughly ten feet by ten feet. It was damp and smelled musty, like rotting soil. It wasn't a nauseating smell, rather a scent of organic decomposition. The odor reminded Hansen of his al Qaeda cell, minus the reek of piss and shit.

He and Sinclair would spend the next several days in this room. It would be cramped, but to avoid detection early deployment to the den was necessary. The Park Service and Secret Service, according to Sheriff Fielder, wouldn't begin full scale security measures until the day before the president's arrival. However, the Park Service's visit about the missing driver had convinced them to initiate their plans a little early.

The room was tight, but despite its small size the sniper den had several advantages. Running water was its primary asset. This meant the two men didn't have to carry several days' supply of water in with them. It would be hot in the shed and staying hydrated was important. The shed also had several pipes and ducts running out to the exterior of the building. A twelve inch wide pipe penetrated the wall roughly forty eight inches from the floor. They had removed this pipe, creating a foot wide hole in the wall. They concealed it with camouflage netting. Unless someone was looking directly at the shed from close range, the hole was virtually impossible to see. The shed was set back from the park road a fair distance and shielded from direct observation by a beauty strip. A beauty strip was a park euphemism for a string of trees or bushes that hid park facilities or maintenance yards from public view. In this case the beauty strip would also obscure the Secret Service's ability to see a potential threat.

Inside the shed, Hansen set up a small table and placed the TAC 50 caliber sniper rifle on top. He set his Marine Corps issued backpack on the floor, removed a tripod and mounted the rifle to it. Sinclair employed a laser range finder to determine the distance to target.

"Two thousand nine hundred and eighty five yards to target," Sinclair said.

Hansen let out a whistle. "That's a fair distance. More than two hundred yards farther than the longest ever kill shot."

This shot would stretch Hansen's skills. But he had the right weapon, the right ammunition, and the proper scope. The president would be a fixed or slow moving target, which was also to his advantage. If this shot were about one mile he would guarantee a kill. However, in this case wind was a significant variable. Moving up their deployment to the snipers den had prevented them from deploying wind sensors between them and the president's podium. Precise information related to distance and wind speed led to a solid adjustment of the rifle's scope. Even a slight miscalculation of wind speed or direction would cause him to miss his prey. He hated uncertainty, but in this case it couldn't be avoided. There simply was no way to know which way the wind would blow. Ironic that all this effort could be wasted on a slight breeze.

Over their first meal in the shed Sinclair and Hansen went over the plan. Hansen would wait until the end of the president's speech, when he was expected to make his way through a receiving line. The disadvantage of waiting until after the completion of the speech was that the president would be a moving target. However, Hansen had shot running targets from over a thousand yards. He figured he could hit a walking target at roughly double that distance. The advantage of waiting for the end of the speech came from the president's departure plans. According to the Park County sheriff, the president was expected to immediately board his Marine One helicopter for the short trip to a Jackson Hole fundraiser. In order to meet the tight timeline and discourage unwanted press questions, the helicopter rotors would be fired up as the president shook hands. The noise of the helicopter, while masking annoying press questions, would also cover the report of the rifle. The Secret Service would eventually figure out the source of the shot, but he and Sinclair would be long gone by then.

Chapter 36
Middle East, Midnight

It could have been any city in the Middle East. Broken and war torn dwellings littered the little town. A cliché really. Sand and palm trees dotted the landscape. The heat was oppressive, even at this late hour of the night. The moon shining behind a thin veil of clouds provided enough light for a hidden bomber to see his target.

Soldiers up ahead appeared to be on patrol. A few were on foot, the rest in an armored Humvee. The troops were investigating recent terrorist activity, a fire-fight that led to the capture of other rangers. This and other patrols were there to rescue their comrades. And if they could root out the terrorists, so much the better. But it was an impossible task, for as soon as one terrorist was killed two more were created. They were like rabbits. No, more like rats. Rats, rabbits… it didn't matter. That was how the Army saw him, his family and friends. They were pests to be exterminated.

He watched his targets through high powered binoculars as they approached a road intersection. He had picked this spot because it was not uncommon to find garbage piled up at intersections. Abandoned cars, power poles, trash cans and other assorted debris offered plenty of places to hide a bomb. Countless places for the Army to search.

The Army bomb detection units were quite good at finding hidden improvised explosive devices, or IEDs. The obvious solution was not to hide them, but where to hide them. Where wouldn't a soldier expect to find a bomb? A place where he would let his guard down and miss the obvious.

It had been a major breakthrough to place bombs in the bodies of dead dogs and cats. There was no end to the dead animals littering Middle Eastern streets. Soldiers, at least at first, paid these ubiquitous carcasses no heed. This lack of attention came at many a soldier's peril. That changed quickly and once again the terrorists altered tactics.

The patrol moved cautiously toward the intersection, looking for disturbed ground that might indicate the recent burial of an IED, or wires protruding from an unlikely source.

The patrol rounded a corner and immediately came under fire. Small arms, machine guns and rocket propelled devices fired at their rear. The foot soldiers dove for cover while the Humvee sped up the street to get out of the line of sight of rocket propelled grenades.

Racing up the street, the Humvee took fire from its right, forcing the corporal behind the wheel to make a sharp left down a deserted street. Another Humvee sat smoking in the street up ahead. It appeared to have been caught in the same crossfire and suffered a worse fate. Smoke and fire billowed from its engine. The destroyed Humvee wasn't going anywhere.

For now the rescue team was safe and out of the direct line of fire. The rangers on foot had driven back the first set of attackers. These U.S. Forces traveled down a set of back alleys to rejoin their separated counterparts.

The commanding officer, a captain, ordered his patrol to spread out and take defensive positions. He radioed in his situation and advised his superiors that he had found the missing patrol.

Pulling out his night vision binoculars he trained them on the smoldering Humvee. It was a mess. No one could have survived in the vehicle, which appeared to have taken a direct RPG hit. But then he saw it. Movement in the cabin, as if someone were struggling to sit up.

"I think someone is in there," he whispered to his lieutenant.

A muffled cry of agony wailed from the vehicle. There was someone in there.

"Damn it," the captain yelled. "There are survivors." Turning to his lieutenant he ordered his men to crawl in to get a closer look.

Before the team could set out for the ruined Humvee, machine gun fire erupted from several of the abandoned buildings. It was nearly impossible to tell from what direction the shots came.

"Get under cover," the captain yelled. Men dove everywhere.

Machine gun fire continued to strafe the alleyway. It focused on the single remaining target, the downed Humvee.

Shots pelted the vehicle. Plinkty, plink, plinkty, plink, plink.

"God damn it! They're shooting at the men trapped in the Humvee," the captain shouted over the din. "We need to ID the source of the weapons fire now! Those men can't last much longer!"

It took the rangers a few seconds to locate the fire sources. "The shots are coming from three spots. Two windows down the right and a doorway on the left," a forward private reported over the radio.

"Okay, here's what we're going to do," the captain shot back. "Squad two and three take out the threats in the windows, squad four stop the fire from the door."

Machine gun fire and rocket propelled grenades erupted from the three squads. Explosions ripped apart the targeted windows and door.

Fire ceased from all locations except from one of the windows.

"Close that window, Sergeant," the captain ordered.

Readying his rocket propelled grenade launcher the sergeant fixed his sights on the open window and waited.

A head popped up within the window and continued to spray the alleyway with bullets. Rangers returned fire, causing the enemy sniper to duck behind cover. The sergeant pulled the trigger. Whoosh. The grenade rocketed toward the window leaving behind a smoke trail in its wake. The grenade entered the window, exploding on the far wall. Debris and material shot out, while a giant cloud of smoke and flame erupted from the roof. No one could have survived the explosion.

"Cease fire," the captain commanded.

Except for the noise from the burning

buildings and bombed out Humvee, the alleyway was quiet. No gunfire, no explosions. Nothing.

It appeared all clear. But one could never be sure. Further, it wouldn't be long before this firefight attracted more of the enemy. Time was running out.

The captain took out his binoculars, training them on the Humvee and focusing on the driver. He was slumped over, but did appear to be moving. "Squads two and three move up, secure the Humvee and get our men. Squad four ready covering fire. Now!"

Squads two and three broke into a full run, dashing the twenty or so yards between the ranger's covered positions and the Humvee. The lead sergeant reached the downed vehicle first, followed by the rest of his team. Resting his back on the Humvee's rear bumper, the sergeant quickly peaked through the rear window.

"What do you see sergeant?" the captain inquired.

"Three men. Two appear dead, but the driver's still moving," the sergeant reported. "I'm going up to the driver's door to get the man out."

The sergeant dropped down on his belly and crawled to the door. Rising to his knees, he reached for the door's handle and opened it. Inside, the driver was still alive, however, he was bound and gagged, unable to escape the vehicle. His eyes flashed panic.

"What's the holdup, sergeant!? Get that man out of there," came the captain's voice over the radio.

"I can't, sir. The man is bound and gagged.

He appears to be chained to his seat. I'm going to need some bolt cutters."

A chill went through the captain. "Get out of there sergeant. Now!"

The sergeant never heard the captain's order. The Humvee went up engulfed in a ball of flame. The two forward squads were obliterated as were the captain and his men. When the smoke cleared, the bodies of thirty rangers littered the alleyway.

The bomber watched the drama from his safe vantage point, pleased with his work. Use the Americans' values against them. Never leaving a man behind was an American strength, but also a vulnerability. The Americans would now think twice about retrieving downed comrades, which could undermine morale, weakening combat effectiveness.

The bomber packed away his materials, including the cell phone he used to detonate the bomb. A good day he thought, climbing down from his perch to the city streets. A crowd of onlookers was building now, drawn to the area by the explosion. The bomber slipped into the crowd and disappeared.

Joseph Hansen woke up, sweating, and coughing. It had been a dream, one he'd had several times before. He was tense and in need of some water. His flashbacks were getting worse. The nightmares were coming more often and leaving him drained every time.

He coughed. His head was pounding. Reaching for a napkin, Hansen blew his nose.

246

Blood poured from his nostrils. It had to be the park's high altitude and dry air. Wiping his noise and downing a gulp of water, he swallowed a couple aspirin. He lay back on his cot. It would all be over shortly.

Chapter 37
Grant Village, NPS Housing, June 30, Evening

When Cole joined the Park Service he had been told he would live on property with multi-million dollar views. That may be true, but they didn't mention the nearly worthless accommodations. His lodging was an Eisenhower era single wide trailer. Trailer 51. It had seen better days. The trailer was cold in the winter, hot in the summer. The shower leaked into his closet and he often shared his living quarters with mice, squirrels, and the occasional raccoon. Not all park accommodations were as bad as his, though. Many were more than adequate. But the Park Service charged rent for more regular housing and often required staff to take a roommate. Cole's willingness to live in the trailer eliminated both of these requirements.

As he switched on his TV, an MSNBC news program came on. The reporter was going on about the failing health of the vice president and speculating on his stepping down.

Cole moved to his desk, flipped on his computer. It would take a while to boot up. He opened a beer and drank a gulp while he waited. His dog Jake, an Alaskan malamute, was rolled up next to the desk. Jake had traveled with him to every one of his duty stations, but it appeared the dog liked Yellowstone the best. He picked up the TV remote and turned up the volume. The MSNBC reporter continued her story on Vice President Winfield's health.

"The Vice President is 68 years old and has

experienced several health challenges over the past three years, including his battle with liver cancer. The White House tells us that his cancer had been in remission, but a recent physical revealed its return. Let's turn it over to Chuck at the White House. Chuck, what can you tell us about the VP's health, the possibility of his stepping down, and any possible replacements?"

"Hey, Grayson? You in there?" Agent Harris yelled from outside.

Cole opened the trailer door, revealing Harris clad in a spandex jogging outfit. "Harris, good to see you. Come on in. How's the victim?" He was referring to the hiker they had found shot a few days earlier.

Harris climbed the steps to the trailer and entered. "It looks like she may live, but it will be a long time, if ever, before we can get any information." She looked around the trailer. "Nice place you got here," she said sarcastically.

Harris could see down the hallway into Cole's bedroom. The bedroom closet was visible through the bedroom door. Despite the clutter spread throughout in the rest of the trailer, the closet was an example of military order. His ranger hats were hung on the wall in a hat frame to keep them flat. His uniform shirts and pants were pressed and on individual hangers. Cole's several clip-on ties hung from individual hooks on the back of the bedroom door. Cole may not care about the appearance his surroundings gave off, but he did care about the impression his uniform and approach to his job left on others. In work Cole liked perfection.

"It's home," he replied. "Like a beer?"

"No thanks, do you have any water?"

"In the fridge. Help yourself."

Harris retrieved the Brita water pitcher from the refrigerator, poured herself a glass of water and sat on the couch. A few dirty dishes were stacked in the sink, laundry heaped on the washing machine, and unopened mail was on the kitchen table. "So, I assume there is no Mrs. Cole."

"No," replied Cole. It wasn't that he was opposed to marriage. Cole had had several girlfriends, but Park Service life was difficult on relationships. A ranger's career, while appearing romantic, often required numerous moves, in some cases to very remote duty stations. Very few women, at least the ones Cole met, were willing to cut themselves off almost entirely from civilization. So while he'd had his share of relationships, they were what he called cruise ship romances. They weren't destined to last.

"How about you? I don't see a ring. No Mr. Harris?" Cole asked.

"There was someone, but . . ."

"I didn't mean to pry," Cole apologized.

"No, it's all right . . . my fiancé was killed during a criminal investigation," Harris offered. "I've spent the last several years working to forget the past and have devoted all my effort to becoming an FBI agent. Not much time left for dating."

Harris removed her baseball hat. Her raven hair fell about her shoulders, framing her face. She was fit and had obviously taken care of herself. She was beautiful.

Harris looked up at him with a tilt of the head that made him wonder if she could tell he was checking her out. He became very self-aware. "Ah, would you like something to drink?"

"Got something." Harris replied holding up her glass. "Remember?"

When she moved closer to him, he froze with indecision. Was she sending a message? His computer chimed, having finished warming up. Saved by the bell.

He turned down the television and launched his email program. Opening the inbox, he found an urgent message from the national crime lab.

To: Ranger Grayson Cole, Yellowstone <Grayson_Cole@nps.gov>

From: FBI National Crime Lab, Quantico VA jwhite@fbi.gov

Ranger Cole:

The national crime lab has completed the analysis of the sent materials. The following are the results:

The patch is a U.S. Army issued American flag. However, a civilian can acquire it from nearly any army surplus store. The flag is affixed with Velcro to a soldier's helmet, backpack or uniform. The patch is contaminated with dirt, petroleum products consistent with motor oil, and gun powder. A minor amount of genetic material was found on it, but tests to determine their origin have been without result.

The second item is a dosimeter badge. It's used to measure radiation exposure levels. The badge was designed for medical professionals by a company out of Kansas.

Must be for the X-Ray techs at the park's lake health clinic, Cole thought. He continued reading.

The meter's blinking light indicates it has been exposed to a high dose of radiation. The Kansas company reports that anyone exposed to the radiation levels indicated by the meter would be experiencing signs of radiation sickness.

The Kansas company also believes the meter may have been tainted at manufacture. As such, it is being kept at the crime lab in a secure container. The flag will be returned to the park.

Please let us know if there is anything more we can provide you.

Sincerely,

James White

Cole printed the email and handed it to Harris. "What do you think?" he asked.

She skimmed the email. "It's quite a coincidence that a highly radioactive dosimeter is found at the same time NEST believes a nuclear attack may be imminent." She looked up. "However, I can't quite place the flag. How does it fit into all this?"

Cole leaned back in his chair. He pulled up an image of the flag patch on his computer. Where could it have come from? U.S. flags and radioactive badges. He didn't like it one bit. And

with the president arriving in a couple of days…
no this was definitely not good.

Chapter 38
Grant Village, Hell Hole Bar, June 30, Early Evening

Cole sat at his regular booth nursing a pint of Strider Beer. The bar was crowded with its typical customers. A couple was playing darts, two Park Service maintenance workers were shooting pool, while a handful of locals moved about the dance floor. The bar's front door opened. Agent Harris walked through. She was wearing a summer sun dress. She surveyed the crowd, a large smile crossing her face when she spotted him.

Cole gulped down what remained of his beer and signaled the waitress for another. Harris pushed her way through the throng, stopping at his table.

"Hi there, Ranger. May I join you?" She asked.

He sat there amazed. In his many years at Yellowstone no one had ever asked to have a drink with him.

"Certainly," he modestly replied. Cole found himself straightening up in his chair as Harris glided into the booth. She slid in close to him. Her sweet smelling perfume filled the air.

The barmaid arrived at the table. She looked at Cole, then at Harris, then back at Cole. "What can I get you two?" she asked, drawing out the word two in a friendly, sarcastic jab at the ranger.

"Another Strider pint, please? Harris, what would you like? I'm buying."

"Do you have any Honey Jack?" Harris asked the barmaid.

254

"We do."

"I'll have a double shot, please."

A wry smirk crept across the waitress' face. She winked at Cole as if to say, watch out cowboy it could be an interesting night. Then she turned to get the drink order.

Harris turned her complete attention to him. "So, I was thinking about this bar, the Hell Hole. I read on the outside plaque that its name has something to do with a Yellowstone mountain man. What's the story?"

"Really?" Cole asked. "You want to know about Colter's Hell."

"Yes, why is that surprising?" she responded.

"To be honest, I got the impression you were uninterested in park history."

The waitress returned with the drink order.

Harris took her double whisky. "Down the hatch," she said in a mild toast before gulping the sweet drink in one swig. She signaled the barmaid for another.

"Careful, Harris," Cole warned. "Yellowstone's altitude can cause drinks to sneak up on people."

"Call me Dianne. Thanks for the tip, Dad," she continued with a playful salute.

The retort produced a blush from Cole.

"So are you going to tell me about Colter's Hell or what?" she probed.

For nearly an hour, he recounted in detail, metaphor and literary flair the story of John Colter, his exploration with the Lewis and Clark expedition, his life-risking adventures through

Yellowstone, and eventual return to civilization. Cole explained the dubbing of Yellowstone as Colter's Hell by Easterners, and the recent scientific discoveries that gave more significance to the nickname. Throughout the story, Harris watched him closely.

"Why do you love this place so much?" she asked.

"Well, I guess because Yellowstone in particular and the parks in general aren't just pretty places or old buildings," Cole explained. "They are the physical expression of the ideas and hopes America holds sacred."

Cole realized he should stop himself, that Harris would start looking at him odd like everyone always did when he got on a roll. But he couldn't help himself. "For example, take Gettysburg National Military Park. Sure, the actual site, the battle's events and the artifacts contained there are important. But it's the values, such as the belief that all men," he caught himself "and women..."

Harris tipped her drink to him.

"Are created equal. That is at the heart of the Civil War. That idea is what the NPS is trying to protect. Unfortunately, it's difficult to put a value or idea on display, but we do our best."

Harris downed her shot and ordered another. "So what's the value being guarded here at Yellowstone?"

"There are several. But before I give you my thoughts, I'd be interested in what you think."

Harris apparently was not expecting to have the question turned on her, but she took up the challenge. Biting her lip, Cole could see she was seriously pondering the question. After a few moments she said, "For me, I think the most import value protected here is that parks create a promise across generations of Americans."

"How so?" he asked.

"Well, from what I've learned during my time here in the park, Yellowstone was established when America was expanding rapidly. Government efforts had been focused on transferring federal resources such as farm lands, minerals, and timber into private hands like the railroad companies."

Now it was his turn to be impressed. "Go on," he urged.

"Yellowstone and its surrounding lands could have easily been homesteaded, or reserved for mining or timber production. However, thanks to a select few forward thinkers the country said no. Rather, the nation put aside short-term wants by reserving a select portion of the public land for protection, for current and future generations."

He watched Harris as she explained her take on the importance of national parks. He was struck by her simple beauty. The way the raven hair fell over her shoulders. Her hair was pulled back in a ponytail revealing her beautiful face. The dress she wore exposed her shoulders. She continued to speak, but he found himself distracted. He watched her mouth as it formed the words. He was drawn to her eyes as the excitement and emotion of her thoughts came out. He noticed the nape of her neck and bare shoulders. The hint of a sun tattoo could be seen peaking over her right shoulder. Cole thought about how nice it would be to kiss it.

"Hey, you paying attention?" she asked.

Cole, embarrassed to be caught in his dreamy state, fumbled for his beer. "Yes," he stammered, downing a swig. "Sorry, please continue."

Harris downed another shot before continuing her story. "Our ancestors did the hard part in establishing the park system. Our job in many ways is simpler. We merely have to pass it along unimpaired to the next generation. In other words, the parks are a pact between the past, the present, and the future. How cool is that?"

Regaining his composure, Cole let out a long whistle while clapping his approval. "Very impressive, Agent Harris. I like it very much. May I steal it for some of my ranger talks?"

"Be my guest. Okay your turn."

Cole responded without missing a beat. "For me one of the most important things about Yellowstone is what it can teach us about humanity's place in the universe."

"Oh, I can see this is going to be deep."

"Not really," he began. "See, here at Yellowstone, the Park Service is charged with managing forces which currently are beyond civilization's ability to control." He went on for the next ten minutes explaining about the Yellowstone super volcano and the killer that lived a mere three miles below their very feet. "If this volcano begins an eruptive cycle like that of six hundred thousand years ago there is nothing we can do to stop it."

"Let's hope Yellowstone's cycle is late," Harris kidded.

Harris watched the park ranger as he explained the intricacies of plate tectonics and volcanology. She was struck by how arresting Cole truly was. She hadn't noticed before, what with his always being in the dorky Park Ranger uniform. His sharp facial features and his soft square jaw were attractive but not intimidatingly so. His brown eyes with flecks of green were captivating. As Cole spoke, Harris could see his eyes were obviously windows into a caring soul. His chest and arms were just the right size. Neither too skinny nor too muscular. There was nothing she hated more than a steroid body. She had seen plenty of that at the FBI academy. But above all, she was drawn to his hands. They were masculine, but not rough like a cowhand. She pondered what it would feel like to have them exploring her body.

Cole noticed Harris wasn't paying attention. His lecture must be too esoteric. He had the tendency to drone on when talking about humanity's place in the universe. He went on unabated, however. "We are not the most powerful force on the planet. Not by a long shot. There are few places where one can learn this lesson more powerfully and clearly than here at Yellowstone. This realization helps me put things in perspective."

They sat there for hours, just talking. The conversation waxed and waned from their childhood, early career, what they wanted to be when they grew up, and on and on. They talked politics, spirituality, and their favorite books and movies. They had much in common and shared many similar values and thoughts. They found the banter back and forth came easy. The drinks didn't hurt either. Yet, it was the bartender yelling last call that pulled them from the conversational trance. It was only then the two realized the bar was nearly empty. He had to go way back to his academy days for the last time he had closed down a bar.

Saying their goodbyes to the barmaid, Harris and Cole headed into the dark night. The moon had risen among an infinite blanket of stars. The stars looked as if someone had dipped a hand in white paint and smeared the night sky. Harris had never seen so many stars. It took her breath away. She was starting to understand why Cole loved the parks so much. "I don't get many nights like this back in D.C.," she said, the shots helping to loosen her tongue.

Then she realized Cole may think she was referring to spending a night at a bar with a guy. What most would call a date.

"Yeah, a very beautiful night," Cole responded, his meaning seeming to be as vague as hers.

After a quiet ten minute walk, the two arrived at her walkway. An awkward moment passed before she took the initiative. "You want some coffee?"

"At this hour?" Cole replied.

"I wasn't thinking we'd really drink any coffee," she said. She headed up the walk to her door. The walk seemed to move underneath her, as if made of Jell-O.

Cole hesitated for a moment before following. Thoughts of past girlfriends raced through his mind. He'd had his share of relationships, all of which had ended badly. He had convinced himself that it was the women's fault for their ultimate demise. But with the help of some of his friends, Cole realized it had been really his fault for their failure. "What was the common denominator about these women?" he'd been asked one time by a buddy.

"They were all stupid," Cole had replied sarcastically.

"I doubt it," came the friend's retort. "Although they did like you, so we would have to question their judgment. Try again."

After a bit of thought, the answer hit Cole. "Me?" His friend had nodded his agreement, placing his index finger squarely on his nose.

Cole had realized then that it wasn't the women's fault for the failed relationships, it was his. He had no trouble attracting women, keeping them was another story. If Cole was honest with himself it wasn't that the women couldn't handle the constant moving or the being cut off from civilization, it was being cut off from him that ultimately made each of them leave. Cole knew he was afraid of the emotional connection, the fear of hurting the ones he loved if something happened to him. His friend pushed him on this as well. Shouldn't he let the women worry about themselves being hurt? They were adults, right? Could it be something else holding back his relationships with women? Again, Cole had been forced to look deeper into his fear. He could face down charging bears, rapel off sheer cliffs, and fight intense wildfires without so much as batting an eye. These things weren't scary. Committing to someone, really opening up, letting go, that was scary. And why? When he really looked at the problem, it came down to his fear about something happening to that person, to the person he loved. What if they were hurt or killed? So Cole wasn't so worried about *their* pain after his injury or death. No, if he was truly honest he couldn't bear the thought of *his* pain if he lost someone he truly loved.

"That was life," his friend had said. "Sorry, Grayson, but life is about pain and loss. There is no way around it. Holing up in the Yellowstone outback, burying yourself in your work, pressing your uniform and clip-on ties, fighting the bad guys won't save you from this fate. It merely means you face the pain alone. Get over yourself, Grayson, and live a life, or you're going to end up a bitter and lonely old man."

Cole knew getting involved with a colleague may not be the smartest move. It could end badly. But it occurred to Cole that it had been a long time since anyone had shown interest in him. It also occurred to him that it could be a long time before it happened again. Besides, he had decided to risk the pain. He didn't want to die alone, and if he did he wanted to say he at least tried to have a meaningful relationship.

Chapter 39
Over Yellowstone Park, Marine One,
July 4, Afternoon

Two pairs of helicopters traversed the
Yellowstone sky. To the average person the
tandem helicopters might garner the occasional
glance. National Parks were no stranger to
helicopters, both public and private. But two of
these helicopters were different. For one, they
were being escorted by two Army Sikorsky Black
Hawks. The four were the only aircraft operating
within a ten mile circle of the park's West Thumb
Geyser Basin. The two other helicopters were
Sikorsky VH 60N White Hawks emblazoned with
the Seal of the President of the United States. The
president always traveled with two vehicles for
both mechanical and safety reasons. The White
Hawks could travel five hundred miles on a single
tank and surpass 180 mph. All helicopters ferrying
the president were equipped with LADAR, an
advanced early warning system that could detect
biological and chemical threats. Radioactive
sources, however, were not detectable. LADAR
also wasn't designed to sweep an area the size of
Yellowstone.

No one other than the Secret Service and
the pilots involved knew in which vehicle the
president traveled. This basic safety precaution
was instituted to keep assassins always guessing.

President Paine looked out the helicopter's
left side window, the entirety of Yellowstone
Lake's eighty five thousand acres opened below
him. The enormity of the lake hit him as he took

in the size of the lake's West Thumb. At roughly three miles across, the West Thumb would be among the park's five largest lakes. Yet, it was merely one small appendage of Yellowstone Lake. Yellowstone Lake was twice the size of Washington D.C., and yet was just a small part of the entire park, whose boundary roughly followed the boundary of the Yellowstone caldera--the mouth of the super volcano.

The president cast his gaze out his helicopter's large cabin windows to the distant horizon. Everywhere he looked, the faraway mountains, the lake below, the millions of trees, the miles of rivers, all were within the mouth of a massive volcano. The president had visited other volcanoes, both in his private and public life. When he was younger, he had climbed the glacier encrusted and snowcapped Mount Rainier in Washington State. He had visited the buried ruins of Pompeii at the base of Italy's hard scrabble and scarred Mount Vesuvius during the meeting of the G5. He had toured the shrines surrounding the conical Mount Fuji as a part of a trade mission to Japan.

All very impressive volcanoes, yet kittens compared to the monster he was staring at now.

He hadn't really appreciated the power of the earth until he had toured Mount St. Helens and its blast zone during one of the 1980 eruption memorials. The 1980 blast, he had been told, had leveled hundreds of square miles of virgin forest, buried several miles of surrounding streams and rivers in hundreds of feet of mud, and killed fifty seven people. He had stood in Mount St. Helens' blast zone, taking in a full sweep, all three hundred and sixty degrees of the devastation. One ranger at the volcano had told him the power unleashed by the eruption was equivalent to forty thousand Hiroshima bombs. Paine could believe it, and standing on the volcano's pumiced plain he had felt for the first time the unimaginable power of the earth. And the St. Helens eruption was but a firecracker compared to the bomb under the nation's premier park.

Rainier, Vesuvius, Fuji, and St. Helens had craters hundreds of yards to a few miles across. The volcanoes' magma chambers, although capable of releasing catastrophic forces, were believed to be of typical size. The West Thumb of Yellowstone Lake, an ancient caldera in its own right, was larger than the craters of these other volcanoes combined. But the West Thumb was a mere divot of the actual Yellowstone crater. Scientists feared the magma chamber was equally monstrous, and that humanity might not survive its next eruption.

On the flight into the park, the superintendent had been good to point out the Yellowstone crater's boundaries, way off in the distance. The president hadn't been able to identify it. The crater rim was just too far away.

The superintendent went on to explain that the Yellowstone plateau, smack dab in the middle of the Rocky Mountain range, was uniquely devoid of high mountain peaks. Scientists didn't believe this had always been the case, and that past eruptions may have blasted any mountain peaks in this area of the Rockies to bits.

"The West Thumb of Yellowstone Lake is directly below us, Mr. President." The park superintendent, a middle aged woman explained. "Beyond," she pointed toward the east, "is the rest of the lake, the largest high alpine lake in the world."

President Paine remembered the conversation he'd had with Secretary Matson about the potential Yellowstone eruption. The size of the lake below him finally revealed the scope of the threat facing the nation. The president let out a long whistle.

***

Marine One banked to the left and made a slow turn over the West Thumb, giving its passengers an excellent view of the approaching geyser basin, their final destination.

A stage and podium could be seen out on the lake shore.

A large crowd was assembled. Local and national cable news programs were covering the event live, tracking the president's arrival. What viewers at home couldn't see was all the security in place to protect the president, starting with the Secret Service, which would control the president's movement to and from the helicopter. The Secret Service would also be responsible for monitoring the event's immediate vicinity and the attending crowd.

The Secret Service treated these outdoor events as modified storm stops. A storm stop was a presidential trip where the Secret Service was unable to control all access to the president and sweep the entire area for potential threats. The

Service had tried to talk the president out of the trip, but he would not be denied the opportunity. Failing to change the Commander in Chief's mind, the best the Secret Service could do was mitigate the risk to their boss. The Secret Service's protection plan called for a focus on the inner circle of security extending from the podium out to three hundred yards. The Service would have visible agents surrounding the president, both on and around the stage and even in the crowd. These agents would be monitoring the crowd, searching for people acting abnormally. Anyone with their hands shoved in their pockets, rapid movements of their eyes and hands, excessive sweating, or wearing sunglasses on a cloudy day could all produce extra attention from the Secret Service. Even though everyone in attendance that day had been specifically invited, the Service could not assume safety or let down their guard. A jackal, the informal name the Secret Service gave to would-be assassins, could be anywhere.

The Park Service, augmented by the FBI and local law enforcement, would be responsible for security from where the Secret Service stopped out to two miles from the event. This meant that rangers would be staffing road blocks on all roads leading to the West Thumb Geyser Basin as well as on horseback patrolling the nearby backcountry. Just to be safe, the NPS closed all backcountry campsites within the two-mile security zone and placed non-law enforcement rangers at these sites. FBI sharpshooters were set up on nearby hill tops, while Park Service and sheriff patrol watercraft kept park visitors from boating too close to the

proceedings. Meanwhile, the Air Force and
Marines patrolled the sky, insuring free airspace
above. Ever since 2009, when two partiers crashed
a White House state dinner, the Secret Service had
doubled its efforts to make certain that no one
showed up at presidential events uninvited.

The Yellowstone security plan, including
the president's arrival and departure, was a
precisely choreographed military operation. It
rested on two assumptions. First, it expected any
attack on the president to take place from a
relatively close range. Thus the Secret Service's
blanket coverage of the hot zone. Several weeks
prior to the president's arrival, Secret Service
agents conducted advance sweeps. Agents scoured
every square inch of the West Thumb's parking lot,
warming hut and board-walked geyser basin. The
agents searched the entire ten-acre site for hidden
bombs and weapons. The area's garbage cans and
recycle bins were removed, manhole covers were
welded shut, and even trailhead map donation
boxes, large enough to conceal a small pipe bomb
or grenade, were removed. Nothing could be left
to chance.

Outside the hot zone was the exclusion
zone. Here the plan assumed attackers would have
to get past road blocks, patrol boats, and aircraft to
get to the president. Would-be attackers would
have to cover great distances and overcome
multiple defenses to make their attack. Distance
meant time. Time gave the Secret Service the
ability to whisk away the Commander in Chief.

Unfortunately, assassins were already in the
exclusion zone and they had no intention of going

anywhere.

Chapter 40
Sniper bunker, July 4, Afternoon

Charles Sinclair watched through high-powered binoculars as the president's helicopter made its landing in the West Thumb ranger station parking lot.

The time was finally here. In a few short moments the Paine administration would be over and a significant step toward Christ's return would be taken. Sinclair put on his crusader robe and handed another to Hansen. Sinclair couldn't help but be struck by the unfolding sweep of history. For nearly a thousand years the hated Muslims had held the Holy Land. The Defenders 1307, his knights, would bring this darkness to an end and usher in Christ's return to begin his millennial earthly rule.

Some in his inner circle questioned his vision, his mission. The recent public failure of a doomsday prophet weighed heavily on their minds. Didn't the Bible say no one can predict the time of Christ's return? Sinclair agreed. But the Bible also foretold that the Lord would only return when the Jews had reclaimed the Temple Mount. This would never happen if President Paine's two-state Middle Eastern plan was adopted. The president must be stopped.

Some also thought him crazy for actually staying in the bunker during the presidential attack. Didn't he risk everything if the attack failed and he was caught? No, he was implementing God's plan. He would be rewarded in heaven. The potential loss of a few billion, his freedom, or even his life was nothing compared to spending eternity with the Almighty and being the catalyst for the thousand year reign of heaven on earth.

Besides, Sinclair had no doubt the plan would succeed. Yet, part of his confidence came with his being in the bunker. Hansen was the best, but Sinclair had lingering doubts about the captain's full commitment to the cause. He couldn't quite put his finger on it, but Hansen had seemed distant, distracted, harried of late. His sleep was disturbed and he barely ate. Sinclair would be there to make sure Hansen didn't lose his nerve. To make sure he pulled the trigger.

Sinclair watched as Marine One made its slow approach to its landing zone. An ideal time to take a shot, Sinclair had thought. Wouldn't it be that much easier to hit a large, slow moving target from a great distance than a small target from the same distance? Hansen had educated him on this matter.

Hansen's TAC 50 sniper rifle could take down a standard helicopter. But Marine One wasn't a standard helicopter. It contained state of the art weapons and armor. A 50 caliber bullet may not penetrate the helicopter's armored hull, let alone bring it down. Yet, even if the bullet did destroy Marine One, the president might survive the crash. Finally, they couldn't even be sure which helicopter held the Commander in Chief. There were two copters with the presidential symbol emblazoned on their side. The president was likely traveling in one of these. However, there were two Army Black Hawks mirroring the presidential helicopters' approach. The president could also be on a Black Hawk. Misdirection was a prime component of protection for presidential travel and happened more than the public would guess. Dick Cheney even rode in the back of an ambulance to an event where he had to pass through large protesting crowds. Taunts and insults were hurled at the Vice Presidential limo as it passed by the protesting crowd. No one in the raucous crowd batted an eye as an ambulance, which actually ferried Mr. Cheney, traveled the same route not ten minutes before.

All these variables, Sinclair came to understand, made taking down the president on Marine One highly unlikely.

Marine One was on its final approach, the aircraft's rotor blades kicking up dust and debris from the parking lot. Its three escorts broke off at the last moment and headed to a nearby secondary landing spot. Marine One hovered a few seconds, allowing the cloud of rock and other hazardous materials to die down. Then it slowly touched down without the slightest disturbance to the main cabin. A perfect landing.

After Marine One's rotors came to a complete stop Marine and park ranger honor guards took up their positions. Half a dozen Secret Service agents also moved into position near the helicopter's main doors. A reception line of invited dignitaries, including the Governor of Wyoming, formed just beyond the reach of the rotors.

"Son of a bitch," Sinclair exclaimed.

"What's that?" Hansen asked, a small hint of concern in his voice.

"Oh, nothing." Sinclair said, embarrassed. "I can see the reception line forming to meet the president and our good governor is at the front. I gave money to that bastard's campaign."

The helicopter's foot-thick door opened, extending a small ramp. For a few moments nothing happened. Finally, the president emerged, heading down the ramp followed by the Yellowstone Superintendent and the president's Chief of Staff.

Six Secret Service agents immediately flanked the president in a classic diamond formation. These were the president's personal protection detail. The most dedicated agents, literally willing to lay down their lives for their boss. Their job was simple. If a danger presented itself the personal protection detail would surround the president and get him out of the area.

Although not visible, Sinclair knew these men were heavily armed. Most likely they carried the FNP 90 submachine gun. This machine gun was compact and easily hidden under the agent's business suits. The FNP 90 fired small 5.7 mm rounds designed to fragment in the person hit. This reduced the potential for collateral damage to the president and innocent bystanders. The guns were no threat to Sinclair or Hansen, however. Their range was much too limited to reach the sniper's bunker.

Sinclair watched the unfolding drama through his binoculars, which were equipped with state of the art lenses covered in non-reflective materials. Many a sniper had betrayed his location by sunlight reflecting off their binoculars.

Not today. They had thought of everything.

He turned to Hansen. "Let's go through the plan one last time."

Hansen didn't answer.

"Joseph? You there?" Sinclair asked.

Hansen's eyes were closed. His lips were moving. A quiet mumble escaped his lips. When he finally did respond, he coolly and simply said, "What?"

"Not a good time to lose your concentration, son. We are about to shoot the most powerful man in the world. I need your head in the game," Sinclair scolded.

"I wasn't daydreaming. I was praying."

"Okay. Doesn't hurt to seek the blessing of the Almighty. You mind if we say a prayer together?"

Hansen hesitated. The billionaire could see Captain Hansen was considering something. Sinclair knew snipers went through a set of rituals prior to their shot. Some were quite superstitious about disruptions to the pattern.

"Never mind, sorry I asked," he apologized. "I didn't mean to interrupt your routine."

So they waited. Sinclair trained his binoculars upon the presidential dais. The president was fifteen minutes into his speech. How long was the bastard going to speak? How long did it take to announce the dumping of your loyal vice president for a politically self-serving new running mate?

The president's decision to dump his vice president only confirmed Sinclair's belief that the Commander in Chief lacked honor.

Hansen was seated behind a table with the TAC 50 caliber sniper rifle mounted on top. He had kept the rifle scope's cross hairs fixed on the back of the president's head since he had landed. There was always an off chance the president's schedule would unexpectedly change. Sinclair's instructions were clear. If the president veered from the expected he was to take the shot. Sinclair wouldn't miss his opportunity to serve God because of a presidential change of plans.

"I wish we could take out Governor Carson as well. That S.O.B. has sold out his party, country, and God to be Vice President," Sinclair cursed. "He too has shown his true colors and deserves to die."

Killing the president would likely precipitate a constitutional crisis, Sinclair knew. The chain of succession would be in doubt, especially with the vice president having been dumped from the ticket minutes before. Sinclair had spoken to legal experts, asking, hypothetically of course, about possible confusion over who would take over the executive reins if the president were to die prior to Election Day. The experts had advised that the Speaker of the House would be next in line to the Oval Office.

This pleased Sinclair. The speaker was a strong, God-fearing conservative. The new president would set the country right with the Lord.

"All in good time," Hansen responded without moving from the scope. "All will be held to account."

Through the scope Hansen could see the

crowd applauding and Secret Service personnel moving into new positions near the rope line. "It appears we are getting close to the end of the speech. Reshoot the laser range finder. I want to make sure the scope is dialed in properly."

Sinclair stood up, retrieving the range finder. Moving it up to his eyes, he looked out of the small secondary window and measured the distance between the bunker and the president. "Two thousand nine hundred forty nine yards," Sinclair announced.

Hansen adjusted the data on his scope to incorporate the new information. "Please stay on the finder for the duration of our action," he commanded. "I may need you to re-measure the distance."

"Will do."

The president's speech finally came to an end. Sinclair could see the governor through the range finder being called up to stand next to the president. The president and the potential new vice president shook hands and raised their clasped hands in the air. The audience, even at this distance, could be seen to stand, applauding the spectacle.

The president stepped down from the stage. The Secret Service agents moved into flanking positions around the president. The six agents were there to protect the president by eliminating a threat and moving him to safety. If the worst happened, the PPD was prepared to take a bullet to save the president's life. *You elect, we protect* was the Service's motto. The agent's presidential huddle made it hard for Sinclair to see the target. Hansen had anticipated this and said it wouldn't be a problem. The ammunition in Hansen's rifle was powerful enough to go through six inches of concrete. Even if Hansen's shot had the misfortune of striking an agent first, the bullet would easily pass through with enough force to still kill the president. If Hansen's shot hit an agent in the head it could easily take it clean off. The president may just as easily be killed by the force of being struck by one of his agent's skulls as by the bullet. Wouldn't that be something?

The president walked down the stage ramp to the visitor rope line. The time was getting close now. Dozens had pressed up against the barriers to shake hands with the most powerful man in the free world and his new running mate.

Just then Sinclair had a curious thought. Did the president know he had only seconds to live? Did CNN, MSNBC, FOX and about a dozen other television crews covering the event live have any thought they would soon cover the story of the century? The assassination of the president, live and in HD. Did the Secret Service realize its greatest protection failure, the shooting of JFK, was about to be surpassed?

It was a mystical moment for Sinclair. He had waited decades for this moment. His plan had been meticulous. He had spent hours, no days, going over every detail. He had recruited the best for the job, especially the man set to pull the trigger. The chess board was set. With one more move it would be checkmate for the Paine administration and the forces of evil.

Sinclair's head felt light, his stomach tight.

An anxious calm washed over him. He imagined this being the feeling signaling the rapture, the lifting of the worthy to heaven. Could the rapture begin with Paine's death? He was ready, so ready, to leave this sinful world and be with God in eternity.

The president moved along the line, shaking every hand thrust in front of him. In the background, Marine One fired up its engines. The helicopter rotors began to turn. Even at nearly three thousand yards the helicopter engines firing up, although very faint, could be heard in the bunker.

Now was the time.

Sinclair remained on the range finder. He could see the president reaching the end of the line. Sinclair heard Captain Hansen's measured breath. Sinclair knew the sniper's ritual was to take three controlled long breaths and hold to lower his heart rate, firing between beats. Hansen held his breath. So did Sinclair.

A beam of sunlight cut through the overcast sky, illuminating the president in a wash of light. Surely a sign from God. This was the moment. Sinclair stayed on the range finder. The president was clearly illuminated now. God was confirming Sinclair's faith. Paine had to be removed. Paine was the obstacle to God's plan on earth. The president was so exposed Sinclair almost believed he could make the shot.

The anticipation, the years of planning were coming down to this moment. He felt himself grow lightheaded. Steady, Sinclair told himself. Concentrate, just a few more seconds.

The president continued to move down the
line. He was nearly at the end. Sinclair's sense of
joy changed. He started to worry. The Secret
Service appeared to pick up the president's pace as
he neared the end of the line. The agents could at
any moment break off the proceedings and head to
the copter. If that happened all their efforts would
be for naught.

Take the shot. The president was getting
away.

Calm down, he told himself. Hansen was
in charge. He knew what he was doing. Perhaps
there was a puff of wind or the president's body
was turned in an awkward angle that prevented the
shot. Hansen was the better judge than Sinclair to
determine when to shoot. But still, it seemed like
Captain Hansen was nearly out of time.

Hansen continued to hold his breath. He
was the sniper, trained by the greatest military in
the world. But something was wrong. The shot
should have been taken.

Take the shot.

The president shook the last hand and
waved to the crowd. The Secret Service hustled
him toward the helicopter.

"We can't wait any longer," Sinclair yelled.
"He's getting away!"

BANG!

The rifle's report was deafening. Sinclair
fought the urge to cover his ears, staying on the
rifle scope. Time seemed to slow down. It
appeared to take an eternity for the bullet to cover
the nearly three thousand yards from the bunker to
the president. Finally the bullet reached the target,

striking the president in the back of his left shoulder. Through the laser scope, Sinclair could see the president's body spin in reaction to being struck by the bullet. He went down to the ground before anyone could react.

For what seemed like another eternity, nothing happened. The scene around the downed president was calm. Then almost as if reacting to a hidden cue, all hell broke loose. Like ants reacting to someone kicking their ant hill, people scattered everywhere. The president's personal protection detail immediately surrounded and secured the area around their Commander in Chief, their previously hidden submachine guns now held at the ready. Through the throng Sinclair could see the downed president. It was over he thought. Hansen had done it! The president was dead. Christ's rein on earth would surely begin soon.

Sinclair's joy was short lived.

Through the laser scope, the billionaire could see the downed president stir. "No, it can't be!" Sinclair screamed. But it was true. The president hadn't been killed. He was very much alive.

Two agents, one on each side of the president grabbed an arm and hustled him to the now fully warm Marine One helicopter. The agents sprinted the president to the helicopter and up its extended ramp, basically throwing him into the cabin and slammed the door shut. The helicopter went wheels up before the door handle locked into place.

The president's helicopter screamed out of West Thumb, immediately joined by the three helicopters that joined in on the inbound flight.

"You missed him!" Sinclair screamed turning to face Hansen.

Only Hansen wasn't behind the scope. Panic gripped Sinclair. Adrenaline shot through his body. Something was terribly wrong. Captain Hansen was face down on the floor facing east. His eyes were closed, a peaceful, almost angelic smile on his lips. A small cell phone was held in his right hand.

Chapter 41
West Thumb Geyser Basin, July 4, Afternoon

Grayson Cole watched Marine One lift off and head due west, rather than south toward Jackson Hole and Air Force One. Cole watched it disappear over the nearby hills. It was joined by the duplicate Marine One and the two Army Black Hawks. His entire experience with the White House had been one unforeseen event after another. A change in flight plan was the least of these twists. As the helicopter quartet disappeared over the horizon, Cole returned to the job at hand. The remaining crowd had just witnessed the president of the United States being shot right in front of their own eyes. The crowd was in a state of panic, men, women and children running everywhere. Cole could see Secret Service agents securing the scene with machine guns at the ready. Air Force F-16 fighter jets screamed overhead while sheriff and Park Service patrol boats raced across Yellowstone Lake looking for the possible assassin.

The Secret Service had reviewed with the National Park Service its responsibility under a shots-fired scenario. The situation called for the Park Service to keep the remaining public and VIPs from leaving the scene, as well as prevent terrified people from running head long into a geyser or hot pool.

Fellow ranger Jennifer Chin ran up next to him. "Sir, there's an emergency call for you at the ranger station."

"Thanks, Jennifer. Take over here." Cole

sprinted to the West Thumb ranger station. He picked up the nearest phone receiver on the nearest desk and punched the blinking line. "Cole, here."

"Grayson, this is Harris. I've got some new information to pass along regarding the radiation contaminating the smuggler's sub, the Ryder, and Sinclair trucks."

The president had just been shot and there were still safety concerns related to his trip. Cole half thought she was kidding.

"NEST has completed an analysis of the radiation and it appears to be from weapons grade plutonium and not from medical or other non-military sources. Also, all three vehicles are contaminated from the same source. In other words, there is a high probability these three vehicles all carried a nuclear weapon. The same nuclear weapon."

"How's the president?" Cole asked.

"He's going to survive," Harris replied. "The bullet went through his sports coat just over his left shoulder. Other than destroying his coat and being shaken up a bit, he'll be fine.

"Is the president aware of the situation with the atomic bomb?" Cole asked.

"Yes. The Secret Service alerted him a few minutes ago. The president and Governor Carson are racing due west to an undisclosed location. They hope to escape the nuclear or eruptive fallout if there's a blast.

"Has NEST found the bomb?" he asked.

"No. The Justice Department has just dispatched the NEST teams."

NEST teams were elite squads of military personnel highly trained and equipped in nuclear weapons detection, recovery and disposal. Cole could sense this conversation was heading in a bad direction. He placed his hat on the desktop and took a seat.

"The president determined that the federal government's immediately available resources should be deployed to the nearest vulnerable metropolitan areas. Since the sub was found in Oregon and the Ryder truck in eastern Washington, the west coast's teams are on the ground in Portland and Spokane."

"And when should we expect a team here in Yellowstone?" Cole asked.

"That's the problem," Agent Harris continued. "The remaining teams are on the east coast. They are mobilizing right now and are expected to arrive in Yellowstone in twelve hours. Unfortunately, the president fears we don't have that long."

The Park Service ranger academy provided its cadets with valuable law enforcement theory and concepts. However, it was the instruction and lessons on maintaining a calm temperament that would be most important in this matter. Cole needed to keep his faculties if he and his ranger corps were going to protect the public from this new threat.

"One more thing," Harris continued. "The FBI has issued an A.P.B. for one Jamil Ali Hussain. I'm faxing you information on him right now."

The fax machine at the West Thumb

ranger station rang and began to download the
transmission. He took the fax from the machine.
Basic information like height, weight, and age were
all included on the sheet. There was also a grainy
low resolution picture. The image was of such
poor quality it could have been anyone.

"We believe Jamil is the cell leader of this
operation. He is al Qaeda and should be
considered extremely dangerous."

Cole wrote down the name.

Harris continued. "It looks like it's going
to be up to you and me here in Yellowstone. We
need to think fast on where to look for the bomb."

He thought for a moment. He should ask
something, but what? He would have to close and
evacuate the park, but where would he look for an
atomic bomb? He didn't even know where to
start. Nuclear weapons were a bit outside the scope
of his training.

"Dianne?" Cole asked. "Has the FBI
considered why al Qaeda would detonate an
atomic bomb in Wyoming? The only metropolitan
area is Bozeman, about fifty miles away."

Bozeman was the center of central
Montana, but hardly a city that if destroyed would
bring down the United States. Rather, like the
bombing of Pearl Harbor, it would only increase
its wrath. So why here? And more importantly,
where in the park?

Cole tapped his fingers on the desk, when
he looked down at the desktop. There was an
assortment of books, magazines, and videos strewn
across it. Obviously this was an interpretation
ranger's desk. Interp rangers were the flat hats that

led guided hikes and gave campfire programs. On top of the heap of magazines was a copy of *National Geographic*. The cover story was on the Yellowstone super volcano and its destructive power.

"Dianne, meet me at the West Thumb ranger station. I've got an idea," Cole said, hanging up the phone. He didn't know where to look for the bomb, but tapping the cover of the magazine with his index finger he realized he knew someone who might.

Chapter 42
Sniper Bunker, July 4, Afternoon

Hansen was in a daze-like state, similar to a narcotic high. Through the haze he could hear a voice calling his name. Was it the Almighty? "I'm here," he whispered, still lying face down on the ground.

But the voice wasn't heavenly. It sounded hollow, desperate, more like a shriek. Hansen's mind began to clear. He was still in the bunker, and Sinclair was screaming.

"Joseph, what the hell are you doing? The president has gotten away!" Sinclair cried, his face twisted with panic and anger.

Hansen ignored Sinclair's ranting. He slowly pulled himself up to stand. He checked his body. No injuries. He was still intact, no visible signs of trauma. This wasn't right, he knew. Then he realized he was holding something in his hand. The cell phone. Of course. He flipped open the cover. The phone's display blinked to life.

"The phone has power," he mumbled. "Why are we still here?"

"What?" Sinclair answered.

Hansen looked at the display again, and then it hit him. He had no signal. His phone couldn't find a tower. Fear gripped him. All the years of planning, all the sacrifice, all the death, and the plan failed for a lack of a few cell phone bars. How could this be?

Sinclair moved to him and grabbed him by the front of his jacket. He shook him violently. "Snap out of it! What the hell is the matter with you? You missed the opportunity to kill the president!"

Hansen dropped the phone and pulled a handheld Taser from his pocket. In a swift, blinding move, he shoved the device's prongs into Sinclair's chest. The billionaire's body went stiff as electricity raced through it. He withdrew the Taser, and Sinclair fell to the floor. The shock left the old man dazed, drool dripping from his mouth.

"Joseph, why?" was all Sinclair was able to get out in a heavily slurred manner.

Hansen squatted, aligning his face in front of Sinclair's.

"My name is not Joseph," he screamed with a contempt that had been building for years. "My name is Jamil Ali Hussain."

Sinclair's eyes went wide with fear.

"Joseph ceased to exist the day I was exposed to Allah and the one true faith of Islam during my time in Afghanistan," he stated. Spittle flew from his mouth.

Sinclair remained confused. "But we were to kill the president. To take down his administration."

Hussain gave Sinclair another jab with the Taser. His scream filled the bunker. "Idiot," Hussain shouted. "You don't get it do you? I don't want to take down the president or the administration." He moved his face closer to Sinclair's. So close that the downed man would feel his breath on his cheek. "I want to take down the entire United States."

Again, Hussain paused, letting his words sink in before continuing. "I've infiltrated your organization to use its resources, contacts, and facilities, as well as used your blinding hatred for the president to put me within one final step of achieving this goal."

The cell phone failure was a minor setback. He could still manually trigger the bomb. But he would have to act fast.

Hussain began to cough, hacking up red phlegm. He spit it out. Blood. It was all blood. This, along with the recent hair loss, confirmed his suspicion. Radiation poisoning. Perhaps he didn't have as much time as he hoped. He would have to move quickly. With Allah's help he could still make it.

Hussain gave Sinclair a final jab with the Taser. The old man barely responded this time, now nearly unconscious. His breathing was labored and irregular.

"You'll burn in hell for this," Sinclair wheezed.

"Perhaps," he said, pulling a large hunting knife from his belt. He held it mere inches from Sinclair's eyes. "However, I know one thing for sure . . . you're going first."

Chapter 43
West Thumb Geyser Basin Ranger Station, July 4, Late Afternoon

Cole punched a new phone line and dialed the number for the Yellowstone volcano monitoring center. A receptionist answered the phone, "Hello, National Park Service."

"Jessica Drummond, please," he said.

A moment passed. "Dr. Drummond here."

"Jessica, Grayson Cole."

"Hey, Grayson what the hell is going on down there? I just heard on the radio the president has been shot? Is that true??"

"Look Jessica, I don't have time to chat and I've got a bit of a situation here and need your help."

"Sure," Jessica replied all kidding gone from her voice. "What is it?"

Cole took a breath, not really sure how to proceed. "How's the caldera doing today?"

"Pretty normal," Jessica replied. "Nothing out of the ordinary. Geyser activity, earthquake activity, and gas venting all are within the normal range."

"Good to hear."

"Now, the Hayden Valley dome continues to grow, pushing Yellowstone Lake to the south."

"Could that be the sign of a pending eruption?"

"Not likely. While the dome continues to grow, its expansion is at a slower pace. All signs indicate the growth cycle is subsiding."

Cole let out an audible sigh. "Good to know."

"However," Jessica continued. "This assumes no unforeseen events, like a large earthquake or a meteor strike."

He swallowed before asking his next question. "Could a nuclear explosion trigger an eruption?"

"What? You can't be serious."

"Please humor me."

"Well, I guess it's possible. A large enough atomic detonation in just the right location could trigger a cataclysmic eruption."

"Where might that location be?"

There was a pause on the line as Jessica thought for moment. "It would have to be a spot where the crust is thin, I suppose. It would probably also help if it were a site of recent or new geothermal activity. And while we're speculating, it would probably need to be a spot not normally frequented by the public. It's kind of hard to place a bomb when surrounded by thousands of visitors."

"Hmm, would you please run a park analysis of potential sites with those parameters?" Cole asked.

"Give me a second to pull up GIS."

GIS stood for geographic information system. It was a computer program that generated maps from data such as earthquake activity and location. "Okay. The computer generated several sites, six to be precise."

"That's too many. Can you narrow it down more?"

"Not with GIS."

"Okay, then give me your best guess. If

you wanted to ignite an eruption of the Yellowstone caldera, where would you place a nuclear device?"

Again the line went silent as she thought before answering. "I'd place it at the Centennial Geyser Basin," she said. "The earth's crust is the thinnest there and thermal features have recently developed. This is an indication that the crust is weak and fractured. Finally, the area is extremely remote and sees limited visitation. That's an excellent location for a bomb... hmm, that's curious."

"What's that?" Cole probed.

"The Centennial Geyser monitor in the basin is experiencing a sustained power loss. It's probably nothing, dirt or something on the solar panel. I'll send a crew to check it out next week."

Cole knew they probably didn't have that much time.

"Grayson, what's this all about?"

"Thanks, Jessica, you've been extremely helpful," Cole answered, hanging up the phone.

He ran out of the West Thumb ranger station toward his Jeep. Harris was just arriving.

"Come with me," he yelled to her. "We've got to go now!"

Chapter 44
Centennial Geyser Basin, July 5, Early Morning

There were many disadvantages National Park rangers faced enforcing the law. Unlike their big city counterparts, park rangers often worked alone in extremely remote locations. Backup could be hours or even days away. Park rangers seldom had state of the art equipment or weapons.

The Park Service also had an extremely limited staff. Cole had a total of twenty four law enforcement rangers at his disposal. There were more than 2.2 million acres to cover, or one officer for an area four times the size of San Francisco. Fortunately, this proportion wasn't normally a problem. Most park visitors congregated in the front country, and not surprisingly, so did most crime. Knowing this, Cole sent his troops to the Old Faithful, Canyon, Mammoth and Lake Villages. These areas would be thoroughly searched. Rangers set up road blocks at all park entrance stations. Everyone in the park was being evacuated. No new visitors would be allowed in. It was the best use of the Park Service's available ranger force and would protect the most people.

Meanwhile, the Secret Service and local law enforcement were combing the West Thumb area for clues to the attempted presidential assassination. Harris and Cole wouldn't get any help in their current search. They were on their own.

But Cole and all park law enforcement enjoyed significant advantages over their urban counterparts. Park rangers lived in the parks, giving them a better understanding and appreciation of potential crime scenes. In more traditional law enforcement settings, criminals often knew the crime scene better than the police. Big city police officers often didn't live in the communities they patrolled, meaning they had a limited understanding of these places, the people and their normal activity. This helped the crooks.

National Parks were a different story. Rangers like Cole lived, worked and played in their parks. He had been stationed at the West Thumb district for several years. During that time he had explored all of the park's front country sites and much of its backcountry. Ranger Cole enjoyed an advantage even at the Centennial Basin. Early last year, Cole had been on the basin's first survey team. He knew the area as well as anyone.

Park rangers also had access to roads and trails closed or unfamiliar to the general public. At the Centennial Geyser Basin it was no different. The Centennial Geyser Basin was located on the shore of Shoshone Lake. In the distant past, the Park Service had built a road to provide quick public access to a lakeshore campground. Over the years, however, diminished road maintenance budgets forced the Park Service to focus its resources on more heavily used roads and front country areas. Consequently, the Park Service had removed the road from park maps and closed it to the public.

Public access to the Centennial basin was now only on foot, a several hour hike. Cole and Harris could be there in fifteen minutes using the closed road.

The Centennial road was in poor shape. Similar to the Bechler road. Potholes were everywhere. Vegetation was growing in and around the road, making it resemble a wound slowly healing. It was obvious no one had driven the road in sometime. Cole stopped the vehicle and pulled it off to the side of the road about three hundred yards from its dead end. If someone were already in the geyser basin, Cole didn't want them to see or hear his vehicle. Harris and Cole would travel the rest of the way on foot.

Walking around to the back of the jeep, he opened the hatch. In the back were additional weapons and tools. Cole handed Harris a bullet proof vest and donned one himself. The vests were hot and uncomfortable to wear, but many a law-enforcement officer owed his life to this body armor. Next, Ranger Cole grabbed a Taser, radio, and flashlight, placing them on his belt. Finally, he grabbed his 12 gauge shotgun, a Standard Remington 870 P. He cursed that he hadn't placed his high-powered, fully automatic AR15 in the vehicle. But he had lent the rifle to another officer who had yet to return it. Cole loaded eight slug rounds into the shotgun. Slug shells had more stopping power than regular shotgun ammunition. He figured he would need the extra firepower. Along with his service pistol, he and Harris had more than a hundred rounds of ammunition. As he surveyed the basin, he hoped it wouldn't be necessary.

The Centennial Geyser lay at the heart of the expanded Centennial Geyser Basin. For beauty and predictability it rivaled Old Faithful.

Centennial Geyser was unique as well. It was a combination hotpool and geyser. Its source was a sixty-foot deep pool. Unlike other thermal features, the sides of the Centennial pool were devoid of bacteria. Bacteria in the water gave the park's hot springs their distinctive, blue, red and brown colors. Water temperature was the crucial factor in bacterial growth. The hotter the water, the less bacteria. And the less bacteria, the clearer the water. Centennial was clear to the bottom.

Centennial Geyser's eruptions were fairly regular. Roughly every two and one-half hours a column of boiling water shot two hundred feet into the air. The eruption typically lasted two to three minutes, drenching and quickly killing any soaked plants. In a couple of years the geyser would kill all of its surrounding vegetation. Between eruptions, the geyser's pool churned and bubbled with an obvious fury, like a child building to a tantrum. The sulphur and other volcanic gas caused the bubbles that gave Centennial Geyser a continual dragon like roar. In short, the area was loud, wet, and foul.

Armed, the two officers set down the road. It was dark, but they couldn't risk using the flash light. Anyone in the basin would surely see the light. They also couldn't make any noise. That too would alert someone to their presence. The need for silence made Cole nervous. Yellowstone was full of several man-eating predators, including some very large bears. Many a visitors had lost their lives failing to let bears know they were coming. Startling a bear was one of the quickest ways to get oneself mauled or killed. Cole didn't

share this fear with Harris. He knew she had
enough on her mind.

They walked to the end of the road and
took cover behind a tree. Before them was the
Centennial basin, roughly the size of a football
field. The moonlight gave the area an eerie glow.
Enough light was cast to see major obstacles, but
not enough to illuminate the many thermal
features. They could be heard, but at least they
were extremely difficult to see.

The geyser basin's young age complicated
the matter. Much of it was forest covered. From
his survey work, Cole knew there was an older,
extinct geyser cone nearby. It would provide a
perfect hiding spot to survey the entire basin. He
lifted his high powered binoculars to his eyes and
scanned the basin, looking for the sensor that Dr.
Drummond mentioned was losing power. He
found it. Zooming in, he noticed a small briefcase-
type object tied into the sensor.

He handed Harris the binoculars and asked
her what she thought of the briefcase. She agreed
it was suspicious.

Chapter 45
Centennial Geyser Basin, July 5, Early Morning

It was well after midnight. The moon was at its apex but providing scarce light. Hussain had been walking for nearly seven hours when he finally topped the last hill into the basin. He was exhausted. A long hike wouldn't normally tax him, but the radiation poisoning had weakened him. That didn't matter, his quest was nearly over. A few more minutes and he'd be basking in the glory of Allah.

He had spent the last several hours avoiding helicopter and ranger patrols. Secret Service helicopters had passed nearby a couple times but the park was so large he hadn't really needed to hide from their search. They had a huge amount of territory to cover. Besides, Hussain knew law enforcement would be looking for an assassin trying to escape the scene of his crime. They'd be covering the roads and park exits. Law enforcement wouldn't guess that the assassin had a plan B which called for heading deeper into the park's backcountry.

The night vision goggles provided Hussain the vision needed to complete his task. He looked for the briefcase. There it was, right where he had left it.

The basin appeared empty. Hussain did a quick scan of the area. Nothing appeared out of the ordinary. He wanted to take the time to be sure, but the radiation was taking his strength and he had to move fast.

Surveying the basin one last time, Hussain

was struck by the odd path his quest had taken. Fifteen years had led him to this thermal feature on the shore of one of Yellowstone's high alpine lakes. It was a stark juxtaposition. The area was the epitome of tranquility, beauty, and calm. A slight breeze blew against his face. It was quite lovely. But in a few minutes the gates of hell which lay just beneath the earth's surface would be released upon it, America and the enemies of Islam. He was grateful and humbled to be the instrument of the great Satan's destruction.

The ground crunched under his feat. Hussain knew the danger of walking in geyser fields. The ground could give way at any step. Time was running out, however, and Hussain had to take some risks.

The briefcase appeared unmolested. No one had touched it since he had set it in place days before. Flipping open the case's top, Hussain saw the bomb's power level was full. The computer screen's cursor blinked ready, meaning the arming codes could be entered. Hussain's fingers raced across the bomb's keyboard. He brought the device online. The arming screen went blank, with a small hour glass indicating the program was loading. The screen cleared and asked for the first code word.

Hussain typed, SUBMIT. Pressing enter, the computer went through another loading sequence. The screen cleared. The second and final screen came up asking for the last code word. Hussain again began to type.

Chapter 46
Centennial Geyser Basin, July 5th, Early Morning

Ranger Cole and Agent Harris watched a hiker move through the basin. He was wearing night vision goggles and had a pistol on his hip. Not your typical park guest for sure. Immediately, Cole was suspicious. He watched the hiker head straight to the edge of the Centennial Geyser and its sensor array. It couldn't be a coincidence. When the hiker opened the case, he could wait no longer. "Get ready," he whispered to Harris.

Cole raised his shotgun to his shoulder and took aim at the intruder. "Police officer. Get on the ground," he commanded from behind the cover of the extinct geyser cone.

The intruder spun and capped off two shots toward Cole. One passed through the geyser cone and struck him in the right shoulder. The bullet proof vest prevented the bullet from entering his body, but he lost his grip on the shotgun. Stumbling back, he fell.

Harris had taken cover behind the geyser cone. She had never been under live fire before. But she quickly recovered her wits and returned fire.

Harris's shots drove the suspect from the bomb. He dove behind a stand of lodge pole pines. Harris kept firing, emptying her clip. It was dark and she fumbled replacing her magazine. She dropped her spare clip. It hit the ground with a clank. "Damn it," she cursed. She took her eyes off her attacker to find her magazine. She slapped it into the butt of her pistol and looked to relocate the attacker.

The suspect had moved and was now nowhere to be seen. She frantically searched the area. A small baseball-sized object rolled to within a few yards of her position. A flash bang grenade. "Shit!" Harris dove for cover.

The grenade went off, blinding and knocking her senseless. As she stumbled to the ground she lost her grip on her pistol. It fell into the inky blackness of the Yellowstone night.

Cole's arm was numb. He watched Harris go down. He scrambled to remove his pistol from its holster. His right arm wouldn't function. His Maglite six cell flashlight was digging into his left side. He was helpless. He heard the crunch of approaching footsteps.

"Ranger Cole. I should have known. Is Agent Harris with you? I'm sure she is around here somewhere." The voice was surely that of Joseph Hansen.

"You are under arrest, Captain Hansen," Cole said still lying flat on his back, sensation slowly returning to his arm.

"My name is not Hansen. I am Jamil Ali Hussain."

Cole continued to reach for his pistol until a boot came down on his right hand. Cole couldn't stop the cry that left his lips.

The dark figure standing above him reached down and removed his pistol from its holster and threw it into a nearby hotspring. Next, the figure seized the shotgun, emptied it of its shells and smashed it against a tree. Returning to Cole, the man now going by Hussain stood over him. He pointed his pistol directly at Cole's head and prepared to fire.

BANG! BANG! BANG! BANG! BANG!

Cole winced, expecting to feel the searing pain of gunshot wounds. But the agony didn't come. And the pops sounds more like firecrackers. Harris?

The explosions took Hussain by surprise as well, pulling his attention from Cole.

Seeing the opportunity, Cole snatched his flashlight. Maglite's were the choice of many law enforcement officers because they were durable and cast a strong light, but more importantly in a pinch they could be used as a club. With his left hand, he swung the flashlight and struck the outside of Hussain's right hand. The force produced a loud crack, breaking several bones. The pistol flew from Hussain's hand and struck the ground, discharging a round.

Hussain staggered off, holding his hand. Cole scrambled to his feet. Snapping on the light, he shined it directly into Hussain's eyes. Night vision goggles are excellent in low light conditions. In daylight or bright light they could be blinding. The flashlight beam would be like a searing blast from the sun.

Hussain screamed again, throwing off his goggles, now blinded. Cole didn't have much time to contemplate the situation, and threw himself on the attacker. Both tumbled to the ground, mere feet from the rumbling Centennial Geyser.

As if on cue, the Centennial Geyser

erupted to life. It sent a column of searing hot water hundreds of feet into the air. Boiling rain poured down on the two men. Yet, Cole kept his wits and landed two quick punches to Hussain's jaw.

Hussain pulled the Taser from his belt and jabbed it into Cole's chest. His bullet proof vest prevented the Taser's prongs from making full contact with his skin, but still the device produced a significant jolt. Grabbing Cole by the shirt, Hussain pulled the ranger toward him, slamming his forehead into the ranger's nose, followed by a loud crack.

Hussain shoved Cole back, causing him to tumble to the ground. Hussain pounced, kicking Cole repeatedly.

Cole struggled to catch his breath. The fight was going badly and he still had little feeling in his right arm. He couldn't take much more punishment.

Hussain lifted his foot. It was obvious he planned to bring it down on Cole's face. He caught the downward thrusting boot. Holding firm, he twisted the foot, hyper extending it, producing intense pain and stress on Hussain's right ankle and knee. Hussain stumbled back.

"This ends now," Hussain screamed. "America will be destroyed, its time is over. Allah and Islam will take their rightful place in the universe."

Centennial Geyser continued in the background. Hussain's body was a shadow against the cascade of searing water erupting a mere few feet away.

Like a devil possessed, rage burned within
Hussain. His body was wounded, yet ready to
thrust one last time at the ranger.

He pushed off with his right foot, releasing
his pent up fury. But the lunge didn't get the
acceleration he had expected. The ground gave
way under his foot, throwing him off balance.

Scrambling to get up, the ground
continued crumbling, a large hole developing near
his feet. It inched toward his knees. Hussain
began to panic. He had to get up. But the ground
continued to give way. A large section dropped
out under his chest. He sank, only able to stop his
fall by grabbing a nearby tree. The hole had grown
to the size of a large pick-up truck. He dangled
from the tree, his right hand hanging at his side.
Steam and smoke shot up from the new crater,
choking his lungs, burning his skin, and stinging
his eyes. Boiling water stewed and bubbled mere
yards from his feet. He was staring into the guts of
the Centennial Geyser and it was churning away
with a vengeance. He struggled to pull himself
out. His twisting and turning loosened the tree's
roots and it slipped, dropping Hussain closer to
the boiling tempest. He froze, realizing he was
trapped.

Cole witnessed his attacker's fall and leapt
to save him. Diving toward the hole, he grabbed
Hussain's arm about the wrist just as the tree lost
its hold.

Cole' upper chest, arm and face were over
the hole, the Park Service tie dangling from his

neck. The belching smoke scorched his exposed skin. He was in a difficult spot and couldn't hold on long. Thinking fast and still holding Hussain's right wrist, Cole extended his left arm out to Hussain. . "Take my hand," he yelled over the roar of the geyser. Cole could see Hussain's eyes. They were filled with murderous rage. "Take my hand," he yelled again. "We don't have much time!"

Hussain didn't take the extended hand. Instead, he grabbed Cole's hanging tie to pull Cole in with him. Hussain's move caught Cole by surprise, causing him to defend himself by letting go of the terrorist's wrist.

"Allah Akbar," Hussain yelled, giving the tie a violent yank.

His entire body was now supported by the tie. As expected, he began to fall. He and the ranger were being pulled to their death.

Hussain was in a free-fall now. Only seconds before he hit the water he still had the wits about him to look up into the eyes of his defeated opponent. But he wasn't there. How could this be? His mind raced. He looked to his hand. In it was a *clip-on* tie.

"AAAAAAA!" was the last Cole heard from the hole. No splash came. The roar of the geyser drowned all other sound out. Nor did he hear any scream. Hussain would have been boiled alive almost instantly. As his body broke the surface, he may have had an instant of awareness. But he would have been dead in seconds.

Cole dragged himself back from the crater,

moving to safer ground. The Park Service would be unable to retrieve the body. Over the next few hours, all muscle, tendons and other internal organs would be boiled off the skeleton. A scattering of bones would be all that remained of the man determined to destroy America.

Centennial Geyser continued to erupt in the distance. Geyser streams were normally white, but even in the pale moonlight a hint of pink could be seen in the water column. He tried not to think about the color's source.

For what seemed like an eternity Cole lay on the ground. Finally pulling himself up, the tunnel vision that had constrained his reality for the duration of the fight was dispersing.

Where was Harris? Scrambling to his feet, Cole ran back to the extinct geyser cone where the two had originally taken cover. "Harris!"

"Over here," came a weak reply.

Cole followed the voice to the downed agent. She was on her back. She struggled to get up. Cole quickly figured out why she was having so much trouble regaining her feet. Shifting geyser basins often kill and expose the root systems of surrounding trees. Several tree roots near the Centennial Geyser were sticking straight up from the ground. The flash bang grenade caused her to fall into a clump of exposed roots. Several had impaled her left shoulder, pinning her. She was unable to get up.

Hurrying to her side, Cole cursed. "Hold on."

"Did we get him?" Harris asked through her fog, a pack of firecrackers and lighter lying

306

near her right hand.

"Yes, we did. Thanks for the help." Cole soothed. "But. . ." Cole trailed off.

"What's the matter?" Harris asked panic rising in her voice.

"I lost my favorite tie," Cole joked. "Now lay still, you'll make the wound worse."

An ambulance arrived fairly quickly. Paramedics were stationed at the Old Faithful Inn a mere thirty five minute ride away. The EMTs stabilized Agent Harris, freed her from the roots, and whisked her away to Jackson Hole Hospital.

Cole was now all alone again. Centennial Geyser had long ago ended its eruption. Its subterranean chamber would take time to refill. All was relatively quiet.

He slowly walked over to the small suitcase sitting next to the geyser monitor. A small computer screen was active, with a top line reading: Initial Password. *Submit* had been entered on the line next to it.

Below this a blinking cursor prompted: *Enter password for final initiation.*

Chapter 47
Grant Village Ranger Station, July 12, Late Afternoon

It had been a week since Cole's encounter with Hussain. He was at his desk typing a report regarding the events of the past few days. This would be the first one he had ever filled out that required a top secret classification. Few outside the National Security Administration or the Defense Department would ever read it.

There was a knock on the door. "Grayson?" a woman's voice asked.

In the doorway stood Agent Harris. Her left arm and shoulder were heavily bandaged and in a sling, stitched cuts marked her face, but otherwise she looked no worse for wear.

"Harris," Cole shouted. He bounded to his feet and enfolded her in a warm hug. She took the opportunity to plant a deep kiss on his lips.

Pleased, but slightly confused Cole asked, "What was that for?"

"For saving my life, for saving the country, for making me a better agent. For everything," Harris confessed. "I came to Yellowstone with a giant chip on my shoulder. You were gracious and patient with me. I thank you for that."

"You're welcome," Cole replied. "Let me get you a seat." Cole pulled out a chair for the injured agent and helped her into it. He pulled his chair from behind the desk, allowing him to sit next to her.

Harris went on. "This isn't merely a social call, however." She pulled a letter with the Office of the President printed on it from her briefcase and handed it to him. "I'm here on behalf of the President of the United States to offer you the thanks of a grateful nation for a job well done. Your efforts prevented Jamil Ali Hussain from detonating a nuclear device, which our experts believe could have initiated an eruption of the Yellowstone caldera, quite likely destroying much of the United States."

A flush of red crept across Cole's face. He wasn't used to being thanked for doing his job, especially from the President of the United States.

"As you know, the NEST team recovered the nuclear device planted at the Centennial Geyser Basin," Agent Harris continued. "It was disarmed and transported to a secure location in Nevada.

"The remaining NEST teams have swept Spokane and Portland, as well as Seattle, San Francisco and Los Angeles, for good measure. All came back negative. It appears our bomber focused on the park."

"Lucky us."

"In addition, I know you're aware that Charles Sinclair's body was found last week in one of his outbuildings. A 50 Caliber sniper rifle was found in the shed as well. It appears Charles and Captain Hansen had been planning to kill the president during last week's trip," Harris said. "We're chasing down leads on any additional conspirators."

"What a week," Cole retorted. He was going to say more, to let slip what was on his mind, but bit his lip instead.

"What is it?"

"I just don't get it." he answered.

"Get what?"

"It looks like Jamil Ali Hussain and Charles Sinclair were intent on taking down the United States, going so far as to kill the president and ignite a volcanic eruption."

"Yeah, so?"

"But both of these attempts were doomed to fail from the start," Cole said.

"Well, of course they were doomed to fail. Cole and Harris were on the job," she joked, thumping herself on the chest with her fist.

"Of course," Cole said with a smile. "But that's not what I meant."

"All rright. Go on then," she encouraged.

"These two attempts to destroy America were doomed from the start because they were based on a false premise. A premise that assumes the United States is a single person or group of people, or even a place for that matter. America is none of these things. Rather, she is an idea. An idea that humans should be free, free to decide who they are and what they will become. That's what Hussain and Charles were trying to kill. But an idea can't be killed by violence or explosives.

Agent Harris paused for a second, almost as if she wished she didn't have to utter what she was about to say.

"No mention of these events will appear in your official record. The evacuations of the past week will be attributed to unusual earthquake activity. Due to high levels of radiation, Centennial Geyser will be closed to the public. The superintendent will amend the park's compendium, closing the area for scientific reasons."

Harris went on, "The president has determined this attack to be a national security matter. I must swear you to secrecy."

Cole figured this would be the case. It was probably safer to classify the entire event as top secret and, for the good of the country, pretend it never happened.

A cold feeling spread through him. Cole realized this couldn't have been the first time such an attack had been attempted on the United States. How many other evacuations, fires, or natural disasters were covers for failed nuclear attacks? He would never know.

Epilogue
Pyongyang, North Korea, July 14, Morning

Park Jae-keunt sat outside the supreme leader's office. Park was the North Korean chief intelligence officer in charge of all foreign covert operations. He had been waiting outside the leader's office for nearly an hour.

A brawny, stern faced guard sat at a desk next to the office's large oak double doors, staring straight ahead. The phone rang on the guard's desk. He lifted the receiver without taking his eyes off Park.

"Yes?" the guard answered. "Right away." He returned the receiver to its base. "You may go in," the guard grunted.

Park entered the office. Walking the two dozen paces to Kim Jong Un's desk, his steps clicking on the marble floor, Park placed his briefcase on the ground. Opening it, he retrieved a large report and placed it before Kim Jong Un. Park bowed and retreated.

Un was engrossed in his computer screen, reading the latest foreign newspaper reports.

Un finally pulled his gaze from the monitor and addressed his intelligence chief.

"Well?"

"Operation Dragon's Fury failed," he said.

"Obviously. As no Western media has reported either a nuclear blast or volcanic eruption in the United States," Un said, pointing to the large TV screens hanging on the walls. "What went wrong?"

The security chief shifted his weight from

one foot to the other. He was nervous. "The
operation failed for three main reasons. First, it
was situated well within the United States. This
made significant North Korean involvement and
support impossible. Moreover, America's nuclear
detection defense is more sophisticated than we
anticipated. This alerted law enforcement and
defense department personnel to a potential threat
almost immediately. Finally, this operation was
dependent upon Jamil Hussain, a foreign devil.
His religious fervor gave him determination, but
also appeared to cloud his judgment."

Un paused for a moment to take in the
information. He leaned back in his chair, tipping
his head back to stare at the ceiling. The dear
leader was surely worried that North Korea's
involvement in the failed attack may be uncovered.
He knew the bomb could not be tracked to his
country. North Korea had been careful to build it
with stolen Russian components and more
importantly nuclear fuel. Park wished he could be
at the State Department meeting where the
Russian ambassador would have to explain that
uncomfortable reality. But those involved in
carrying it out may have talked. Un would surely
make sure all involved would be taken care of.

"Did Jamil ever suspect he was working for
us?" the leader asked.

"He had no idea he was working for us and
not Al Qaeda. Our recruitment and grooming of
him was painstaking and flawless. Yet, any
American investigation will turn up al Qaeda's
fingerprints on the operation. North Korea cannot
be tied to it in anyway. However, we were still

dependent upon Hussain's skill and resources. Too many variables were at play to guarantee success."

Un leaned back in his chair, a smile creeping across his face. "We knew it was a long shot when we initiated this plan my friend."

"Yes, we did my leader. However, I'm happy to report that phase two of our plan is ready. We merely await your approval."

Park pulled another report from his briefcase and handed it to Un. The supreme leader opened it to its title page and read.

"It's called operation Clean Sweep," Park continued. "Like Dragon's Fury, it presents North Korea with little risk, but the opportunity to cripple, if not destroy, the United States. However, Clean Sweep is not hobbled by the drawbacks of Dragon's Fury. The intelligence and military give it a high probability of success."

The smile on Un's face grew. "When trying to kill a bear with a bee sting, it's helpful to have many bees."

Now, here's a special preview of the next
book in

Sean Smith's

National Park Thriller Series

Grayson Cole and the Lost Cause

The riveting follow up to

Unleashing Colter's Hell.

Prologue
Sharpsburg, PA, September 13, 1862, Mid-Morning

The morning was growing hot--hot and muggy to be precise. Not yet 10 a.m. and already the temperature was pushing eighty degrees. The wool uniforms the Union soldiers wore weren't helping either. Why the commanding generals insisted upon wool even in the height of summer heat was beyond Sergeant John Bloss. Bloss, along with Corporal Barton W. Mitchell, were with the Indiana 27. They'd spent the better part of the morning moving munitions and supplies up the Smoketown Road. At least that was what they had been ordered to do.

A large thunderstorm, the type that normally built up during hot, humid summer days had dumped buckets of rain through this part of Pennsylvania the day before. The Smoketown road was little more than a mile long mud streak. The muck was several feet deep, making the road to Sharpsburg nearly impassable.

Sergeant Bloss sat under the shade of a nearby Pitman tree, his back propped up against its trunk. Corporal Mitchell lay prone on the ground. Both men were covered in mud to their knees. Their supply wagon lay stuck in the mud up to its axle. No matter how hard the men dug, pulled, or even swore, the wagon wouldn't budge. Hours of effort and the two managed to only move the wagon a few feet.

Bloss could see the wagon mules were growing weary too. Before resting in the shade, the men had unhitched their team, watered them and turned them loose to rest in a nearby field.

The sun would be at its zenith soon, Sergeant Bloss observed. He removed his hat and wiped the sweat from his head with a handkerchief he had pulled from his pocket. Whitman, still prone on the ground, opened his canteen, swigging down a large gulp of water. He poured the remainder over his head and face.

"You better save that water, Corporal," Bloss ordered. "I fear we're going to need every drop on this trip to Sharpsburg."

"What I wouldn't give to be back in Indiana at Barton Lake right now," Whitman replied. Bloss knew what he meant, but he was too hot and tired to mutter a word. He merely dipped his head in a meager nod of approval. Both men were exhausted, not just physically but emotionally too.

Bloss and Whitman were friends from before the war, each enlisting the same day the South fired on Fort Sumter. That was what, eighteen months ago? But it might as well have been a century. They were veterans of how many battles? Ten, fifteen, more? He had stopped counting long ago. What had started out as a quest for adventure had turned into a quest for survival. There was little glory or adventure in this war.

The experience might have been different if the war had been going well for the North. It wasn't. General Robert E. Lee, Bobby Lee as his men called him, consistently bettered the Union's Army of the Potomac. President Lincoln went through general after general in a desperate

attempt to counter the Confederate leaders'
success. To no avail.

Sergeant Bloss noticed Whitman's rifle lay
out of reach. It was common knowledge that
these roads were patrolled by Confederate cavalry,
sentries, spies and scouts. An out-of-reach rifle
may as well be an unloaded rifle.

"Retrieve your weapon," Bloss ordered.
"It would be mighty embarrassing to your family if
you turned up dead a mere few feet from your
rifle."

The corporal must know Bloss was right,
but he just lay there, unmoving.

"Get it moving man," Bloss stated more
forcefully.

Whitman grumbled his approval, slowly
pulling himself from his comfortable position.
The heat continued to rise, and he nearly stumbled
getting to his feet. He appeared to move in slow
motion and it seemed to take all of his energy to
shuffle over to where he had discarded his rifle.

Reaching to retrieve the weapon, the
infantryman paused, noticing a carefully packed
bundle on the ground. It appeared to be three
cigars wrapped in several expensive looking papers.
Whitman picked it up, forgetting about his rifle for
the moment. A small box about the size of a deck
of cards lay near the bundle of cigars as well.

Sergeant Bloss watched the private's
progress with only passing interest. "Whatcha got
there?" he asked.

"Not sure, Sergeant," came the reply. "But
I think it's important."

Corporal Whitman handed the bundle and

the box to him. The burly veteran placed the box in his pocket. He then untied the string that held the bundle of cigars together. Unwrapping the paper, the sergeant studied the three cigars. They appeared to be southern made stogies. REL was stamped on the wrapper. Sergeant Bloss handed the cigars to the corporal. "Here, hold these," he said.

Turning his attention to the wrapping paper, the sergeant was stunned to discover its actual contents. It wasn't a wrapper at all, but rather General Robert E. Lee's battle plans for the upcoming engagement. There in the sergeant's hands were the strategies and tactics of the Army of Northern Virginia. He couldn't believe his eyes.

The sergeant took a moment to take in what they had found, nearly forgetting about the small box that had been found with the plans. Folding up the battle plans, he placed them in his breast pocket. He retrieved the box from his pants pocket and slowly opened the lid. Corporal Whitman leaned in close to get a better view. Both stared into the box in wonder.

"What do you think this means?" the private finally said with one of the REL cigars hanging from his mouth.

"I think the North has just won the war."

ABOUT THE AUTHOR

Sean Smith is an award winning
conservationist, whose work has been seen on
CNN, heard on NPR, and covered in the New
York Times and National Geographic.

Sean is a former park ranger who worked
at Yellowstone, the North Cascades, Glacier, and
with the Forest Service at Mount St. Helens. He's
also an accomplished artist, as well as a private pilot.

Recently, Sean began writing political
thrillers set in National Parks. His goal is to
entertain his readers, but also educate them on the
challenges park rangers face every day protecting
America's heritage.

He currently lives in Western Washington
with his wife and two children.

- Contact Sean at:
  seanwrites@yahoo.com

- Or visit:
  SeanDavidSmith.blogspot.com

- Like him on Facebook, search for
  "Unleashing Colter's Hell"

- Or follow him on Twitter :
  @parkthrillers